Johnny Talon and the Goddess of Love and War

by

W.B.J. Williams

Johnny Talon and the Goddess of Love and War

Cover Art by *The Wild Rose Press, Inc.*

The Wild Rose Press, Inc.
PO Box 708
Adams Basin, NY 14410-0708
Visit us at www.thewildrosepress.com

Publishing History
First Edition, 2024
Trade Paperback ISBN 978-1-5092-5385-2
Digital ISBN 978-1-5092-5386-9

Published in the United States of America

Dedication

To all who helped me with bringing this story to life, especially Leonid Korogodski and Wendy Delmater Thies.

To my two daughters, Kayla and Hannah for your love and support.

Especially to my darling wife, Margo, without your love and support none of this would be possible.

Chapter 1

A Hot Proposition

In the shadows of the flickering fluorescent lamp, I fumbled with my key until it inserted, and I felt the latch turn. I was too tired, too drunk, too disgusted to do much more than find my bed, so I took off my hat, kicked off my loafers, and shed my coat still damp from a typical San Francisco fog. I tossed the coat and hat onto the back of a kitchen chair. I made my way through the kitchenette with its smell of stale tobacco, banging into one of my chairs. The noise of it hurt more than the sharp stab on my stubbed toe. I'd have a devil of a hangover in the morning.

My bed creaked under my weight, and I thought once more about starting a diet just to dismiss it as tomorrow's problem. I noticed the light under the bathroom door as I dropped my socks onto the floor. I silently cursed the electric bill I'd have next month, I rose to go in there and turn it off. Before I could do more than stand, someone opened it. Those curves, silhouetted in the light of the bathroom, certainly belonged on a woman.

"Hello Johnny," she said.

Kind of recognizing her voice, and enjoying the seductive tone, I could barely manage to speak. "Hi."

"You don't remember me, do you?"

"I can't see your face in the shadows, and I'm a bit drunk so I'm not certain about your voice."

I reached over and turned on the lamp on my nightstand. While the shapely petite blonde in the clingy black dress brightened my room like a diamond in the mud, I did not recognize her, and I was certain I would have remembered a face like hers.

"I'm afraid I don't recognize you. Wish I did. It would help if you told me who you are, why you are here, and how you got into my place."

She lifted an arm gracefully above her head, taking a dancer's pose, and said, "I'm Eve, from heaven. Does that help?"

A dim recollection of going to a strip club pierced my soggy mind. I'd passed some time there drinking before heading to the failed stakeout. "The dancer, I remember now." I also remembered promising to help her with something, but not what. I had to cut down on the whiskey.

"Look, Eve, I was drunker than I am now, but I do remember I promised to help you with something. However, this is not my office, and I still don't know why you're here or how you got in."

She slid out of her dancer's pose and took a step towards me. "I also need a place to crash, and I took your offer to help in any way you could seriously. Look, if you can't—"

I put a hand up to stop her from continuing her thought. "I only have the one bed. If it can wait until morning, we can discuss your case over breakfast." The smile that returned to her face broke my drunken heart, as it didn't hide the tears that I could now see in the pale-yellow light. "Thank you. I don't mind the floor."

"Nonsense. I may be a drunk, but I don't ask even unexpected guests to take the floor." I lay down on the floor as if to demonstrate my willingness right away. If she said anything else, I don't remember it.

****

I was back in the theater, watching the same surreal drama I'd seen awake, but the production made more sense, though none of the actor's feet touched the stage. I looked up to see if the woman with the blue hair was in the balcony, but instead, my mark sat there with a sly smile on his greasy face. Jack the Fish, looking as slippery as ever with his slick black hair and his blue silk suit. Figures that I'd dreamed my stakeout had been successful. I got up from my seat and found myself climbing stairs made of air up to the box with no clear goal in mind but nailing that bastard to the wall. Jack didn't seem to notice me, his eyes on the woman lip-syncing to the music on stage. I climbed over the railing to find him gone, but a note was left on his seat. I picked it up and put it in my pocket without reading it.

Hoping Jack had left through the normal exit, I opened the door in the back of the box to find it opened on a plaza surrounded by buildings with red tile roofs. Most of the buildings had only three walls, some only had one wall with a door. Men and women in various states of undress wandered across the plaza, in and out of those wall-less homes, but always through the doors. I looked back through the door I'd come through and no longer saw the theater but a large laboratory where men in lab coats examined some shells, while women wearing only ornate feathered hats waited along the walls.

I went up to one of those women to ask her if she knew where Jack the Fish had gone, but before I could ask my question, she put her finger to her lips.

I woke to find Eve in my arms on the floor with a blanket over us both. She must have lain down next to me after I passed out. As she was even more naked than the women in my dream, it took me a while to fall back asleep. I tried to recall what she said in our conversation to keep my mind off the scent of her hair and the warmth of her bare hips under my right hand. At some point exhaustion took me, and I don't recall any more dreams.

****

I woke again hours later, stiff on the floor, a warm ray of sunlight on my face. Eve was still wrapped in my arms, asleep. I slipped my arm from under her head, carefully pulled the covers off me, and pushed myself up as quietly as possible. Puzzled as to how I had become naked, I needed a leak, a shower, and an explanation, but the latter could wait. Once in the shower, the throbbing in my temple increased in tempo and sharpness. I opened my mouth and let some of the hot water stream down my throat to ease my dehydration. I started to lather up my hair when I heard the door to the bathroom open. Whoever Eve was, she was full of surprises. Glad of the frosted glass, I closed my eyes and started to rinse off the coconut scented shampoo that always reminded me of Gladys. As long as Eve didn't flush, I'd be fine. For the life of me, I still couldn't remember her problem. I needed to cut down on the booze.

Clean and rinsed, having heard her leave the room, I turned off the water and stepped out of the shower to towel off and flush. While rubbing the scratchy cotton across my skin to dry myself, I thought of ten witty things to say to her as I left the bathroom, but the smell of fresh coffee removed all thoughts except a tall cup of

Joe. I pulled my threadbare blue robe on and left my bedroom to find her going through my fridge.

"Not much for privacy, are you?" I asked, hoping to learn more about her thought processes.

"I'm private in the things that matter. You don't have much food."

I guess she didn't consider that perhaps my standards were different than hers, or perhaps she thought the things that went down in the strip club removed the need for such barriers. I wish I could remember it better. "I wasn't expecting company. There should be enough eggs and bread."

"I found that. I was looking for some butter."

"I doubt you'll find any of that. I'm trying to lose a couple and cook fat free. Let me boil the eggs. We can use jam on the toast and discuss your situation after we eat."

She closed the fridge and turned to me. Last night I hadn't noticed the blood on her dress. What kind of trouble was she in?

"How about you dress while I cook," she said.

I never regretted more that the door to my bedroom would not close properly as when I disrobed and dressed. Trouble she might be, and likely in worse, but she was more beautiful than a spring tree and I was not as hard as I once was, at least not all of me, and at that moment I wished that part of me was less so. I focused on the smell of toast and hot metal, hoping to forget that the room had been filled with the scent of her but moments ago.

I returned to the kitchen to find the table set and the toast ready for the jam. She had her back to me, so I let myself watch her move as she cooked. Every move she made reminded me she was a dancer. I enjoyed watching her reaching into an overhead cabinet, adjusting the stove, or simply shifting bare feet.

With two hot, steaming coffee mugs in hand, she came to the table and sat, giving me a chance to study her face. Her left eye betrayed hints of a recent black eye, and there were faint traces of what would one day be crow's feet at the corners, placing her age, in my estimation, in her early forties.

"Not finding any milk, I imagine you like your coffee black," she said.

"I do. If you want, I have sugar." I tapped the sugar bowl with my knife.

"No, I'm okay, though I do wish you'd had some skim milk."

"I'll get some later. From the look of it, I'm going to need to get into your apartment and bring you back some clothes. You'll not want to go out in the daylight with that amount of blood on you."

"Could I stay here for a few days?" She took a sip of the coffee, made a face, and took another.

"Yes. What happened?" I fished a pen and pad out of my coat pocket.

"Before I get into any of that, how much to take my case?"

"What is your case? Protecting you or investigating something? I'm not a bodyguard."

She shook her head. "You really don't remember what we discussed?"

"No."

She dug into her eggs, talking between bites. "My ex disappeared about two days ago with his new fling and just about all of my savings. I'm just trying to get back the stuff and the money. The gal can keep him if she still wants him."

"So, where did all of that blood on your dress come from?"

Her eyes finally met mine. "I think he got word that I was after him and sent a goon to beat me up. Came at me with a knife."

I put my pen down. "That's not your blood. Did you have to hide the body?"

"I didn't kill him. I tried to trail him, but he evaded me, so I came straight here."

"Kung-fu?" I put some eggs on my fork but watched her face.

"Vajra-mushti with the comb I wear in my hair."

She obviously assumed I knew what Vajra-mushti was, while in fact I couldn't even pronounce it. I moved on. She was lying about something, as no one hires muscle for some stuff and petty cash.

"Good place to hide a weapon, especially for a dancer," I said, hoping to draw out more information.

"Exactly." She drank some more coffee and scowled.

"Do you have any leads I can follow?" Now I was fishing.

"We have the blood of the goon on my dress. That's about it right now."

"Okay, first thing we do is to get you an outfit you can wear in public without attracting the cops. Then we'll see where that blood leads us."

"You're taking my case without asking for a fee?" She stared at my face as I swallowed some eggs. A bit bland, I must remember to get some salt next time I went to the market.

"You're asking me to take on a case based upon a

7

drunken promise without any knowledge of me, my firm, my methods. That's a lot of trust in me. How much do you have?"

"Nothing. He took everything."

"Okay, how much did he take?"

"Everything."

I was thrilled at the precision of her answer. "All right, my fee is one percent of what I help you recover." If I was right, her reluctance to tell the truth meant she'd lost a lot and she didn't want me to fleece her.

"That's an odd fee." She looked at the cup of Joe, shrugged and drank some more.

"I'm an odd man. I don't like to work on absolutes, so I work on percentages. Let me tell you a few things about my methods. I'm not the typical gumshoe, though I will use those methods when they are likely to produce results. I'm a surreal detective, which means while I deal with the facts, I deal with them both in my conscious rational mind and in my subconscious. I'll follow a dream as quickly as a lead; my actions often seem irrational. I'll pursue a non sequitur as if it was a hot tip. I will take you to strange and unexpected places in my pursuit of the truth, and of the thief. You still want me to take the case?" I took a long sip of the coffee. Just the way I like it, dark and bitter—like life.

"Yes, actually more than ever."

She'd kept her gaze steady, so she was likely leveling with me. "Okay, then let's start with some basics. First, I have to imagine Eve is your stripper name. What is your real name?"

"Eve."

Like hell it was. She was good at lies. I took a sip of the coffee. "Last name?"

"Hennessy."

"Like the drink?" I stared at her, hoping to catch a hint of the lie. I wouldn't want to play poker against her. "Where are you from?"

"Portsmouth, New Hampshire."

Slightly surprised, I wrote that down. "Is stripping your only job?"

She straightened up and leaned forward on her elbows. "No, I'm a corporate lawyer who pulls in six figures. Of course stripping is my only job." She took a sip of the coffee and grimaced.

"Ever turn tricks?"

"Stopped doing that years ago."

Truth! Wonder why. Everything else I asked her about herself was met with a sarcastic stone wall. "Under the same name?"

"Yep."

"Anyone in your life? A husband, boyfriend, girlfriend?"

"My wife is dead. My last boyfriend stole everything I have."

I took a sip to delay the question. "Wife?"

She smiled. "Yes, I swing both ways."

I tapped the pen on the pad. "No, I mean can you tell me a bit more about her?"

"I'd rather keep that private. I don't think it will hurt your chances of finding Fred."

"Fred is your ex?" I wrote down his name.

"My, you're good." She took a long sip of the coffee, hiding her expression.

"I could do without the attitude. I am trying not to make any assumptions."

Eve looked down at the table. "I'm sorry, just don't

like talking about myself and so I get defensive."

She didn't like telling the truth much either. "No problem. Just remember the more you level with me, the quicker I'll get your stuff back. What was his last name?"

"Stone."

"Fred Stone?" I tried not to chuckle. "Smells like an alias to me."

She shrugged her shoulders, the first bit of body language she'd displayed since I started with my questions. "That was the name on his driver's license."

"What is his phone number?"

"Don't know."

I took a sip of my coffee to relax. "Let me guess, it was on your cellphone which he stole."

"I'm not good at remembering things like phone numbers. There are reasons why I used to turn tricks, and now I take my clothes off for a living. I'm no good at anything else."

She didn't change her expression, so I had no idea if I'd touched a nerve. "Do you know where he works, or in what field?"

"He always kept that vague, but he was in some high-tech startup. I think he was in sales."

"Do you remember the name of the company?"

Again, the shrugged shoulders. "'Fraid not. His laptop had all sorts of stickers on it, but none come to mind. Keep in mind we were only living with each other a few weeks, and I'd only known him about six months. Frankly, when we were together, we didn't spend a lot of time talking. He worked days; I worked nights. We only saw each other at odd times, and we spent that time in bed."

I realized I'd been doodling and stopped myself.

"How did you meet him?"

"Supermarket actually. I'd gotten to the register and realized I'd left my wallet at home. He paid for the groceries."

I closed my notebook. "Okay, that's enough for now. We need to get you some clothes. What size are you so that I can pick you up an outfit, or are you going to tell me where you live so I can bring back some clothing?"

"There are no clothes at my place. He really did take everything. Also, I lost my keys in the fight."

"That didn't keep you out of my apartment. I'll need to look through your place in any event for evidence."

"We'll go there together, later. I'm a size four, and wear size six shoes. Just add it to the bill."

"Bra?" I asked.

"Don't bother. I only wear them when I have my period."

****

I bought her some light gray yoga pants, a long-sleeve t-shirt, a jacket, some socks, and a pair of sneakers, figuring she'd be comfortable and not think I was thinking what I was thinking whenever I looked at her, even though she was likely very used to that. I returned to my apartment to find Eve in the shower with the bathroom door open. The place smelled good, and I felt a cool breeze. She'd aired out the room to get rid of the smell of cigarettes. I tried not to look while I laid the clothing on the bed and tiptoed back to the kitchenette. I forced myself to read the paper while the water stopped running, trying not to think of her as I could hear her moving around while she dried and dressed. She might take her clothes off for a living, but while she stayed with me, she would have what privacy I could give her, even if she didn't seem to care about it. After reading every part of the paper, including the funnies twice, she finally came into the kitchen, a hint of her scent the only thing to let me know she'd entered the room.

"What does my horoscope say?" asked Eve.

"How would I know? What is your sign?" I answered without looking up.

"Gemini."

I glanced over at her, wearing only a smile that didn't meet her eyes and a towel wrapped around her hair. She certainly got my pulse up. I quickly glanced back at the paper. "Let me find it. Here: 'Your tendency to leave things unfinished will be your chief challenge. While you want to skip off to something more fun, stick with the unpleasant tasks you find yourself in the middle of. It will be worth it.'"

I glanced at her face to see her smile fade.

"Okay, now what does yours say?" she asked.

I put the paper down. "No idea. I don't even know what sign I am."

"When were you born?"

"I'd rather not say."

Tears welled up in her eyes and she wiped them away with the back of her hands. She was good at manipulation, that was certain. "Look, I don't pay much attention to that stuff," I said, trying to sound reassuring, but I didn't want to talk about myself at all with a client who lied as often as she had.

She grabbed the paper from me. "It's important to me that I know what your horoscope says. Please tell me when you were born."

I wasn't going to win. "April 1."

"Oh."

"Oh, what?"

She pushed the paper back at me and sat, head in her hands. I looked down at the paper to find what sign that was and then read, "Now is not the time to be taking on new projects, no matter how attractive. Say no and be firm about it."

"This is nonsense. Get dressed and we'll get started."

"But—" There were actual tears rolling down her cheeks. Was she crying at the thought of me not taking the case?

"No buts about it. I'm as good as my word. Besides, helping you is not a new project. I agreed to this twice last night. Until I've helped you get your money back this is the only case I'm working. Now, get dressed and let's get going."

She sniffled and I gave her my handkerchief, which she used to dab her eyes. She played the damsel in distress perfectly. I found myself watching her sway into the bedroom and dress.

"It fits perfectly," she called out to me as she laced up her sneakers.

Yes, it does, I thought, but why is it now black? I could have sworn I bought light gray.

I fished in my pockets for my receipt and pulled out both the receipt and a note card which was not there yesterday. The receipt confirmed my memory; I'd bought gray sweats, but on her they were black. I put the receipt back into my pocket and opened the note. Just a drawing of a fish in a silk suit, no writing. My dream had given me my mark, as a mark. I folded the paper and put it back in my pocket. Until I was done with Eve, Jack the

Fish could wait. I'd consider it an IOU.

Eve looked stunning in those sweats as she rejoined me in the kitchen holding a bag. "I put the dress in here. Let's go."

Chapter 2

A Fine And Quiet Place

I stopped walking so suddenly that Eve walked into me. I found an old red Fiat Spider with a beige ragtop where I'd left my car. What the hell was going on? No way anyone stole what I drove. All I'd had to drink was coffee, so unlike last night I was stone sober. The plates on the car were mine. I tried my key and the door opened. This made no sense. I caught a whiff of sea air, so much nicer than the stale beer and weed I remembered of the car I drove home. My key turned in the ignition and I started to drive to the best forensics lab that would work on credit without a clue as to what was suddenly going on with my car.

"This is a fun ride," she said. "You should let the top down on mornings like this."

The unusually warm sunlight had me rolling down my windows. "Good idea. I'd love to say it's my car, but it isn't and I've no idea how to work the top on this thing."

"You got an antique as a rental? Impressive."

"More a loan than a rental."

She flipped up her visor. "I don't understand."

I hit the brake as I slowed to the bottom of a hill. Sure enough, the light turned red as I got there. "I'm not certain I do either. Last night I drove a Ford to the

15

stakeout and drove a Chrysler home. My key seems to work in whatever car is parked where I left the car I drove last. I guess I'm just driving what I find that has my license plate. I guess my car is becoming an extension of my method."

"That is weird but does explain your behavior back there. Where are you taking me?"

The light turned green, so I glanced to ensure no one was running the light and give it some gas. "There is a forensics lab that I like to use. I'm going to ask them to examine the blood on your dress, to try to track your assailant and through him find your ex. Once we've dropped that off, I'll take you to your place, and see if we can find anything."

"Is it a surreal forensics lab?"

Was that a tease or a real question? I didn't know her well enough to tell, I couldn't read her face or tone. "Is anything real? They don't follow my method is probably the best answer I can give you. Their techniques are classic science-based forensic analysis."

The lab was out in the burbs. I did enjoy the drive, especially after we figured out how to let the top of the car down. The warmth of the sun felt good on my shoulders. I parked the car and was making my way around to be the gentleman and open the door for her when she swung herself out, now dressed in a blue mini skirt and pink t-shirt with a rude slogan.

"How did you do that?" I asked, locking the door.

"Do what?"

"Change your outfit."

"What do you mean?"

"Look at what you're wearing." I pointed, as if that would help.

She glanced down at what to me were the most lovely pair of legs I'd laid eyes on and shrugged her shoulders. "That's so weird, I put on the black sweats you bought me."

"That's part of what is odd. I bought you light gray sweats."

She smiled. "Perhaps my clothing is like your car, an extension of your method."

That sounded like a well-aimed barb. Good to have a client with an active sense of humor. I was used to what folks think of reality bending in odd directions while on a case, but this case was going above and beyond the call of bent reality. I knew there were important things to understand in all of this, but what things exactly I wasn't certain.

"My car doesn't change while I'm driving it; or at least it hasn't yet. Anyway, let's get going. Wondering about the imponderables is something we can readily do while walking. Both will lead us someplace, perhaps where we intend to go."

The lab was on the third floor of an older building—where the elevator was often broken, and the halls were not air conditioned. South San Francisco summers weren't much, but in that mild heat the climb up became quite the workout. I was sweating a little when we got to the landing.

"You're certain there is a crime lab here?"

"Yes, right this way." I started walking to the right.

While the halls were dim and hot, you felt like you stepped into a refrigerator when you opened the door to the lab's office. The place used to be a doctor's office, so it had a waiting room with old magazines and a window where a receptionist sat. I took the bag containing her dress to the window hoping that her dress was still a dress and the blood was still on it. Unfortunately, the woman behind the window was still Gladys.

"Hello Johnny. It's been a long time since you darkened my door."

It would have been a lot longer if she hadn't worked at my favorite lab. "Hello, Gladys. How are things?"

"Actually, they're good. I got me a man, moved in with him about three weeks ago."

I forced a smile. She still wore the same perfume and its elegant scent of sandalwood and vanilla clashed with her everything. "I'm glad for you." Poor guy must be a saint. Still, I had to admit that she looked happy, was wearing less makeup, and her face was less gaunt.

"That your client behind you, or your latest lover? Hey, blondie, you better be careful with Johnny here. He's big on promises and small on delivery if you know what I mean."

I rubbed my face. "Look, Gladys, I'm sorry it didn't work out between us, but I honestly did try. Can we just keep this to business?"

"All right, business. What you got for us?"

I took the dress out of the bag and handed it to her. "There is blood on this dress. I need to know who it belongs to."

"Lost the body again?"

I stiffened. "I never lost a body, and in this case there is no body to lose, yet. The thug we're looking for assaulted my client; it's his blood."

Gladys took a long look at Eve, who was reading the newspaper clippings on the wall.

"Her ex?"

"No, her ex hired muscle to take her out."

"I'm impressed. She looks like nothing more than a common whore."

I ignored her, hoping Eve hadn't heard. "What's the backlog?"

"A month."

"A month!?" I couldn't keep the shock and disappointment from my voice. They used to work much quicker than that, and I had no other lead to work on.

"You don't exactly pay promptly."

"And if I pay up front?" I leaned forward on one of my elbows.

"She's that good in bed?"

"Look, Gladys, she's a client, not a lover."

She leaned backward, relaxing in her chair. "You pay up front, we'll have the results by end of day."

"How much?" I reached in my pocket for my checkbook.

"Four bills."

"Take a check?"

"From you?"

"Look, it's good, and I don't happen to carry around that kind of cash."

I opened my check book and wrote the check, which I then tore off and handed to her.

She snatched it out of my hand. "If it bounces, I'm going to take this dress and hold it over a Bunsen burner myself."

"It's good."

"It better be." She pulled a machine from under her desk, set it on top and ran the check through it. A few minutes later she handed it back to me. "Well, we have reformed ourselves. You can keep this as a receipt. Not a lover, just a client, and you can produce four bills without worry. Well I'll be, Johnny. It looks like you're growing up a bit."

I forced a poker face. "I'll be back at the end of the day for the results."

Eve followed me out of the office without a word, but that only lasted until we were in the hall. "Well, Johnny has quite the history. Will super bitch in there actually do the work?"

"Gladys, a super-bitch? Yeah, I guess you could say that. From her perspective I really did her wrong. However, I trust her and the entire lab to pull together anything that can be learned from that dress of yours—- and do it fast. Now, on to your place."

This time the car was an old Citroen, somewhat rusted around the bottoms of the doors.

"I'm impressed, you weren't just telling me a story about your car changing shape each time you drive it. Shame, this is a bit of a step down from the sports car," said Eve.

I held the door for her. "With any luck, it won't be ours for more than this drive." I got in, the interior smelled of old tobacco. Sure enough, the key turned the ignition. I just hoped I would never get towed, as I'd not know what car to retrieve from the police. "What is your address?"

"575 Leavenworth, near O'Farrel."

I shrugged my shoulders and sighed. "Well, the car matches the neighborhood."

****

The Sonny Hotel still had the steel gates rolled down when I pulled into a parking spot between a lavender pimped-up Cadillac and an old rusty Chevy.

"Posh neighborhood," I said as I opened the door.

"I like it. People are honest here: no pretense, no masks." She got out and I did a double take. She was in a long silk gown, cut low in the front and clinging like my gaze to her curves. I'd gladly walk back to the lab just to keep her dressed like that.

"What is it?" she said, "You're staring at me."

"Look at your outfit. It's stunning on you."

"I preferred the mini skirt, or the sweats. I could fight in that if I had to. The skirt on this would get in my way. Follow me."

She took me down an alley off of Leavenworth. Stepping gracefully over a pungent pool of vomit, she went straight to a weathered wooden door, its blue paint peeling and cracked. She took her comb from her hair, pressed the image of the blue dragon, and a thin chamber opened. She turned the comb over so the key that she hid in it fell into her palm, closed the chamber, and unlocked the door.

I wondered briefly if she remembered lying to me that she'd lost her key, and how much else she'd told me was true. I followed her up the stairs to an interior door with a combination lock. She punched in the code, opened the door, and I followed her into a room that looked like the inside of a cloud. Everything was white. White mosquito netting draped over a white circular bed in the center of the room. White walls, white diaphanous curtains, white linoleum, even the door handles on the two doors which exited the room were white. The place smelled of sandalwood, although I couldn't see any incense burners.

Other than the bed, she had no furniture.

Eve said, "Please excuse me as I get changed. While

I'm grateful for the sweats, I'm a bit freaked out by what's happening each time I'm in your car."

"No problem." I was finding the changes a bit disconcerting as well, but I was more interested in knowing that she'd lied again when she'd said everything had been taken. The more lies she piled on, the more I began to wonder if I was being played, and what her game was.

Not closing the curtains, Eve stripped bare, the dress becoming gray sweats as they hit the floor. She walked to one of the two doors which she pulled open; she stumbled backwards screaming. I forced myself to look past her naked body to see that behind that door was a corpse. I stepped closer to take a look. The body was propped in a sitting position, legs crossed, holding his head in his lap on a silver tray. The lack of blood told me that whoever had done this killed him elsewhere then brought this here for her to find. The lack of any odor indicated this was done very recently.

I turned to Eve, who was holding herself and shaking. Thinking she could use a hug to help pull herself together I went to her and wrapped my arms around her. She uncurled, turned to me, and pulled me tight while she sobbed. I ignored her nudity by running my mind over the facts and came to two conclusions: that was likely her former boyfriend, and whatever he took from her was valuable to someone who was very dangerous. She'd obviously not given me the full story, but I'd worry about that later.

When she quieted down, I asked, "Was that the guy you wanted me to help you find?"

She nodded. "He was a rat and a thief, but he didn't deserve this."

I wanted to say, *No one deserves to have their head handed to them on a silver platter*, but I restrained myself. Instead, I said, "Look, Eve, we're going to have to call the cops. I think that would go over better if you put some clothing back on."

"All my clothing is gone."

Then what were you expecting to find in that closet? Was the corpse another setup and her reaction the best acting job I'd ever witnessed?

"Can you wear the things I picked up for you?"

She nodded, pulled herself away from me, and put back on the gray sweats which immediately turned pink. Even staring at her I missed the transition.

Once she was dressed, I went back to the corpse. I knew the cops would dust for prints, so I used a pen to push back his jacket a bit to see if there were any papers. I found an envelope in his breast pocket. I carefully pulled it out, and then let his jacket close.

"It's probably nothing, but it might help." I tore open the envelope, pulled out a single folded page. I unfolded it: blank. No writing on either side. "Someone has a sick sense of humor." I put the paper back into the envelope and slid both into my pocket. I'd look this over for lemon juice or other secret messages later. With any luck, I won't have to wait for a full moon.

"Now, the police are going to have a lot of questions for us both, is there anything you haven't told me?" I asked.

"Nothing."

This girl would win at poker every time. I suppressed the sigh. "Okay, time to bring in the cops."

I did a lot of work in the Tenderloin, so I had the local precinct on speed dial. For the same reason, the desk clerk must have known my number.

"Hi Johnny. Lose the corpse again?" said the desk clerk.

"Actually, no, and as a matter of fact, there is a corpse right here that I thought you guys would want to take a look at, but I can hang up if you're not interested."

"Cut the crap, Johnny. Can't take a joke? Where are you?"

I gave her the address and hung up. I was getting pretty tired of the lost corpse joke. There must have been a donut shop nearby that I was not aware of because San Francisco's finest arrived just five minutes later, sirens blaring.

Eve stuck her head out of the window and called to them as they exited the car, "Up here boys. Come around back and use the blue door. It's open."

I rolled my eyes as I recognized one of the cops. Greg O'Neil. Hard-nosed veteran who hated private dicks. He'd enjoy making my day hell.

They came running up the stairs; Eve opened it for them just as they reached the top.

"Thank you, officers, for coming so quickly," she said.

"No problem, Eve. Glad to help you out. Where's the stiff?"

They knew her by name? Did she do private shows for the precinct or something? Or were there corpses turning up in her closet on a frequent basis?

She pointed over her shoulder. "There, in the closet."

Glad to be ignored, I stayed in the background as Greg took pictures of the dead body. I didn't know the other officer who took out a pad and pen.

"About what time did you find the body?" he asked.

Eve shifted her stance to show off the curve of her hip. "I don't have a watch or a clock, but I'd say it was about ten minutes before we called the precinct."

"Did you touch anything in the room, or the body?" asked the cop.

She put her hand on her chin as if thinking it through, and batted her eyes at him as she said, "No, I didn't touch anything except the door through which we came, the closet door, and the floor." Astonishingly, they didn't ask me. I decided not to volunteer anything. I'd dust the paper for prints myself.

The officers started taking photographs, taking measurements, and had just finished drawing the infamous chalk line when two men from the coroner's office showed up. Eve took my hand as they laid Fred out in a body bag and then walked him down the stairs.

After the body was gone, the officers turned their attention back to Eve. "Did you know the deceased?" asked O'Neil.

"Yes, he was my boyfriend for the past six months."

"Did he have any enemies that you know of?"

She flashed him a smile. "No. Everyone liked him."

"Was he in trouble or in debt?"

I was very familiar with that shrug by now. "Not that I know of. He didn't do drugs either," she said.

"Okay, don't think of leaving town any time soon. We may have more questions for you."

She shifted back and forth from one foot to another. "I'll be around, but I'm going to be staying elsewhere. I can't live in this apartment after today."

The officer closed his notebook and smiled. "Just let the folks in the precinct know your new address."

I watched the officers leave but held my questions until they'd driven away.

"They should both be fired," I said under my breath tapping my pockets for some cigarettes, irritated I couldn't find any.

"Why?"

I brushed my hair back from my forehead. "Neither of them asked you key questions. Things I wish I knew myself: where and when did you last see him alive; did the two of you have a fight; did you know where he was going; was that your silver tray, amongst others. The most pressing question to me was of the things you own, what was he trying to steal and failed to find."

Eve froze. Her lips quivered, tears welled up. Her voice was barely a whisper. "How did you know?"

"You wouldn't let me enter this apartment alone. You were afraid I'd find it, and then there is the body and the fact that you were looking for clothing in that closet when you told me he'd stolen everything. I'm hoping that is because you purchased something after the theft, but still, you're not exactly being level. As for your boyfriend, he may have thought he'd taken everything except the bed, and I imagine he tried to take even that. However, I don't think it's your bed he missed. To my knowledge, the things he didn't get are your bed, your comb, and the dress you were wearing when you came to my place. Is there anything else, something you haven't told me?"

She wiped her eyes with the back of her hands and sniffled. "How about I take you out of here to some place where we can sit and talk where the stench of death doesn't linger," she said with just enough of a sob that I listened.

****

The car was an old-fashioned olive-green jeep, no doors or roof, a white number painted on its olive frame. Glad the warmth from the bright sun had held, I got in. Sure enough, the key turned.

"Where to?" I asked, putting the car into gear.

"Holy Cross Cemetery in Colma."

That was her idea of a place where the stench of death didn't linger? The white noise of the wind blocked out everything else while I drove. I wanted to say I was dying to ask her why the cemetery, but that would be disrespectful. After handling a corpse that had his head handed to him on a silver platter, I was getting a bit allergic to morbid puns. Thankfully, there were no funerals, so I had no trouble finding a place to park. There were always tourists, but that day there were few cars parked, giving us hope of a fine and private place to talk. If I had been a cat, I'd have died from how curious I was.

I followed her lead. Her outfit had shifted to a full-length black gown and a black hat with a long black veil. The smell of freshly cut grass reinforced the peaceful feel of the place. Under my breath, I hummed an old Johnny Cash song, which ended conveniently as we came to a stop at a small tombstone. While questions clamored for attention in my thoughts, I forced my mouth into a respectful silence.

She knelt in front of the stone, placing her hands on either side of it, whispering some words that I could not catch. Behind me I heard a scream that froze my blood. I wheeled, pistol in hand to find myself staring at an orange skinned parody of a man with horns and fangs. I braced and fired at its orange face, my bullet placing a third eye between the two it came with. Unfortunately, this neither killed it nor gave it enlightenment. Instead, two others materialized behind it.

"You dare to attack me here!" screamed Eve, suddenly naked, blond hair free and blowing in the wind as she took her comb from her hair and held it in front of her, knees bent, ready for a fight. The demons raced towards us, screaming. I pocketed the revolver, crossed myself, and settled into a Tai Chi stance. All three seemed to want a piece of Eve, so I threw myself on the closest one, pummeling it with kicks and punches, which seemed to be doing nothing much while Eve's comb was making them bleed. The demon I was vainly trying to pull off of Eve caught me on my side with one of its claws, tearing right through my clothing. I screamed as the pain seared my side but redoubled my efforts.

I was not letting it through to overwhelm her.

"Jesus, Mary, and Joseph! Back to hell with you," said a gentle voice behind us and the demons disappeared in a puff of sulfurous smoke like in some old movie. Eve and I wheeled and dropped our guards. Somehow, she was once again dressed in mourning. A white-haired priest in the traditional black suit complete with the old-fashioned roman collar and wide brimmed black hat hobbled towards us, leaning heavily on a black hawthorn stick.

"Saints alive I tried to get here sooner, but I'm not as quick on my feet as I was. Those three were lying in wait for you, Eve. They're likely to try again."

I never would have guessed her to be friendly with a catholic priest. I kept my mouth shut despite my growing sense that everyone knew Eve, and that she needed me as much as that proverbial fish needed a bicycle. I took a quick look at the scrapes on my side, they weren't as deep as they felt. I'd live, and not need more than first aid.

"Father Donn," she said, "how kind of you to help. I think they were trying to keep me from revealing to Johnny why I need him to help me bring back what was stolen from me, and why only he can do this."

He turned to me and took off his hat. "Johnny, I've not seen you in Church as of late."

How he knew I was a lapsed Catholic, I couldn't guess, but I wasn't going to deny it. "Father, I've not been able to bring myself to attend Mass since the pedophile scandal."

"Yes, we are all sinners, and all in need of the dear Lord's forgiveness." He raised his stick and tapped me with it. "The innocents need you, Johnny, those poor kids and those poor folks growing up with such a wrong burden imposed by vow breakers, and they need you too. They need your prayers and suffer greatly the lack. You're wounded, let me wash it clean." He took a flask out of his breast pocket, unscrewed it, and poured it over the tear in my side. The scrapes frothed, and the pain stopped as I watched the flesh close over the wound.

"Thanks, Father. Holy water?"

"Irish whiskey, blessed over breakfast," he said, putting the flask back into his pocket.

"I ain't no saint myself, Father." I wanted to urge him that this was no time to be arguing about these things, but I doubted he'd let go of the subject so easily. "But what has this to do with why Eve needs me or what they're looking for?"

"Johnny, you're a detective, a specialist in figuring out who's done what and why. This places you in contact with wicked people who do evil within the world. I'm worried about your soul, young man."

Eve pressed herself against me like we'd been lovers as she straightened my lapel. "I need you, Johnny."

Uncomfortable with being attacked by demons, by having a strange priest preach about my eternal soul, and with the erection that was pressing to join with her through our mutual clothes, I took a step back and wiped my face with my hands.

"How about we start with why we're here."

Eve bent over, picked up a small stone, and placed it on top of a tombstone with the word 'Jessica' carved onto its surface. "This is the grave of the last person I loved, a beautiful woman who gave me so much. She also left things for me in her will, along with a warning that some people would stop at nothing to lay their hands on them. My former boyfriend took those things when he stole from me, or at least I no longer have them. I don't know what he did with it all, nor why people would kill to possess them."

"Tell me about her." The more I could learn about her relationships, the easier it would be to untangle this mess.

"Actually, I brought you here so you could talk to her yourself."

"Look, Eve—" I began, but Father Donn interrupted.

"It's okay, Jessica. They're gone and can't hear what you want to say. Eve's brought Johnny and he's willing to listen."

"Thank you, Father, and a blessing to you and your parish."

I'd never heard a voice like that before. If speech

was music with the fragrance of flowers, that would approximate her words. I could feel them along my spine and never felt so alive with joy.

I turned to see a lovely ghost that stood over the grave. "It is a pleasure to meet you. How can I help Eve?"

"They don't know what they have, though they have it all, without knowing amongst all the things they have, one is no thing, and there is no other thing like the one no thing in all they have. Only you can retrieve them."

Riddles. Just what I should have expected. What did I do the other night, stumble into a postmodern fairytale? Was that it or was there more?

"How can a thing be no thing?" I asked, despairing of an answer.

"When it contains a soul. In this case, mine."

With that, she was gone; only the faint hint of flowers on the wind was left. Well, riddles or not, the only lead I had was blood on a dress. I looked over at Eve, on her knees, arms wrapped around herself as she sobbed. It had taken a lot out of her to bring me here. I looked around for Father Donn, expecting him to be her comforter, but he'd disappeared during the seance, so I had no recourse except to lift Eve to her feet and hold her while she sobbed.

"When we fought, she used to say to me that my nothings were her somethings, and her nothings were my somethings and that is why we were fighting."

"While I hate to bring up practical things, our only lead is the blood on that dress. We need to get back to the lab before it closes."

Nevertheless, she hadn't exactly answered most of my questions. Part of me felt wonderful; part of me felt like I was being had.

She rose, face mottled with tears. "You're right, let's go."

Chapter 3

A Fine Mess

The car, a black Cadillac right out of the sixties, waited for us in the parking lot. I'll give her credit; Eve opened the passenger door without pause and slid onto the seat. I did likewise, grinning like a kid in a candy store when I got in. I settled into the driver's seat and breathed deeply the new car smell. My smile was so broad it hurt when the key started the car. If I drove it to a used car lot and sold it, I could make a fortune as the car was showroom condition. Instead, I drove back to the lab using the traffic as an excuse not to think of cars, dresses, demons, and riddles. I might have wondered if I was dreaming it all, except for how raw my knuckles felt from the pummeling I'd given the demon. Surprisingly, my side felt as good as new, only the hole in my shirt remained of the attack.

After we'd parked and walked away from the car, I glanced back at it for one last lingering look. I'd always wanted a car like that, ever since my uncle's wedding when I was a kid and rode in the back of one. Well, better to have driven a classic caddy once than never at all. Eve looked like she was both annoyed and amused when I turned and skipped to catch up with her. Her mourning garb had changed back to the light gray sweats, like all the magic of the day had fled with the sun as clouds gathered.

"You liked that one."

"When I was six, my uncle got married. I was in the wedding party and rode in the back of a car just like that. I adored my uncle. He was cool: drove a motorcycle and was a captain in the army. I always wanted to do the things he did, especially drive a '67 caddy."

"Johnny, sometimes you surprise me. Is this the building?" she pointed.

"Yes, let's go in."

The building's halls and stairwells hadn't gotten any cooler in the hours that had transpired since we'd dropped off her dress, so we were quite the sweaty pair when we got to the door to their suite. Like with everything else, the sweat looked good on her. Suddenly her face was hidden behind a long black veil. She was dressed in mourning again. How that happened with me by her side looking at her I'll never know.

I turned the knob and knew my mistake as I heard a second click. Heat followed by a flash of blinding light. Eve and I were both thrown backwards.

I woke moments later. Eve lay senseless by my side. Around us was the debris of the bomb shattered door, but not a cut on either of us. I rose and raced into the inferno, covering my nose and mouth with a handkerchief. The fire was licking the walls of the waiting room with the remnants of the bomb hanging from the side of the doorway I'd entered through. I kicked down the inner door to the lab, swallowing bile when I found Gladys' bullet-ridden body on the floor. The walls, monitors, computers, microscopes were all shattered by bullets.

I was no fool. I knew that the folks in the lab could have been working on a mob case and word got out. I also knew what my gut was telling me as I stared at the body of a woman who once loved me. I also knew that our still being alive was yet another cryptic clue to what was going on. I didn't need to remember fighting demons to know that I was next. I felt Eve take my hand in hers.

"Johnny, we've got to call the police."

"Yeah, but while we wait for them, we're going to search the lab and the bodies. If I know Gladys, she found a way to hide the evidence and I want us to find it, not the cops." I dialed 911 and gave them the skinny. "They'll be here in under ten minutes. We've got to work fast."

I found a box of gloves that wasn't splattered with blood and pulled out two pairs. Tossing a pair to Eve, I slid on the other and went to work.

"What are we looking for?"

"Thumb drive. That's what they've used in the past. Also, your dress and any samples they may have taken, but I expect those are long gone."

I wiped tears off my cheeks. I knew the shaking in my hands was anger, not grief. I had to have this under control or I'd be useless with a pistol.

"Found one!"

My relief flooded me with tears that broke anew along with my voice. "Where?"

"Let's just say I hope this thing is water resistant."

"When we get to my place, we'll put it in a baggie with some dry rice. Works every time."

"You mean she—"

"No, I've no idea what she did, and I really don't want to know. Just I've had issues with electronics getting wet. While my gut tells me you found the stick with the evidence we need, we should keep looking to see if there are any others."

The police and fire came in with sirens blaring so we had time to get rid of the gloves before they got up the stairs. They took us downtown for questioning, which took hours and went nowhere. Thankfully, the cops in this precinct didn't know either of us and had no agenda against private dicks. We told them nothing of the demons, changing cars and dresses, or of the thumb drive.

After they let us go, as we got to the car—an old Honda—Eve said, "Look, Johnny, I'm no fool. I know that no money gets a man to put his life on the line for a client."

She was missing something very important. "I owe Gladys that we nail their balls to the floor. Now, we can't go to my place, or my office. They're likely watching both. We've got to go into hiding and get a computer so we can read what is on that drive." I never liked it when the folks I was investigating knew more than I did. They knew who I was, who I was doing business with. They certainly knew by now my address and where I kept an office.

****

Thankfully the hotel I found for us had a computer available to its guests. The thumb drive was quite dry by the time we tried it, and it had the information we'd hoped for. We had the name and address of the muscle who had tried to kill Eve the other night, as well as the hospital he checked into after the fight.

His name was Sean Hanrahan, professional muscle with a rap sheet as long as the night. What I found fascinating was that he was a mixed martial arts champion. Reading his fight record, he had never lost a bout, yet Eve had bested him the other night. This was important somehow.

I gave the hospital a quick call, but he'd checked out earlier that day. I printed the information and then headed up the elevator to our room. I remembered that neither of us had any night clothing or toiletries, went back down to get us some toothbrushes and toothpaste, as well as combs and brushes. I figured we needed a more permanent location, but this would do us for the night. When I got back into the room, Eve was naked, on the bed, watching TV.

I showed her the supplies I picked up and went into the bathroom to brush my teeth, hoping the focus on simple grooming would reduce the swelling in my pants. I also wanted to get out of my clothing and didn't want her to think I was either hoping or presuming anything. Trouble was my anatomy was.

I stepped out of the bathroom, and she got off of the bed and entered it. While she brushed and washed, I undressed, putting my clothing on the desk. I then grabbed a pillow and spare blanket, laying them on the floor. I think if I'd liked her less, I'd have chosen to join her in the bed.

"Well, I'll be, Johnny. I'm flattered."

"Sorry about that."

"It's an occupational hazard. Look, Johnny, I know you want to be all business, and a gentleman, but please share the bed with me. I need to be held."

After the day we had shared, I shouldn't have been surprised. I just never thought my embrace would offer comfort to a woman who could defeat an MMA champion. "You don't mind this thing poking you?"

"Oddly enough, that will help."

"All right. One more thing. I have very vivid dreams, which I use in my case work. Having you in my bed may impact those dreams—and my work."

"I'll take that risk."

I climbed into bed. She turned off the light and snuggled into me. I could feel her breathing change as she fell asleep rather quickly. It took me somewhat longer; I was far too aware of her, her scent, her touch, and each place I rested my hand that wasn't under her pillow felt too forward. However, exhaustion took me all too soon, and I slept.

****

I strode through a ruin, tall grasses growing from the tops of ancient red brick arches, mostly collapsed. I walked a cracked red brick street with the shorter grass growing through the crannies tickling my bare feet. This made me look down to see that the rest of me was as bare as my feet. I came upon a woman whose face was turned away from me. Her skirt was rags, and she wore nothing else, though she held up an ornate silver mirror. I tried to call out to her, but my voice had no sound. In the air near to her was a silver necklace strewn with diamonds in the shape of a bird with wings spread, and a thick diamond bracelet.

I stepped nearer to the woman, coming closer to both the necklace and bracelet in the process. I was not surprised that they floated; things do that in dreams. What surprised me was that they pulsed. I could feel it as I neared them. I went to touch the necklace, but the pulsing was too intense. It had a heat to it, so I pulled my hand back. I tried to touch the bracelet next, and as my hand moved closer, I could tell that from a distance the pulsating seemed to come from both. Close up, only the necklace pulsed. I touched the bracelet and felt myself falling.

****

I woke to find that I'd had an orgasm all over Eve's back. As she seemed to still be sleeping, I rose to get a towel with the idiotic idea of being able to clean her up without waking her. I grabbed a towel without needing a light, so I jumped when she touched me on my hip from behind.

"Where did you get this?" she asked.

"Huh? The towel rack."

"Not the towel silly, but that is a thoughtful gesture. Could you wipe me?"

She flicked on the light and turned her back to me. As I wiped her dry, she held over her shoulder the same bracelet that I'd touched in my dream. "I was asking you where you got this bracelet from."

"I had a dream where I walked naked through ruins, saw a woman with sandy hair who wore only a torn shift which barely covered her legs. She was holding a mirror to the sky. Next to her in the air was a necklace and the bracelet you now wear. I tried to take the necklace, but it was too hot. I was able to touch the bracelet and woke up to find myself creating a mess on you. Sorry about that."

"Don't worry about it. With how often I've been naked around you, I think you're on a bit of a short fuse when it comes to desire. It's not as if you were raping me or anything, you just had a wet dream. You guys all have them. This bracelet matches one that Jessica had left me in her will. It was one of the things stolen from me. Please describe the mirror and the necklace."

I described them to her: the shapes, that they were all silver, the necklace with diamonds and shaped like a

39

bird, and the oval mirror. "You don't think this bracelet was hers?"

"I do, and I think that one of those three objects is the one that Father Donn was talking about. Did the pulsing have a rhythm to it?"

"Come to think of it, yes, it did. The rhythm of a heart."

"Tell me about the woman who held up the mirror."

"The oddest thing was that she wasn't looking at herself in that mirror. The mirror itself was blank, as if whatever it was reflecting had no shape. The woman had light brown hair which flowed loosely from her head, was about a hand taller than you, wider hips and fuller breasts with dark pink nipples pointing out instead of centered."

"That sounds so much like Jessica," she said. "I wish she'd spoken, then we'd know for certain as you heard her voice earlier in the cemetery and would know it if you heard it again."

"In the morning we'll go after that thug you fought. Hopefully we'll get some information out of him." I ran my hand over my face and stifled a yawn.

Eve echoed my yawn. "Let's get some sleep. Maybe you'll have another dream, and frankly, I'm tired."

I decided that I would try once more to return the situation to a more professional one. "You want me to sleep on the floor now that I've—"

My voice dropped off as she took my penis in her hand.

"No, silly. You're just showing me how much you want me in a deep primitive way. It's sweet, but with demons, bombs, and being jumped in the night by thugs trying to kill me, I'd rather you were in my bed. I couldn't abide my dreams if I was alone."

"Okay, but I can't promise that the same or worse won't happen while I sleep."

"Poor Johnny, you're trying so hard to remain a gentleman."

Like hell I was, but I let her think that. I felt like a rapist who had been forgiven. I don't recommend the experience. I knew this was important for understanding what the hell was going on, but I didn't have enough context to know why or how.

She turned off the light and started walking back to bed, still holding me so I had to follow rather closely. She had a firm grip.

"I'm glad you've figured out that despite how frequently I've been naked around you, I really don't want sex right now, but I'm being a bit cruel. While I'm comfortable being naked around people and think nothing of it, you're not. There is nothing wrong with where you're at, nor where I'm at, but it would be wrong of me not to help you relieve the stress of it all. I'm going to do something for you if you're okay with that, and then we'll get some sleep."

That I was okay with.

****

I had no more dreams that night and woke refreshed from a knocking at the door.

"Housekeeping."

"Please come back later," I called out.

I looked at the time. The alarm clock showed only 8:30, and I remembered putting the DO NOT DISTURB on the door, so I figured something was amiss. Eve started to stir as I rose from the bed. I put my finger on her lips and then whispered into her ear that housekeeping was at the door, hoping that she'd draw the same conclusions that I'd done. We both rose and dressed silently.

She'd slept with the bracelet on her wrist. Perhaps what she'd told me was actually the truth for a change.

Once we were both dressed, we went to the door. The space was too narrow; we couldn't easily position ourselves to properly respond to an attack. I motioned for Eve to stand in the restroom, while I peered through the peep hole. I couldn't see anyone. Knowing that if anyone was there, they'd have the advantage, I opened the door and stepped into the hall. Three doors down I saw the housekeeping cart; the housekeeper must have been in that room. Someone had removed the DO NOT DISTURB sign from our door.

Feeling rather absurd, I motioned for Eve to follow me. We made our way to the fire escape stairs and walked the three flights down. As the hotel had a free breakfast, we had some weak coffee, watery eggs, and toast in silence. I hoped no one would notice us if we didn't make a sound.

When we were both finished with the coffee, we strode to the front desk. After we were checked out and in the car, a 1970s Corvette today, she said, "I can't shake this feeling that we're about to be attacked."

"I'm the same way. Must have something to do with how yesterday went."

"Instead of going after Hanrahan, could we go shopping, pick up some things?"

Eve wasn't smiling, not even a fake smile. She wasn't flirting to get her way. Was she serious for a change?

"Afraid?" I asked.

"Somewhat. Also, I'd like some clothing that doesn't change every two minutes. I mean look at me."

I glanced at her and saw what she meant. She was in a high school cheerleader's outfit. "Cute, but it does draw attention."

"Yes, but that isn't my real problem with this particular outfit. Believe it or not, I once wore this or its cousin, and I'd rather not think back to those days."

"There is a story behind that."

"Yes, but not for here and now, and perhaps not ever. The other thing is that I want an outfit that isn't changing on me on its own. Believe it or not, I do not enjoy being naked in public, and want some control on how I present myself."

Evasions instead of lies? A small step in the right direction? "Okay, we'll buy you some clothing."

I couldn't blame her but suspected that the stress I heard in her voice was more related to the unspoken. I drove to the nearest mall, parked, and was about to get out when she whispered, "Put the car in gear and get us out of here."

"But I thought—" I said as I restarted the car.

"I'm naked again, and last time that happened—"

She didn't complete the thought as suddenly a demon stood on my hood. I put the car into reverse, slammed on the gas, hit the brakes, and sped away from the demon which had fallen off the hood.

"Well, that is one thing they do with consistency," I quipped as I wove my way through traffic.

"What is that?" she asked.

"Fall." I pulled the wheel to the right, swerving to avoid an oncoming truck. "I think you had better let me pick the destinations and at random. Two out of the three

43

times you told me where to go we were attacked by demons."

"I think that one was just being opportunistic. I imagine demons hang out at malls. Where better to tempt people?"

I chuckled. I wanted to quip 'strip clubs' but decided that she might be hurt from that jibe. "I think I've figured out a place where I can get you a better outfit without the demons."

"Thanks, as the stuff I'm wearing has a nasty sense of humor."

I stole a glance. The cheerleader's outfit had been replaced with a bridal gown. That bought my silence. I drove to the St. Vincent de Paul at 525 Fifth Street, found parking nearby and helped Eve out of the car, as the long skirt was hard to manage. Thankfully the rain that had threatened all day continued to hold off, as it would have ruined the dress.

We did get some stares as we shopped, and it took some time before we found things in her size. Thankfully they had a changing room. Eve slipped in and I paced. I'd never been good with domestic things, and I'd never felt more married than waiting for her to come out of the changing room. Emerge she did, still in the wedding gown, holding a stack of clothes, but all I could focus on were her tears.

"What gives?"

"Let's just get out of here. I'll explain while you drive."

I paid for the clothing and we got back into my car, now a Le Barron. It took a few minutes to get the fullness of her skirt into the car, but the moment the door was closed, she was dressed in the gray sweats I'd purchased the other day. Once again the transformation happened so quickly that it was as if I'd blinked and she was dressed differently.

I got into the car on the driver's side and just started driving, no clear destination in my mind. Eve was still crying, and I felt it best not to ask questions, but to give her some space. As for me, I was trying not to dwell on the expenses of this case nor the lack of leads. I'd not been paying close attention to the road I'd been driving, so when I came through an overpass and didn't recognize the area, I was not surprised. San Francisco was big enough that I knew I didn't know it all, but that wasn't the problem.

The foliage, the colors, the horizon, the weather were all wrong. There were tall buildings gleaming in the sun in front of us and I knew that the downtown didn't have any of those buildings. I checked my mirrors. The traffic behind me and before me was light enough where I figured I could make a U-turn. I slowed slightly, waited, and then spun the wheel while hitting the brake. We spun around and I hit the gas before the traffic caught up with us, now heading the other way on the road.

"What the hell was that for?" Her voice was hard, no trace of tears.

"Look out the back and tell me where we are."

"Boston."

"What?" I think my voice went up an octave.

"That's what I see. I'd know that stuck-up place in my sleep."

"I'm trying to see if I can get us back to San Francisco. See that bridge up a-head? I drove under it and here we were. Let's see if going under it the other way gets us back in San Francisco."

I hit the gas hard. Thankfully on the other side were the hills of the city by the bay. The long-threatened rain splattered lightly on the windshield.

"Wow," she said. "That was bizarre."

"I wonder if our search to get back your things will take us to Boston and we just missed an opportunity."

"Perhaps. Perhaps not. All I know is that when we find Hanrahan, I may take out some of my frustrations on him. Johnny, I need you to just let me tell you some things and not question them."

I was getting very good at not questioning considering that my business depends on me asking questions, but then again, many of her answers had been bare-faced lies.

"Shoot."

"The clothing we bought in the thrift store was all mine. It has my laundry mark on it. The store tags also show the date of donation, and the date of each price adjustment. They've had this stuff in their store for over six months, but I remember wearing some of these items last week.

"The wedding dress that I seemed to be wearing until a little while ago was Jessica's. She was buried in it. That cheerleader dress, last time I wore it I was molested by my coach, and when I told my parents, my drunk mother threw me out, called me a slut and that I'd ruined myself and the family reputation. There is something very troubling going on here, and a lot of it is very hurtful. Now I'm not a selfish bitch who thinks her inner pain is worse than yours, or poor Gladys. I'm heartbroken over her. I'll lay it on you straight, if it wasn't for your dream last night, I'd run from all of this, find myself a new gig, get started in life again. I'm depending on you in ways that are worse than unfair, and I've not much hope that I can recover any of my funds. Not now, not after seeing that the people who stole from me can bend time. Despite everything, I'm no longer a whore who pays her debts with sex. That is not what last night was all about, and I know damn well that even if you were the kind of man who would accept sex for payment, what we did last night would not begin to cover your losses in helping me, nor the loss of your friend. I know you don't work for free. Are you still on the case?"

I didn't reply right away. I felt she was owed my silence, my thoughts. Frankly, I needed time to think. She was right. I don't work for free and last I checked being paid with sex didn't pay my bills in any event. Bills I had, and plenty. Still, I had recovered some of her clothing, and some of her lost jewelry. While I had no idea how I'd done these things or if I'd be able to continue, I was already out hundreds. I was also very used to reality not being logical. My only hope for reimbursement was to keep helping her. I could put it that way, and part of me wanted to, keep this cold and professional. The truth was far from what I wanted to say and, right then I wanted only the truth. I owed Gladys.

"You've just told me some things that you'd only confide to a friend. Friends help each other out, without expecting to be paid. I know you started out as a customer and I took the job without a fixed fee. I also know that somehow I've helped you recover something precious of Jessica's, as well as some of your own clothing. To back out now would be throwing your trust in me in your face.

"I've no idea how we're going to overcome thieves that can stash their goods in the past, and demonic fiends intent on your death, but I intend to keep my drunken promise. Besides, I owe Gladys."

That sounded much nobler than how I felt when I started speaking, but somehow saying it made me feel better, like I became my inner ten-year-old, fighting dragons with a cardboard sword.

Chapter 4

Three Break Ins

It felt like the right thing to do, so I drove back to the theater where I'd been waiting for Jack the Fish, telling Eve all about why I was trying to catch that slippery bastard as I drove. I paid for two tickets, a bag of popcorn, and two large sodas. The smell of the butter as we walked down the aisle was making me hungry. We made our way through the already dark but mostly empty theater, the show already in progress. We sat and watched, though I would occasionally glance at the empty booth where I'd seen my mark in the dream.

"Softly!" said a tall dark-skinned man with blue dreadlocks sitting in a balcony opposite where the blue haired actress had been in the last show I'd seen in this theater. Eve passed me the bag of popcorn we'd been sharing. On stage a mirror was lowered down, showing in its reflection the audience. Once it rested on the stage floor, a short young woman wearing a brown dress with lace trim, with a matching short brown cape wrapped around her shoulders, the white collar of her blouse pristinely capping an outfit that made her appear as if she'd stepped out of an earlier century emerged from the mirror and went to the microphone. She started to dance while someone else we could not see sang a smoky jazz number in a language I couldn't catch but was likely

French.

"Has Jack the Fish showed?" Eve hissed in my ear.

I shook my head, and whispered back, "Let's get out of here. I need a smoke."

We both rose, Eve munching on more popcorn as we left the theater. The city had cooled with the rain, so I draped my trench coat onto Eve's shoulders as we made our way through the paper strewn street to where we'd left my car. This time we found a Volkswagen Thing with the top up. I slid the key into the ignition and the car started. Eve rested her head on my shoulder as I drove through the cones of light until we neared my place.

"You were right, that was an unusual show."

"Yeah. It runs twice a week. My fink swears that Jack the Fish loves it and goes frequently. I've never seen him there, except in my dream."

"That girl at the end, the one who stepped through a mirror, looked right out of the Edwardian era."

"Edwardian?"

"Yeah, dummy, that is what they call the first two decades of the twentieth century, named after King Edward of England."

I parked and we walked the two short blocks to my apartment building. I didn't intend for us to pass the night there, I just wanted to grab some of my things. If nothing else, I wanted a shirt without a tear in the side. We passed a couple of gals having sex against one of the lamp posts in the gathering fog. "Lovely neighborhood you live in," said Eve.

"How'd you not notice when you came through my window?"

"The way I'd come was not so scenic. I have to admire their style."

"Let's get you upstairs before they notice they have an audience."

The walk up the stairs was somehow more pleasant with her hand in mine, until we reached my door. It had been kicked in.

I stepped through the open doorway to find slashed furniture, stuffing pulled from the couch all over the floor, fabric torn from the bed in ribbons mixed with the stuffing, and everything in the refrigerator, which hadn't been much, on the floor.

"I love their redecorating," said Eve. "Place looks so much nicer."

I went straight to the bath, pulled the lid off the tank and reached in. Thankfully I found the pouch I'd taped there. "They missed this," I said as I opened the sandwich baggie and pulled out a stack of bills. I then went to my other hiding places and found all the cash I'd hid about the place.

"Do you think they marked the bills?" she asked.

"Not likely. I'd sealed each baggie with super glue in a particular pattern. None of that has been broken and would have been hard to duplicate after they'd broken it. I think they were looking for what you have on your wrist or in your hair."

"Could be. Likely now that you mention it. If that is the case, we'll need to make certain that Hanrahan doesn't see it on me when we take him down. The question will be how."

"You could wear a jacket and a head scarf," I suggested.

"Unless the clothing changes to a strapless gown. I guess we'll have to make certain that Hanrahan doesn't tell anyone what he sees. Is there anything else you want to try to salvage from this mess, or should we go?"

"First, I want to grab a shirt if any survived their destruction of my things. I also should let my landlord know about the break in, as well as file a police report, but we don't really have time for that. I know, I'll give my landlord a call and have him contact the police." The last thing I wanted was to deal with the police for the third time in three days. Right then and there, all I wanted was to sleep. "But not until we've gotten some rest. Let's go find a hotel."

Eve said, "Actually, if you don't mind, I want to go to your office first."

"It's three in the morning."

"I know, I'm tired too, but I've got a hunch I want to check out."

Following hunches was my business, but they were usually my hunches. One of the first lessons of working with dames is that they get their way, and the earlier you give into them, the less painful it is.

****

When we got to my floor, to my surprise neither the glass had been broken nor the door kicked in. The lock showed no sign of being picked. I took out my keys and we entered. Everything was as I'd left it the other day. The back room which I shared with my partner, Jim, was the typical mess. From the notes pinned to Jim's cork board, he was after a deadbeat who wouldn't pay child support. All the notes on mine showed my attempts to nail Jack the Fish.

I turned to Eve. "So, what were you hoping to find?" I'd missed something, something important that she'd spotted.

"I was wrong. They've not been here, but then

again, until now, we'd not been here either. Johnny, call your partner and receptionist, tell them not to come into the office. Tell them your case has turned dangerous and they've bombed the forensics lab and tore apart your room, just don't tell them about me. I've got a feeling that the folks who are after me will show up soon after we leave."

"It's just my partner. My receptionist quit last week. You know how to use a gun?"

"No, why?"

"We're not leaving. We're going to wait for them, in here."

"Johnny, please, it's too dangerous."

"That's what they want us to think. I followed your hunch, now we follow mine. I want you to hide behind the desk. When I call for you, I'm not going to use your name. You okay with that?"

"Yes. Call me Ann."

I wondered if that was her real name as I settled in to wait. It took a few long hours, but just before dawn, I heard glass break. They had arrived. From the broken glass, I knew they'd not come planning on planting a bomb, and they had the subtlety of a toddler. Revolver in my hand, I stood to one side of my door. Eve I stationed behind my desk on the floor. With any luck I'd handle them without them knowing Eve was here.

I watched as the knob to my door turned and waited until it opened far enough to grab the arm, pull, twist until his arm was behind him with my gun to his head. He smelled of old spice and fear.

"I've a notion to plug you just because of Gladys," I snarled.

He tried to kick me and failed. "Please, I have no

idea what you're talking about."

I twisted his arm some more. "Then who do you work for?"

"Drysdale," he groaned.

"Tell me more."

"Sam Drysdale, runs a rare collectibles business. He told me you'd stolen a rare bracelet from him, and I was to take it back."

I let up on the pressure of my gun against his head, but kept the tip touching him. "This the first time you work for Drysdale?"

"Yes, and the last. I had no idea it would be so dangerous. I mean who is in their office at this hour? It's as if you were waiting for me. What is this, a setup?"

I pushed the gun hard against his head, ignoring his wince of pain. "I ask the questions. You give the answers. Got it?"

"You're the boss."

"You work for him full time or is this a freelance gig?"

"Freelance. My buddy thought it would be a good opportunity to get in with a major operation."

"What did Drysdale send you here to collect?"

"A thumb drive and a bracelet. He gave me a photo of the bracelet and told me to collect any thumb drives I could find. If you let me reach into my breast pocket, I'll get you the photo."

He started to move his hand to his chest. I said, "Just keep your hand at your side and don't try anything. Were you the guy who broke into my apartment?"

"No, he sent two other guys for that job, but they found nothing, so he sent me here."

Like hell he did. No one tells their staff dirt like that.

I pushed the gun hard against him again. "Where were you to take the goods if you found them."

"His place out in Rinconada Hills near San Jose."

"Give me the full address."

"121 El Porton, Los Gatos."

"Now, sit down."

"What?"

"Sit. Over there." I pointed his head to a row of waiting chairs.

I kept my gun on him as he went for one of the chairs. Once he was sitting, I said, "Hands on the arm rests, and keep them there. Ann, you'll find cuffs in my desk's top right drawer. Cuff him to the chair, legs and arms."

"Heh, that ain't right. You can't leave me like this."

"You better hope that what you told me is the truth," I said as Eve cuffed him.

I picked up the desk phone and dialed. When the desk clerk at the precinct picked up, I said, "This is John Talon over on eighth street."

"Hello Johnny. Lose any more bodies?"

"No, I didn't lose any more bodies. Someone broke into my office. I caught him in the act." I put the gun into my coat pocket after the last cuff clicked shut.

"You're in your office at five in the morning?"

"Yeah, isn't every gumshoe? Anyway, send over a crew to pick him up. He's harmless, but I need him kept off the street for a few days."

"We'll send a car right over."

"Good. I'm not sticking around. Just let yourselves in, would ya? He broke the door, so feel free to hold him on breaking and entering."

"You're not afraid of him walking?"

I gave him a once over, Eve had cuffed him hand and foot to the chair. "No, he'll be here."

****

Tired as I was, I drove to Drysdale's place to get the lay of the land. We found his place in a gated community, so I parked about a half mile away. The rain had stopped, so I figured I'd hop the fence and walk. Eve decided to stay with the car, so I left her with the keys, half of our cash, and instructions to bail on me if I wasn't back in two hours. I was able to move fast and quietly, slipping around the gate instead of fence hopping. His house was no larger than many, and like all the others it had the standard warning about security surveillance. Despite the lateness of the hour, many lights were on, and few curtains drawn, so I was able to get a good glimpse of the inside. I crept up close to each window and took pictures of the interior until I came to a room that was occupied.

In it were two men and a woman who was naked and bound with her wrists above her, tied to the ceiling. The two men were taking turns smacking the woman on her rear and back with what looked to be floggers. I'd no idea if one of the men or the woman was Drysdale, or if the act was consensual, but with each swing my anger at the situation rose. If what they were doing to that woman was not consensual, then I needed to put a stop to it.

I went to the rear door and gave it a try. Locked, of course. Likely, however, the alarm was not active, and I doubted that they had cameras, as I'd not seen any. I broke out my picks and a pair of close-fitting driving gloves. It took me about fifteen minutes before I had the door open. I put the picks away, took out my revolver, and stepped inside. The place smelled of whiskey. I followed the sound of muffled screams until I stood in the doorway of the same living room I'd seen from outside. The woman's back had angry red welts on it, and with each swing she screamed through what must be a gag of some kind.

I held my piece at the ready and said, "The next man who hits that woman loses his hand."

The men turned to face me; their faces were red as her back.

I braced myself to shoot. "Drop those whips and put your hands where I can see them."

"Who the fuck are you?" one demanded, but they both dropped the whips.

"I am me, myself, and I. Right now, if you want to save your miserable hides, you're going to untie that woman from the ceiling and ungag her."

The one man looked at the other who nodded. They both started to rush me, but a quick retort from my pistol stopped them both, one of them now bleeding badly from his shoulder. The other backed up and untied the woman. The moment her arms were free, she kneed him in the crotch, hard. He collapsed in a groan. Obviously, it hadn't been consensual.

"I recommend you use that rope to tie them both up," I said. I made certain that neither of the men moved while she tied their ankles and hands.

"You're not going to leave us like this. I'm shot; I need a doctor," groaned the man on the floor.

"You're the ape who chose to rush me knowing I had a piece in my hand pointing right at you. Didn't your father ever tell you never point a gun at someone if you don't intend to use it? Probably the same way he never told you that real men don't hit women. If you're lucky,

57

your friend here will get out of his rope with enough time to get you the help you'll need. If not, I'll add it to the list of things I'm going to hell for."

The woman had finished her knot work and stood, and I caught a glimpse of her face through her hair plastered to her bruised, tear-strewn cheeks. She reminded me of someone, but her face was too covered by the hair and bruises for me to figure out who.

"I imagine what they were doing to you was far from consensual," I asked.

She shook her head, reaching behind her to undo the gag and screaming in frustration. Apparently, it was locked on.

"I'll cut the lock off later. Do you have some clothing to put on?"

She picked up a pile of rags from the floor. They'd cut it off of her.

"We'll get you something. Come, let's get out of here."

"Hey, what about us?"

"Lady, did they kidnap you?"

She shook her head.

"Did you agree to being tied up?"

Again, she nodded.

"Did you agree to being whipped?"

This time she vigorously shook her head.

"Okay boys, all I'd have you on is assault. Under the circumstances, I doubt much that she'll be interested in pressing charges. If you two can't figure out how to help each other out of those knots before the loss of blood becomes an issue, I'll be surprised."

I gestured for the woman to follow me. The moment we were out of the room, I whispered, "Show me on your fingers how tightly you made those knots, ten for hard, one for easy."

She held up ten fingers.

"Good," I whispered. "We're going to search the house for two things: one is something to cover you in, the other is something of value that a friend needs."

I found her a coat that hung loosely on her, so that it didn't touch her raw back. I also found their safe. I figured we didn't have much longer before they were free, but I would give it a quick go.

No luck there.

With a nervous glance at my watch, I got us both out of there. I'd have to come back for the safe.

As she was barefoot, we had to go carefully on our way back to the car. I kept glancing back, but I could see no sign of pursuit. When we got to the car, I was surprised to find the old Ford Torino that I'd originally purchased, not what we'd driven earlier.

I turned to the woman and said, "Hold still. I'm going to get that gag off of you and then get you some place safe. Then we'll see how I can help you."

As I picked the lock, I heard the car door open.

I took the ball gag off of her as Eve walked over so she stood in front of the other woman. For the first time, I noticed how much that woman looked like Eve: an Eve I'd never been able to picture, one battered and abused, a victim. That wasn't an Eve I thought she could ever be.

The Eve I knew, dressed in the gray yoga pants and shirt I'd bought her, took the hands of the other and said, "Remember this man. When you see him next, it will be at work, and he'll be drunk. He's a detective, a surreal detective. He'll promise to help you and give you an address. Take him up on the offer."

"But how—"

Eve put a finger over that question and said, "I don't know how. Just trust me and do it."

The Eve I knew, or the one I thought I knew stepped back and the other was no longer there. Eve came over to me and said, "In the past, six years ago, right after I said what I said to myself, the two of us and the car faded and I was alone, battered, in just a coat, but no longer frightened. I found I had enough money in the coat pockets to get me home. It took a couple of weeks for my back and face to heal enough for me to go back to work. I never forgot what I told myself, and when you came into the club, I knew that not only could I trust you, but I had to."

That did explain a few things. "Who was the jerk I shot?"

"Not Drysdale. Drysdale always called him Murphy. I've no idea if that was his real name." She leaned her head against the side window.

"How'd you get mixed up in all that."

She yawned. "Look, we're both tired. Drive me to a hotel and I'll tell you the whole thing after some sleep."

I got us to the hotel but had to wake her to get her out of the car. I wasn't much more awake than her and fell asleep the moment my head hit the pillow.

****

I found myself in a large hall, mostly empty. To one side was a group of standing women, all wearing broad brimmed hats with large colorful plumes, but nothing else. On the other side were men, all dressed in dark suits with bow ties, except one, a bald man wearing a brown coat over his suit. He held up a seashell for the inspection of the other men. On the far end of the wall were three large arched windows. Light blue stained glass panes hung along the top of the arch, with a row of darker blue and round glass right below, let in enough light that the gas lamps hanging from the ceiling were not lit. Against that far wall was a table with a number of men sitting, talking to two men who leaned over them, all ignoring the one naked woman who sat on the floor to the side of this table in front of the door, her arms held above her head, wrists shackled. While I wanted to spend my time with the women, I moved over to the men as I saw Jack the Fish among them.

To my surprise, he came over to me and put his arm around my shoulder. "Johnny, so glad you came. I've heard you've been looking for me."

As is often the case with dreams, I found I couldn't speak.

Jack the Fish didn't seem to mind, or notice. "Have you seen the nautilus? It is a beautiful specimen."

He drew me over, and I got a good look at the shell. Much like the necklace in my prior dream, it pulsed, I could feel the heat from it as I stood there.

The man holding it saw me and said, "It looks smooth, no? In fact, it is so coarse that if I were to rub it, my fingers would bleed. Here, touch it and see."

He handed me the fossil and the moment my hands cradled it, the setting shifted. I found myself back in the cemetery, standing next to Jessica's headstone. Of course, I was naked.

A soft breeze: I was covered in goose pimples. I placed the shell on her headstone so that I could wrap my arms around myself and found that the world started to rush at me, hotter and faster toward a noise and a light.

Chapter 5

San Francisco's Finest

I picked up my cell phone from the nightstand. "Johnny here."

"Hello Johnny. It's Detective O'Neil. Since you're working for Eve, we need you to bring her by the precinct later today."

That woke me up. What was I, her lawyer? "Yeah, and just why is that?"

"I found a message on the back of the corpse. I think it might be best if she read it herself."

I sat up. I'd want to see that too. "Okay, I'll bring her by later. Just ask for the desk clerk?"

"No, ask for me. I'll stick by my desk today and get caught up with my paperwork while waiting for you."

"That important?"

"Yeah, it is. Try to get here as soon as possible will ya?"

"Will do."

The copper was being nice, he almost said please. I could hear it in his voice. Part of me wanted to coax it out of him, part of me needed to relieve myself. I decided the second was more important than the first.

I hung up and only then did it dawn on me that not only was the light on in the bathroom, but I could hear the water running. Eve must be in the shower. Hoping she wouldn't mind me using the facilities after the number of times she'd walked in on me, I opened the door to the bathroom and slid in. While the shower was running, Eve wasn't in the stall. She was on the can, cradling her head in her hands. Soap lather clung to her and her hair was tangled in shampoo. She'd been crying.

"Sorry, I didn't—"

"No, it's okay." She rose and washed her face at the sink. Having to go really badly, I sat and let my water out, "Thanks, I needed to use this pretty badly."

"Did you have another dream?"

"Yes. How did you guess?"

She held out her hand to me, one of the fingers now wore a diamond ring. "I noticed this while washing my hair."

"I didn't see no diamond ring in my dream. Was that yours or Jessica's?"

"Let's get dressed and get some breakfast, and then I'll tell you."

That was the first sensible thing I'd encountered that morning. She stepped back into the shower to finish rinsing, so I told her about the phone call from the cops.

"Do you think it could be a trap?" she shouted over the water.

I actually hadn't considered it but did so quickly. "I don't think so. I think if someone was pressuring Greg to lure us in, he'd have found a way to clue me in."

The faucet squeaked as she turned off the water. "Hand me a towel, will ya?"

I opened the door and slid her a towel, trying to look elsewhere. Despite her reassurances, I was none too pleased with myself right then and needed to reduce the stimulus to my libido. I could tell from the soreness of my penis that I'd done something as we slept, but she'd not mentioned it and I wasn't going to ask.

After I'd showered and dressed, we went down to the hotel's lobby for their free breakfast. The supermarket bagels weren't so bad toasted, but the coffee was excellent. There were a few other folks down there, a family with kids making a racket and a few business folks reading the paper while sipping coffee.

We each grabbed our grub and settled down to a table as far away from the kids as we could, relying on the loud television news show to drown out our conversation. As we ate, I told her of my dream. She was thrilled to hear that I'd left the nautilus shell on Jessica's tomb stone.

"That shell was one of her favorite keepsakes. Let's go to the cemetery later to see if it is actually there."

"Think we'll encounter those demons again?"

"If we do, we'll be prepared for them this time. So, what do you want to know about my ring?"

I nodded as I took a tall sip of coffee. "Was it hers as well?"

"This is the ring she gave me when we got engaged. Thank you for bringing it back to me. I had to take it off when I danced, or the men wouldn't let me dance for them. We kept all of our things in lockers in our dressing room. One night, after I'd finished my shift, I went back to find someone had forced mine open and taken everything. The management checked the security tapes but found nothing. All the other girls watched it with me, horrified as nothing opened the door to my locker, as my things disappeared into nothing. Some of the girls were convinced after that that the place was haunted."

"I've no recollection of getting the ring in my

dream, but I've learned that there are connections between things. I let myself follow those connections. They lead to where I need to be."

"You were holding my wrists pretty tightly while you took me. After you came, your one hand reached up and caressed my left hand. I was too focused on the lower part of me to be paying too much attention, but I think that is when you put the ring on me."

"What did I do this time?"

She reached across the table and took my right hand in both of hers. "Let's talk about that some other time. I know you're asleep when you're doing this to me, and I know that each time you bring me back some of the most precious things that were stolen from me. Don't worry about what you're doing; you're hardly in control and I could stop you if I wanted to. Please stop worrying about it. I already told you, I'll let you know if you cross a line."

"I'll try," I lied. "So, we've gotten you some of your clothing, a bracelet, and a ring, but I must be honest with you, I've no idea how." I'd never been more baffled in a case, and I'd little sense of how to proceed. My dreams had always helped me on a case, but never like this.

"Nor do I, but I suspect the sex is part of it somehow. While you're having sex with me, you're reaching through space and time."

I immediately thought of the time we drove through the overpass and found ourselves in Boston. "We did that yesterday while driving, twice, without the sex."

"All I know is that I'm inclined to experiment, so don't be surprised if I get frisky."

With the constant flirtation, frequent nudity, and the many times her hand has drifted onto my lap while I drove, I couldn't imagine what she thought was frisky. "I should drive us to the precinct."

She let go of my hand. "That's my Johnny, always the gentleman. Yes, we should get there as soon as possible."

"When we're done there, I'd also like to find that overpass again, and we definitely need to get back to Drysdale's place. Let's see if we can deliberately step through time. There is something in Boston that will help your case, and I intend to find it. You can tell me how you wound up at Drysdale's while I drive to the precinct."

Hopefully she'd tell me the truth of it.

****

This time a Smart Car waited for us in the lifting fog. Eve fit in easily, but I had a little more trouble getting behind the wheel. Damn thing smelled of plastic. I started to drive to the precinct when an unanswered question came back to me.

I glanced at her as I drove. "Eve, you never did tell me what else your former boyfriend didn't steal."

"As near as I can figure it, you were right when you listed my bed, my comb, and my dress, though when I came to you the other night, I didn't know he'd taken the rest of my clothes. I thought I had a hidden stash still in the place. The dress no longer exists, so I have to imagine that it is my comb that they think they want. I think they already have what they really want, but don't know they do."

"You were able to hurt demons with that comb, so you could be wrong. Might be holy or something like that."

"My comb was given to me by the last john I ever

serviced as his tip. I've no idea of its history, but I gave up prostitution shortly after wearing it. I doubt that makes it holy."

"So, when you went to Drysdale's, you were still a working girl?"

"Yes. Drysdale had paid in advance for sex with him while bound. I'd never agreed to the beatings nor the whipping, but with the gag on, I had no way to stop it, or the other things they did to me. I'd signed on for six months of sexual service while bound, not for S&M."

"Something tells me that while you were in their house, your boyfriend had started to steal from you, which is why we found some of your clothing had been at St. Vincent de Paul for six months."

"No, I distinctly remember wearing some of those outfits last week, and besides, I didn't start dating my ex-boyfriend until years after Drysdale."

"I wonder what made them switch from stealing small things to stealing everything. What caused the urgency? Can you tell me anything else about that comb?"

"The john who gave it to me said it was a key for a lock that no longer existed."

"Could you have heard him wrong? After all, you keep your apartment key in it."

"No, he was very clear on the matter, I remember asking him about it as I found it confusing at the time. It could be what Drysdale is looking for. I do remember that he did a very thorough search of my body when I showed up at his house, even my hair."

"Perhaps he didn't know you didn't have it yet."

I'd reached the precinct and started to look for a place to park. Thankfully Eve's ever-changing outfit left her decently clad, this time in coveralls and a plaid shirt. We walked the two blocks to the precinct holding hands. As we climbed the steps, one of the boys in blue shouted to us, "Ain't that rich, the whore has a boyfriend."

"Ignore them," Eve whispered to me.

"Perhaps that's why he lost the body," sneered a different cop.

The first cop laughed. "He was paying too much attention to hers."

I stepped inside and stopped. All the cops were dressed in clown outfits, with clown noses, and the place smelled of peanuts and cotton candy.

I glanced at Eve and whispered, "Let's say nothing."

"That might be best," she whispered back.

I went to the desk clerk and said to the Bozo, "Greg O'Neil is expecting us."

Without a word to us, he hit the intercom button on the phone. "Greg, they're here."

I didn't know if I was more surprised or relieved that Greg wasn't also dressed like a clown, but he was in the same plaid jacket with brown slacks he always seemed to be wearing when I was around. I was shocked when he extended his hand. "Johnny, Eve, thanks for coming so quickly. Come with me."

I was a little surprised we were doing this at his office, not at the morgue, but with any luck he was going to show us photographs, not the corpse. We went down an elevator to level Q. The door opened and I saw a block of holding cells, but they were not holding the usual drunks.

We walked past a cell containing three women dressed like witches muttering in what sounded like Latin, a cell containing moaning people with peeling skin that smelled of decay who pawed at us through the bars, a cell where a black woman with white eyes and a white mohawk who smelled of ozone sat cross legged, meditating six inches off the floor, and a cell where a creature with a long neck, three eyes and purple skin paced. Eve gripped my hand tightly. I was worried that the first empty cell we'd come to would be for us, but instead we passed through a door at the far end which opened into a white room that had a faint smell of bleach.

It took me a minute to adjust to the bright light of the room. I barely made out a white chest, visible because it had a different sheen than the white floor it rose from, the white walls which surrounded us, and the ceiling which I could only glance at due to how bright it was. Inspector O'Neil took three white coveralls hanging from the wall and handed each of us one, which we put on over our outfits while putting on the third himself. The coveralls fit a bit too perfectly for my taste and covered everything including our faces. The room was very cold; I was glad of the extra warmth. The fronts of the head coverings were a mesh through which we could see, but our faces were now hid from each other. The mesh did make discerning things a bit easier, and I was able to now see the white hooks that the coveralls had hung upon as well as that there were others.

Inspector O'Neil went to the other side of the chest and must have pressed a button I couldn't see because the top slid back revealing the naked torso of Eve's now headless former boyfriend. We were staring at his back, which was covered in writing. I knew enough Latin so I could read it, but the reading was slow. After a few sentences I stopped in disgust.

"That's a Black Mass," I spat, suddenly

remembering the blank paper I'd taken off the corpse.

"Yes, but keep reading," said Inspector O'Neil.

I forced myself to read the mockery. While I was far from devout, reading the twisted text not only made my skin crawl, but I was starting to get angry. Then, towards the bottom of the torso, the text changed to one that would summon demons, complete with a pentagram, the center on the poor man's ass.

"Damnation," I said.

"So it would appear," said Inspector O'Neil, who put his hand on my back, as if offering comfort.

"What is it?" asked Eve.

"The person who wrote this on his back changed it from a Black Mass to a demon summoning."

"That might explain a few things," she said.

"Explain what?" asked O'Neil .

"Not here, let's go someplace less morbid."

****

Inspector O'Neil's office was as dingy as mine with a single grimy window looking over an air shaft and a paper-covered desk with an over-full ashtray next to the ancient computer. The smell of the ashes made me long for a smoke, but I was not asking O'Neil if I could light up. His green vinyl chair squeaked as he thumped into it, tilting it back and turning it so that he could readily see us both.

"So, tell me what that explains."

"Before we had the pleasure to find that corpse in Eve's closet, we were attacked by three demons while visiting a grave in one of your city's fine cemeteries," I said, staring into his eyes, deliberately providing as little information as possible.

He returned my stare. "You expect me to believe

that crap Johnny?"

"I don't expect nothing. You believe what you want. You're the one with a pack of zombies in a holding cell in your basement."

"You didn't see that," he commanded.

"Didn't see what?" I smiled. I could pretend to play the game, he'd not know the difference. I could only hope when all was said and done that I could.

"Tell me about those demons," he said, more gently.

"Three orange-skinned creatures with fangs and claws," I answered, not taking my gaze off of him, wanting him to keep focused on me, not Eve.

"Doesn't sound like demons to me." He leaned his chair back.

I forced a grin. "What do they sound like? Choir boys?"

"Probably just a gang wearing costumes."

"I shot one in the head, but it kept attacking. That sound like guys in costumes to you?"

He sat forward, putting his arms on his desk where I could see them. "I'm going to have to book you, Johnny. Using your ordinance in a cemetery."

I stood up. "Eve, let's get out of here."

"Sit down Johnny. I'm not done with you two."

I remained standing. "Then start with believing us."

Eve pulled me gently back down to the chair. "Greg, Johnny is telling the truth. They were demons and that was not the first time they've attacked me," said Eve, who grabbed a tissue from his desk to wipe her eyes, followed by a fake sob. I had to admire her technique when it wasn't being used on me.

"Okay, let's say that I believe the two of you and there are demons attacking Eve. Why would someone

71

write this on the back of your boyfriend?"

"To summon a new demon of course," said Eve, recrossing her legs. "Father Donn sent the last group back to hell, and I'd dispatched the prior group."

"Dispatched?"

"I don't know if you can kill them, but I got rid of them." She sobbed again, wiping her eyes with the tissue.

"How do you know these demons were different?"

"These were male, the others were female." She grabbed a tissue from his desk, dabbed at the corners of her eyes and blew her nose.

I looked at her, wondering why she'd never told me any of this, and if this was yet more lies.

He leaned forward, eyes on her legs. "Tell me more."

Eve gave my hand a squeeze, leaned back and recrossed her legs. I had to believe she was luring him with lies, and clueing me in to it.

Eve said, "I met Rich about six months after Jess's death. He was the first man to treat me like a woman, not a thing, in a long time. One night he took me to a play— Faustus, I think. Something went wrong and actual demons appeared. The cast tried to go on with the show, but the fumes sent the audience running for the exit.

"Richard and I also ran, but the trio of demons appeared in front of us. We defended ourselves as best we could, but we were outnumbered. Richard hit one with his class ring and it smoked and disappeared. The remaining two became more vicious, and Richard went down just as I found out that if I could pierce the demon's eyes with my comb, it too smoked and disappeared. I leapt between Richard and the remaining demon and we fought until it's foot landed on Richard's hand and she became smoke.

"When Richard recovered, we fought and he left me, but we're still in touch if you need him to corroborate my story."

The smile Eve gave to Inspector O'Neil would have melted any man's heart. She'd fed him a load of bull and expected him to tell her how good it tasted.

"That won't be necessary. We can find you through your business associate if we need to ask any further questions."

Eve and I rose, and she took Inspector O'Neil's hand. "Thank you, Officer. I was angry at Fred when he stole from me, but now I feel very sorry for him. I hope you find his killers."

"Don't worry, we will."

On our way out of the precinct, I noticed that all the officers were now working in their underwear. After the last few days, it was very easy not to stare.

We walked in silence, hand in hand until we were both in my car which had become a '67 Mustang. I tried not to hoot as I unlocked the door which I held open for Eve. Once she was seated, I practically pranced to the driver's side and slid down behind the wheel with a contented sigh. I had a ton of questions I knew I should be asking, but right then all I could do was long to start my drive.

I had one question I had to ask. "You still want to go to the cemetery next? Even after reading that nightmare?"

"Yes. If the shell is there, I want it. Aren't you going to ask me about my performance just now?"

I couldn't get the text out of my thoughts, I wondered if they'd carved that in his skin before or after they'd cut off his head.

"No. I need time to think."

"Thanks, I could use some of that too." Eve pulled her hair back and leaned her temple against the cold glass window.

Chapter 6

One Hell Of A Headache

While I didn't speed on my way to Holy Cross, I took every curve tight and accelerated with joy. I wasn't thinking—I was lost in driving—but I needed that more, or so I kept telling myself. And what could the deepest thinking have even done for me? I had three leads on this case, and they all frightened me.

The first lead was the shell which I'd placed on Jessica's tombstone in my dream. The second was Drysdale's house, if I could get there in the here and now. And the third was the thug, Hanrahan, who wanted my client dead. Not a clue, but also important was the uncomfortable truth that Eve was likely avoiding Hanrahan and Drysdale as much as I was. What would make a girl so frightened of those two as to risk another encounter with demons? Especially since she'd beaten Hanrahan to a pulp when last she'd met him.

I parked. We maintained our silence walking through the graves. The fresh, pine-scented air lifted my spirits. Sure enough, when we got close to her stone, I saw the shell centered in a sun beam from the cloud mottled sky.

"Johnny, it's there. I see it." She took my hand, like I was her lover. In a way, I suppose I was.

"I do too."

"Don't let go of me. Hold my hand tightly when I go to pick it up."

The Bogart fan in me wanted to say, "Sure thing doll," because right then and there I felt like we were in an old movie. Instead, I gave her hand a tiny squeeze and we resumed our stroll among the dead until we stood in front of the tomb stone.

"Jess," she said, "this was your favorite thing in the whole universe. I don't feel right in taking it from you, except I'm trying to keep it from some very bad men. I promise, when we're done with them, I'll return this to you."

She gripped my hand tightly and reached out. She picked up the shell. Nothing happened. Her smile went all the way to her eyes.

"With great relief, I hold again her shell," said Eve, cupping it to her chest.

Just when I didn't think there were surprises left in this odd case, I found something about her statement surprising, but I couldn't put my finger on just what. While I was glad I'd gotten her the bracelet, the ring, and this shell, hopefully we'd be able to retrieve her money. If all I got back for her were her keepsakes, I had no hope of being paid.

"It brings my heart gladness to see thee in joy," I said. Damn, I was speaking funny too. "Shall we return to Drysdale's in this time?"

"Perhaps t'was the better thing to do," said Eve.

"Or are we now cowards, 'fraid of a thug?"

The contractions bothered me, but I had no time to worry that bone thoroughly. Eve took my hand, her smile broad. That was a smile I'd gladly die for, if her smile was for me.

"'Tis not fear but prudent judgment guide us."

Something made us turn.

Three blue female demons rushing us from behind. Why blue?

I let go of her hand and readied myself for a fight. There were three of them again, gruesome mockeries of women. I had a moment to glance at Eve, who'd placed the shell on the ground and had her comb at the ready. Once again, she was naked and a wind I didn't feel was blowing her hair wildly. On a hunch, just before they reached us, I crossed myself like the good catholic I wasn't. Two of the demons made for Eve and the third hit me so hard I was thrown backwards, falling on top of a stone slab.

My pounding head was swimming; I could hear screams of rage from Eve but I couldn't rise. Shadows descended on me and I lost the world.

****

I walked a gray paved path dimly lit by thin lanterns perched on top of tall thin poles. To either side of me were high white walls with trees growing over them on the other side. This wall had many doors in it, all open, showing the bushes and lawn on the other side. In the distance I could see some rolling hills with large Stonehenge like obelisks scattered without a discernible pattern. Perhaps if I could see them from the air?

I turned and saw a woman walking towards me wearing a long black skirt with matching black blouse that hung just off the shoulders. Her flaxen hair, stiffly pulled up, matched the elegance of her dress, which swayed gently as she walked towards me.

I approached her with the intent to ask her where I was and how I could get home when I felt a breeze turn into a rushing wind that disturbed not a blade of grass nor the flow of her skirt and hair. The shades of black and gray blurred and I felt myself being shaken.

****

I heard Eve calling me and I opened my eyes to see her leaning over me as she shook me. Her taut lips and raised eyebrows faded to a smile as she noticed me awake.

"A fine help I've been, laying here while you fought off three demons." I tried to rise, but it hurt like hell and I stopped. "What happened?"

"You were magnificent. The demon that tackled you turned to smoke the moment it hit you. You rose, screaming something in a language that I couldn't recognize and ran at one of the two demons fighting me. You wrestled with it, each of you locked on the other until you pressed your hand on its face and screamed more of that language at it. The demon started screaming, twisting and shaking as if in agony until it disappeared in a cloud of smoke."

"You saw all of that while fighting your own demon?"

"Right after you grabbed the second demon, I was able to claw the eyes of the one I was fighting with my comb. There is something about this comb the demons can't abide."

I tried to rise again, more successfully, and saw I laid in one of three circles of grass that were blackened. I clutched my side from the pain, likely a few bruised ribs. Eve, dressed once more in the gray yoga clothing I'd gotten her, touched me where it hurt. Where she touched me, the pain faded, but I still felt like I was bruised head to foot. The nautilus shell lay where Eve had left it, next to a purse I'd not seen before.

"Perchance, you dreamed while fighting mightily?" she asked as she picked up the purse. "This had been mine before the theft."

"Yeah, verily it is so. Let us leave," I said. "I will share with you my dreams as I drive."

****

My car had become a beige Honda civic, but the keys I carried still fit. I drove us towards the exit from the cemetery, glad to see living people and actual homes again.

"Was that purse one of the other things taken from your locker?" I asked, relieved to be talking more normally.

"Yes, with my license, credit cards, cell phone, cash, and everything else I remember it holding. It's almost as if all we need to do is to get you enough sleep and you'll get me everything they stole from me. The question I have is how you slept while fighting."

"Get me enough sleep, nice thought. With Hanrahan and Drysdale hanging in the wings, as well as demons in the oddest places, it's not as if we're on vacation. They've wrecked my apartment and killed an old friend. They're going to get theirs."

"Agreed. Now, you were going to tell me about your dream."

I told her about the path, the hills, the wall, doors, and trees but she was most interested in the woman and the dress she wore, asking me to describe every detail, including the decorative stitching in the blouse.

"That sounds so much like a favorite dress my mother wore. I'm certain it was her. I've not seen or spoken to her in so long."

Her voice faded. I wasn't certain, but I didn't want to take my gaze off the road to verify, but I think she was crying. I gave her some space as I got us merged on the highway that would take us to Drysdale's part of town.

"Johnny, do you remember that bridge we went under and found ourselves on the highway to Boston?"

"Yes, why?" I asked, dreading the answer.

"I know that this would just be delaying things and all, but would you mind trying to do that again, except if we get through, go on up to New Hampshire? I'd like to find my parents, if I can."

"I'd like to get to Drysdale's place first. The cops will only be able to hold that guy who broke into my place for a couple of days at most, and I'm disinclined to have Drysdale warned that we're coming for him. Likely Drysdale is already suspicious simply because the boy failed to return."

"But you'll try?"

"We have a fairly open-ended agreement, you and I, so I don't see why not. What are you going to tell them about me? Private investigators don't drive their clients cross country to see their moms on a regular basis. It's not likely she'll believe you if you tell her the truth, especially not if you mention how we got to her so quickly."

"I'll think of something. You really think that Drysdale has the necklace and the mirror?"

"I'm hoping, but I really don't know. What I do know is that he's linked to the folks who killed Gladys and he's tried to rob you a second time. If nothing else, it's worth tearing his house apart while we look. I'd like to hope that I don't have to enter a dream state to retrieve everything."

"It's like you're a shaman or a sorcerer."

"With the exception of the bracelet, nothing I've brought back has been something I've been aware of. It's like bringing that back opened some sort of gateway. I've always used my dreams to help me figure out a case. The subconscious can-do things the conscious can't, but never like this."

"Perhaps, or perhaps it is the sex. With the exception of the fight against the demons, each time you've brought something back, there's been sex of some sort involved. It has made me wonder what would happen if we had sex while awake."

"Not this time. This time I fought demons. No sex involved." Why would she think it was the sex? Come to think on it, sex was a bit of an obsession with her.

"True. Still, I wonder what would happen if you acted the way you do in your sleep, but while awake. Perhaps we can try that tonight." She put her hand on my leg and caressed it. At least this time she kept her hand off my crotch.

"I wonder if that might prevent the dream sex from happening and prevent me from bringing something back from dream time." From the corner of my eye, I saw her wipe away tears. I kept driving both the car and my point. "However, the selfish part of me that's complaining about having all this sex with you and not being able to remember a thing is saying we should give it a try."

At this, she picked up her head and flashed me a grin which lit my fires. If I wasn't driving, I'd be looking to tear her clothing off. I was never like this, even with a broad I liked a lot. More importantly, I knew that the reason why I felt this was somehow a key to unraveling some of the lies.

I saw the sign for Drysdale's exit and shifted lanes so I could take it. We were going to have a harder time getting into his place, between the fact that he now lived in a gated community, and he had a state-of-the-art security system which was likely to be active. I started to think of a good story to give the guy at the gate, as there would be no shadows to hide within.

I remembered the name of a neighbor from the other night and decided to use that just as I felt Eve unzip me.

"Please don't do that right now." I couldn't believe myself saying this.

"I think it will help us get in. When he asks for your license, just tell him you can't reach it with me doing this."

If you've never tried driving while a beautiful woman gives you head, I don't recommend it. First, it is harder than you'd think to control the wheel. Second, it is harder to pay attention to what you're doing with your feet than you could possibly imagine. However, with her doing this to me, I drove up to the gate.

I rolled down the window as I pulled up to the gatehouse. A thin young man with long sandy hair looked at us and said, "Dude, you are the man."

I shrugged my shoulders and gave him a sheepish grin. To my surprise, he didn't ask me who we were there to visit, he just raised the gate, giving me a thumbs-up. I waved and drove right through.

****

After I parked, Eve stopped and helped me get myself back together. She playfully patted the bulge in my pants.

"I'll finish with you later. Think you're up to getting

us into his place in broad daylight?"

"If he's not changed the locks," I said, patting my pants to make certain I'd remembered my picks. "It's been six years or one day since we were last there, depending upon when now is. Who knows what we're going to find."

She took her hand off my lap. "Never had to worry about that before. Odd not to be able to take time for granted. Either way, we're not going to know until we try. Let's go."

The one thing our conversation had done is I was no longer embarrassingly excited. We'd parked right behind his house. There were no signs of anyone present, but that was always harder to determine in the daylight. I looked around for the tell-tale signs of an alarm company monitoring the home, but there were none. It took me just a few minutes, and we were in. As no alarms sounded, I hoped that there wasn't a silent alarm of unauthorized entry being sent to the police, but I found no keypad to disable an alarm. Five years ago when I was here last, there had been an alarm, so likely we were here even further back in time. Or was Drysdale very self-confident considering I'd broken into his house already, or had I? Maybe the alarm would be there because of what we do now? Damn, time traveling was too complicated. I couldn't imagine anyone actually *wanting* to do this. Science fiction authors must be nuts.

I felt the lock cylinder turn and opened the door. This was too easy. I looked for signs of cameras and could find none, as if he didn't care if he was burgled again. I stepped into the hall as quietly as I could. Eve's footsteps behind me were barely audible. I retraced my steps back to the room where I'd found Eve. No sign of blood on the carpet. Either they had an awesome cleaning staff, or we'd arrived before my break-in yesterday.

"Notice the absence of blood," I whispered.

"Yes." Her whisper matched mine. "Question is, how far in the past did we go this time?"

"Yeah, that is the question. Let's look for the safe."

We found the safe in the same place, upstairs, behind a mirror in the bedroom. I took a good look at the keypad, noticed the wear pattern and inside of five minutes had opened the safe. Inside were papers, mostly financial in nature, and a safety deposit key. Perhaps that was where Eve's goods were being kept, but not likely.

Eve and I flipped through the papers, carefully keeping their order intact. We found no clues, and soon had everything back in the safe. I'd taken a photo of the key with my phone in case we ever had the opportunity to get a duplicate made.

"Now what?" Eve's tone indicated a lack of hope, or perhaps that was my reading.

I shrugged my shoulders. "Let's keep looking. There could be other places where he keeps things hidden."

About an hour later, in the basement, we came upon space where the wall didn't meet the ceiling in quite the same way the rest of the walls had done. I suspected we'd found a false wall, or perhaps a hidden door. I couldn't find the seam of a door just by looking, but I figured there had to be something. I felt along the wall with my hands until I came to a section where the paint lifted slightly. I found some stiff wallpaper along the edge of the hidden door, painted the same color as the wall. I pressed in on this and it popped out an inch. A latch on the side that had popped out allowed me to rotate the door open.

The room we beheld was a regular pentagon, with a pentagram inscribed in the floor. Candle sconces stood on all the points, and the dripped wax on the floor showed them to be well used.

To one side of the pentagram was a podium with a book on it.

Eve gripped my hand. "Don't go in there. I remember that room, though I never knew where it was. They always brought me to it blind folded. Let's get out, and fast."

I was inclined to agree with her. The room stank with the smell of stale blood, though none could be seen. I didn't want to add mine. However, if we took the book, we might be able to stop the demonic attacks. "Look, I think we should risk it and take that book."

"No, please don't."

"Even if its absence would put a stop to those attacks?"

"I don't want us stealing anything for any reason. I only want us recovering the things they stole from me."

I still don't know if we did the right thing there. I pushed the door closed until I could hear it click back into place. Behind us, I heard another click, that of a gun being cocked.

"Hands above your heads and turn around slowly."

I didn't recognize the voice, likely one of Drysdale's men. We both raised our hands and turned. A sandy-haired punk had a pistol pointed right at us. "So, you found the Boss's hole but didn't dare enter, eh? Open it."

"Look, we meant no trouble," I tried. "We had a tip that some of this ladies' stolen goods were stored in here by the thieves. Obviously, they're not."

"I said open it."

I turned, pressed, and pulled the hidden door open. Depending on how we entered, I might be able to turn this to our advantage, but I was not going to enter that room unless he pressed the issue.

The punk waved the gun in the direction of the damned room.

"Get in there already."

Eve and I stepped forward.

"Not the girl. She comes with me."

Eve gave me a glance, and I nodded, trying to communicate to her not to worry about me. I stepped backward into the damned room, while she stepped forward into a sudden leap towards his side. She pulled her comb from her hair and slashed. I had just enough time to drop and roll as the punk's gun went off, thankfully wide. I rose to see him covered with blood from where she'd slashed him on the forehead. Something ice cold was forming behind me. Without looking I raced out of that damned room, slamming the door behind me.

Eve had her comb against the punk's throat, his head pulled back by her other hand.

"Don't kill me," he pleaded through sobs.

"Why not?" Eve asked.

I raised his gun and pointed it right at him. "On your knees, punk. Hands on top of your head where I can see them."

He dropped, like the good little boy he wasn't.

"Now, where do Drysdale's thieves keep the stash?" I put as much of an edge in my question as I could. I'd be thrilled to have him try something, but I wanted an answer.

"He'll kill me if I squeal."

"Now, ain't that a dilemma. I'll kill you if you don't."

"There's a warehouse on San Pedro street, I'm not certain which one."

I cocked the pistol. "You lie again, and you lose a knee cap. Try me, punk."

"Okay, okay, it's 1313 San Pedro Street."

I hit him on the back of his head, and he collapsed in a heap on the floor. He'd have one heck of a headache when he awoke.

Chapter 7

The Warehouse Of Hell

While I was tempted to torch the place to eliminate that damned room, the punk we left unconscious in the basement didn't deserve that kind of death. We left in a hurry, hoping that he hadn't called in the boss or reinforcements.

Thankfully the punk was overconfident in his ability to handle us and we met no one on our way out. My car had now become a Toyota Corolla. Odd that the car kept shifting while Eve's outfit seemed to have stabilized ever since the last demon attack. Whatever was going on had a consistency to it that was on the verge of being comprehensible.

I knew the street where Drysdale's warehouse was located, as I'd helped the cops with a drug investigation on that same street a few years back. Not a lovely area, but I now had two pistols and Eve her comb. I could only hope that, if the warehouse had her goods, we'd come out to find the car had become a panel truck.

Traffic was the traditional San Francisco jam. Eve tried the radio, probably to reduce the stress, but couldn't find a station she liked and turned it off. As for me, I just tried to quiet my mind, which was racing around the question of why Drysdale was summoning demons and were they the demons that had been attacking us.

I don't think either of us said a word during the hour-long stop and go through the car clogged streets. I finally found a left turn that took us out of traffic and in the right direction. The road was vacant, as if the rest of the city knew better than to head that way. With the sky darkening as we neared our destination, all I needed was the sinister music that started playing on the radio.

"Don't get me wrong, Eve, but could you please change the channel."

"I didn't turn it back on."

"That's odd. Try anyway."

I kept my gaze on the road while Eve hit the buttons and turned the knobs. Nothing she could do would silence that music.

"Sorry, looks like the horror show music is what we've got."

"Well, it's not as if we don't have all the elements of a horror flick, between the sex we've shared and the encounters with demons. Looks like our next stop will be right out of a B-movie." Even the clouds had grown dark, threatening rain.

"If your car transforms into a van painted with groovy flowers while we've driving, I may scream."

"Funny. Whatever happens in this place, we're not splitting up."

"Agreed."

Unsurprisingly, there were plenty of places to park next to the warehouse. I pulled in to the first spot, turned off the car, and we got out. For the first time in hours, Eve's outfit had changed. She was in some kind of skintight black outfit, with a belt containing many unidentifiable objects in it, as well as some throwing stars and a sword. It looked familiar to me, but I couldn't place it.

"Looks like you're dressed to kill," I said, locking the door.

Eve looked down at herself. "A Hollywood ninja. However, you should look at yourself."

I looked at my reflection in the glass and was surprised to see that I was dressed in a medieval tunic and tights, with a sword in my belt. My two heaters, however, were still on me, so I breathed a sigh of relief. "If the danger weren't so palpable, I'd laugh. I think I'd cut off my own leg if I tried to use the sword."

"Shall we?" she asked.

"Yes, once more into the breach."

Eve and I walked side by side, the temperature rising, darkness gathering, and that damned horror show music following us like we had our own orchestra. I grinned as I realized my step was light, I felt like I was ten again, off to kill the bad guys, and nothing could stand in my way. We got to the door and tried to open it. I would have been happier if it had been actually locked. The door opened in, so we let it swing all the way open. The place was pitch black.

"There isn't a flashlight on your belt?" I asked Eve.

"Don't know. Let me check." She pulled out each object and looked it over, but nothing was discernible as a flashlight. "I guess we'll just have to walk along the walls looking for a light switch."

I stepped in slowly aiming a revolver at the darkness while feeling the wall to my left for a switch. I felt one and flipped it. The room was somewhat nondescript to the point of soullessness. Just a gray desk, gray phone, gray chair, gray walls, and even a gray floor. The only thing not gray was the white ceiling with fluorescent lights. Eve stepped in and the door slammed shut behind her.

"I didn't do that," she said, her voice terse and higher pitched than normal.

"Good to know. Can you reopen it?"

She tried the door knob. "No."

"Okay, now we know why this felt like a trap. All we can do is to go further in. I'll cover you. Stand to one side and throw open the inside door."

Eve pulled the comb from her hair and took a step towards the door which burst open and three demons rushed at her. I plugged them with bullets, but like the last time all that did was make them angrier. As two rushed me, I drew my sword and held it as if I knew what I was doing, uttering a silent prayer to St. George.

I don't know how else to describe it other than the sword was using me. I had a back seat in my head as my arms and legs moved, back and forth. With each slash, demon parts dropped to the ground. The demons had no fear, they were embodied rage and kept trying to claw me until they were in pieces.

"I see you've used one of those before," said Eve.

I wanted to take credit, but instead I admitted the truth. "That wasn't me. Someone else was moving this sword."

"That's kinda weird. Can you come with me, or do we have to ask someone else to come along?"

My body took off my now feathered hat and bowed with a flourish that I could never have managed.

"Oh, I see what you mean," said Eve. "Whoever is possessing you, I like them." She knew me well, and it hadn't been a week.

"Come on, let's go slay some monsters and find the

treasure."

She tilted her head and frowned. "Was that you, or the other who is sharing your body?"

"Me. I don't think whoever it is can speak through me, or make the decisions which matter. Let's go."

I wasn't bothered by the possession. After all I had asked for the help. The hall the demons had come through was dark as pitch without a light switch in view from the doorway. I took a small step in and my sword began to glow. "I feel like I'm in some sort of Dungeons and Dragons game." I walked cautiously on the balls of my feet, scanning the walls for arms that would pull us through reality into death.

"Well, at least we won't be needing a flashlight. You do realize it's all some sick male fantasy. The swords are their penises which become magic, slaying demons and rescuing fair maidens."

"Eve, you just destroyed my childhood."

I glanced at her, expecting to see her tight with caution. Instead she had the wildest grin. I think she was enjoying every step we took into danger. I knew my joke was to mask my fear, if only it hid my fear from me.

She nudged me with her elbow. "Come on, Johnny. We women love those magical penises, although some of us like to be ravished before we're rescued. The purity thing is very much a guy thing."

I chuckled, and my heart lightened because of it. "Let me guess. When you were a girl, you liked to play with boys, getting tied up and rescued."

She put a hand on my rear and squeezed. "Sometimes I still like to get tied up when I play with men."

I fought to keep the confusion out of my voice, to

stay professional. "So when you were at Drysdale's, you enjoyed that?" However that last word was an octave higher than the rest of my question.

"No. I'm not into pain. Sometimes, however, I like to be dominated and like to have no control over what's going to happen."

Like we ever have control over what was going to happen, but the talk of sex had put a man back into me and I felt more focused and ready for what harm may come.

We reached a door at the end of the corridor. In the light of the sword, we could see strange markings on the door. Something about them made me sick to look at them, though I didn't understand their meaning.

"Should we leave it closed and go the other way?" I asked.

Eve slid past me to get a better look. "That's cuneiform."

"What?"

"Cuneiform, used in ancient Sumer. Give me a moment; I think I can read it."

I felt so weird, standing next to Eve as she puzzled out the cuneiform while I was holding a magic sword with slain demons behind us.

"Here, I've got it. It says, 'Ph'nglui mglw'nafh Cthulhu R'lyeh wgah'nagl fhtagn.'"

"Don't open that door."

"Why?"

"When I was a kid, not only did I play Dungeons and Dragons, but I read the works of H.P. Lovecraft. If I remember correctly, Lovecraft had that phrase in one of his books, and translated it as 'In his house at R'lyeh dead Cthulhu waits dreaming.' This has got all the elements of a very elaborate prank, but I'm not taking any chances. If I'm right, behind that door awaits madness and destruction."

"I've never seen you frightened before, so I'll take you at your word. Let's go back the other way and see where that takes us."

I realized I was trembling when Eve took my hand. Hand in hand, sword ready, we returned along the corridor, passing the door to the chamber where we'd fought the demons. We walked through a nondescript hall: no doors, no windows, no signs. After a while, I realized that we must have walked further in that direction than the building was wide, and there was no end in sight. Finally, the corridor turned left and ended at a door. Seeing no eldritch writing on it, I let go of Eve's hand and gave it a try. Locked.

"Here, hold this." I gave Eve my sword.

"Charmed, I'm sure."

I ignored her and looked for my lock picks. "Drat. Don't have my picks in this getup. Can you check that belt of yours?"

Eve took out each item one by one, not a lock pick in the collection of oddities. "Shall we break it open?"

I gave it a tap; it sounded like it had a hollow core. "Should bust open easily."

I took a few steps back, squared my shoulder, and ran at the door. It opened on its own just before I would have hit it and I went stumbling into the room and fell onto the hard-gray concrete. Eve extended a hand and I rose. The smell of burnt oil hung heavily in the air. Rows and rows of gray shelves stacked with wooden crates were dimly lit by lamps hanging from the ceiling and the glow of the sword Eve held out to me to take back.

"I've got a bad feeling you're going to need this," she said.

"I've a bad feeling you're right. Let's go see if we can find the inventory for this place."

"What are we looking for?"

"Either a bunch of file cabinets or computers. There's probably an office along the perimeter that has it." The place was massive, but along all the walls the only door we saw was the one we'd come through. We started walking up and down the aisles. Not a computer nor a file cabinet in the place. After we'd come to the end of the last aisle, we both sat, tired, on the floor.

"Any ideas?" I asked.

"We could break into every single crate."

"That could take the rest of our lives."

"I've got nothing better to do."

"Perhaps I've got this all wrong," I said. "Perhaps the inventory is behind that door with the cuneiform on it." I paused, as did my heart. "I'm sorry, but I still don't want to go in there."

"Johnny, I trust you, but I think you're approaching this place and why we're here all wrong."

"How so?"

"If Drysdale is using this warehouse to store his stolen goods, he'd not have such a monster in it. If there is such a monster in it, he'd not use it to store his stolen goods. I'm thinking back to the locked door that opened for us. This room is an elaborate trap, a ruse. If we start searching in the boxes, which is I think what they want us to do, we'll simply waste time until they get here. I've got a feeling that whatever gave us these outfits wants us to go through the other door, and we've got all we need to confront that thing, and we're not going to get back anything else until we do."

"Eve, you hired me to help you get your stuff back, not to fight monsters from beyond the dawn of time."

"Perhaps I hired you for the wrong thing. I've been thinking long and hard about what Jessica said. They've got her soul trapped in something, something I used to have. This comb is the key to releasing her, and they want it from me. I've no idea why, but it is essential that we find that missing something and set her soul free ourselves; and I think the only way we're going to do that is to get rid of those monsters. I know damn well that vague promises of money and some sex doesn't buy fighting monsters. I'm going to go face that monster, taking the fight to hell itself. Are you with me?"

"Yes, I'm with you." I hated myself for saying it. Perhaps next time I should negotiate a more explicit arrangement.

****

It didn't take nearly as long to walk the corridor back to that ill-marked door. Eve took a dagger from her belt and scratched a horizontal line on the door, across this she scratched three lines, the first straight down, the second a v that barely crossed the horizontal line, the third straight down at the end of the horizontal line.

"What are you doing?" I asked.

"Don't know. Just feels like the right thing to do. Ready?"

Another lie? Likely. In for a penny, in for a pound as they used to say, but I still had the enthusiasm of that inner ten-year-old, after all, since I was wielding a genuine magical sword. "Let's do it."

Eve opened the door and we both stared at a place that looked like Los Angeles, only all wrong. First, the round Capital Records Building was right in front of us, only it was twisted. None of the levels were flat, as the structure was twisted to resemble an ampersand. One level spun sideways with sickening green flashes of light in a pattern that was not the Morse code the building's lights usually flashed.

The sky was the white of pus, with black dots pulsing as if a mockery of stars. My nose wrinkled at the overwhelming smell of rotten eggs. Eve grabbed my arm as an immense many-legged creature scampered past us to climb up the green stone road.

I moved to place a foot on that path and felt intense heat and cold flash as if my leg passed through both an inferno and the deep vacuum of space. My instinct was to pull back, but with Eve's hand gripping mine, I stepped onto that road. Eve followed, and as she did so, the pain of the flashing temperature changes dissipated.

I glanced at her to see if she was okay and noticed her holding in her right hand an eight-pointed stone star. "That was on your belt?"

"Yes. Somehow it felt right to grab it before I stepped in. Which way?" she asked.

"I don't know if that question has any real meaning here, but I want to ensure that we'll be able to get back. Let's turn around and see if there is anything definite about where we came from."

From this side, the door seemed to be of the same green stone, open with a brilliant light coming through. "Let's just go forward and see what we find," I said.

She nodded her agreement and off we went. Straight wasn't straight in that place. Our route twisted without us ever feeling we were turning. Periodically I'd look back to ensure that the door was still in sight. We found ourselves on the other side of the bent tower, though still able to see the door as the light traced our path. The door appeared to be in front of us, so we headed towards it as best as we could. When we got to it, we were sideways.

"Shall we pull the door open like this, or lay on our side to open the door?" I asked.

"Hold on to me, I'm going to grab something else from my belt. Hang on tight."

I grabbed her arm as she pulled out a silver Mobius strip. The moment it was in her hand, the door righted itself. Without letting go of the sword or Eve's arm, I touched the door of the building with the tip of my sword to give it a push. It exploded into the building as if my hand was a bomb.

"I didn't mean to do that."

"It happened the moment your sword touched the door. Be careful with that thing down here. We don't want the entire building exploding around us."

"Got it."

With my hand holding her arm as if I was blind and she my guide, we stepped carefully over the debris of the door. On the other side was a single corridor, with doors to either side. I sheathed my sword and tried some of the doors with my free hand, but none of them would open. I wondered if they'd explode like the door to the building had, but I didn't want to cause any unnecessary destruction.

We came upon a door that was open and stepped inside. The room was filled with filing cabinets. I tried each until I found one that opened with only one folder in it. I flipped the folder open and stepped back to let Eve take a look.

"That's my stuff all right."

"Yeah, except they wanted us to find this. Must be a trap," I pointed out.

"I agree, but this entire place has been a setup."

"Yep. Let's go see what we've been setup for."

She picked up the page and we found ourselves in darkness. I grabbed my sword and drew it, hoping the light that had shown in the warehouse would shine here too. It did, though in the light of the sword, everything I saw had an odd sheen to it, as if not designed to reflect light and not doing such a wonderful job of it. Eve folded the page and slid it into a pouch on her belt.

"Let's get back to the warehouse."

Happier words were never uttered. We turned together so I'd not loosen my grip on her arm when, softly in the distance, we heard a noise, like a whistle, "tikili li." We ran from the room stopping as we got to the hall. Coming at us was a large glimmering blob with eyes that kept appearing and disappearing. A tentacle formed from it and reached out to us. Fighting my inability to truly grasp that thing, I slashed at the tentacle with my sword, slicing it from the larger entity. The smell was horrid, like rotten clams, and some of the liquid hit my skin, burning intensely.

More tentacles reached out, these with eyes pulsing along them. I braced myself for the burning to follow and slashed out to slice them off the putrescent mass. Where the liquid hit my clothing, it smoked as it burned, and I wanted to run to keep more of that foul slime from searing my skin. Instead, I roared and charged the insidious slime, slicing off each tentacle until the floor was a pool of noxious liquid with eyes spinning in whirlpools of its own decay. One by one I stabbed the eyes and they went out. Whatever was possessing me was glad that thing was destroyed. Me? I wanted to vomit.

Every exposed part of me was searing and my clothing fell off me in a heap of ash. Eve grabbed something from her belt and pointed it at me. Water flew from it, rinsing my skin of all trace of that thing.

"Thanks! I love those gadgets; how do you know which one to use?"

Eve flashed me a wry grin. "Love your outfit. I've no idea. I just grab and hope."

"With any luck, *that* was the trap. I hope one of those gadgets will sling lead, not only don't I have clothes, I no longer have my keys, wallet, or guns. Maybe you want to turn that water on the floor and wash it clean? That stuff burns."

"It will take more than this thing to wash that floor clean. Let's find another way out."

"Yes, lets hurry in case that thing activated some sort of alarm."

Thankfully, my sword's light was sufficient for us to see by as we raced along the hall until we came to an open door. I quickly ducked inside; Eve followed me close. Too close, actually, as she slammed into me when I came to a sudden stop. In front of me was a petite oriental woman, wearing a French maid's outfit.

"Hi, our master sent us to get you both safely out of this place."

"Your master?" I stammered, not feeling terribly comfortable standing in front of this stranger, dripping wet and naked with a sword in my hand.

"Yes. Please come with us."

"First, tell us of your master," I said.

"He is a scientist studying the caves in Antarctica.

He heard of your incursion into the city of the Elder gods and sent us to help."

"Us?" Eve and I asked together.

"No time to explain. We must flee before one of the great old ones finds out you are here. Follow us."

They led us up a few flights until they opened the door and I could see the ground above us, upside down as if it were the ceiling. The creature that looked like a girl stepped through, and though they looked upside down too, their hair hung towards their feet. Eve and I stepped through, hand in hand, and thankfully also wound up with our feet on the ground.

Chapter 8

Einstein On The Beach

Our guide took us through a torturous route back to the still open door into the warehouse. "This is as far as we will go with you," they said. "We've got to get back to our master."

"You call him your master. Are you his slave?" asked Eve.

"We are his willing and most devoted servant and would do anything he asks of us. We were slaves to the Great Old Ones, but they are mostly gone now. As we were created to serve, we can't be happy otherwise."

My curiosity was getting the better of me, though I wanted to go back through that door to the world I knew where when you went straight *you walked straight*.

"So, there are others like you?" I asked.

"Not as many as there used to be. Now please go, before it is too late."

We stepped through the door and turned to say thank you, but they were gone. I closed the door, wishing I had a way to lock it. "Come on, let's get back to the warehouse and find that crate."

Eve practically pulled me along the corridor, which was cold to my bare feet. "You do realize that even if we find this crate without being interrupted, we'll have no way to carry the stuff out of here. When my clothing disintegrated, so did my car keys."

"Let's worry about that after we find the crate."

The loss of my keys, clothes, wallet, and guns was not the only thing on my mind. Eve not only showed remarkable knowledge of an obscure language, but she was acting as a confident leader. She'd also mostly stopped flirting with me. Other than a brief joke about my outfit that was. She changed the moment we entered that warehouse.

As we got closer to the storeroom, we heard voices. As I'd feared, some of Drysdale's gang had arrived. They'd be none too pleased to find us hanging about the place. Eve slowed her pace, likely thinking the same thing. We finally got to that door, me wishing for both some clothing and a place to hide this glowing sword, but I could tell Eve was expecting a fight, as she'd grabbed the only objects I'd recognized off her belt, a set of throwing stars, each with eight points.

"You know how to use those?" I asked, hoping.

"No, but I've not known how to use anything else on this belt and it's worked out."

"Got it. Stop worrying. Shall we?"

The place was a bit different with the lights on, though no less huge. In the distance, we could hear the persistent beeping of a fork-lift backing up. With any luck, those workers had nothing to do with us, and would not notice us until we were gone. We crept along quietly, but certain of the direction because the lights also illuminated labels indicating row number. The inventory we'd found in the twisted parody of LA indicated that Eve's stuff was on row sixty-nine, so we headed in that direction.

Every now and then I'd hear voices getting closer,

so we'd duck into an aisle and wait until they passed. I only caught a glimpse of the workers once, two large men with arm muscles thicker than my legs accompanied by tall demons that appeared to be men from the neck down, but had the heads and hands of tigers. While I was glad that whoever had possessed me to control the sword seemed to still be around, I didn't want to have to face any of those creatures. I was very glad that they didn't appear to notice us as we crept along the aisle.

Finally, and without much incident, we got to the sixty-ninth row. Eve's crates were supposed to be about halfway down, on the right. We started looking for her stuff when we heard "Hey, you! What are you doing here?" from behind us. We wheeled around and saw the same two men as before, but thankfully without their demon.

"Ignore them," I whispered, "Let's keep walking until we get to your crate."

It didn't take long before a shot rang out, missing us both. We started running. I had no idea what we'd do once we got to her crate, but somehow just getting there felt right. My sword vibrated in my hand with an odd clang; a bullet must have grazed it.

"Their shots are getting closer," said Eve.

"So are we—look."

To our right, about twenty paces away, was a large wooden crate right where the inventory said her stuff was. We ducked behind it on the shelf.

"Push the lid off," I said.

Thankfully the it slid right off.

"Quick, inside," I said, as a bullet came close enough that I felt its heat.

She went in first, and I followed. I found myself

falling at a steady pace in complete darkness so I had no idea how fast I fell. Eve's hand clasped mine, so somehow I'd caught up to her, though that defied Newton's law. But then again, I saw little about this place that seemed to obey the known laws.

Soon I became somewhat accustomed to the dark. We passed a potted plant, which was also falling, but much slower. It smelled heavenly. In the distance below us, I could see a sperm whale, also falling.

"Was that yours?" I asked.

"The plant or the whale?"

"The plant."

"Yes, it sat in the corner of my bedroom."

"Then we have the right crate. With how we're falling, I'm half expecting to see a white rabbit with a watch."

"I never owned any pets, so I doubt it."

I pondered how Eve could not be aware of the rabbit from Alice in Wonderland as we passed a rocking chair, though I didn't understand the whale myself. I just hoped that when we landed, we didn't have to eat or drink anything to get through doors.

Finally, we could see something below us, stars, and we were rushing toward them. A moment later, we were cresting the surface of water, bobbing in the waves of a star lit sea.

****

"I wish I could kick off my shoes," said Eve. "The clothing is so heavy wet. Where is a sudden change of clothing when you need it?"

Rotating to get a sense of things, I spotted an irregular glow on the horizon. "If I'm right, not only is the sun about to come up over there, but there's land in that direction."

"Do you think we should wait until the sun's up to start swimming?"

"I'd rather get to land as quickly as possible. This water's cold. Can you manage?" I asked.

"I'll have to. Let's go."

The light slowly brightened the sky as we swam closer. A red glow with orange halo hung over the land, which remained black, but now we could see buildings against the horizon. I spun around after most of the sky had turned to a deep blue with stars still visible.

Thankfully, we weren't fighting a current and the tide seemed to be moving in, so we had an easy swim towards the shore. Still, I was more than a little tired when the surf tumbled me to the beach, where I lay as the water slid away from me. I rose up on my arm, looking for Eve, who lay face down a few feet from me.

I crawled over to her and felt her pulse.

"Am I dead yet?" she asked.

"No, but you're doing a great job of faking it."

She rolled over and groaned. "Good. Leave me here and I'll let the tide finish the job."

"Then Drysdale wins."

She sat up and spat. "Fuck Drysdale."

We both climbed to our feet and walked out of the tidal plain.

"Can you help me get these things off of me? I want to let them dry in the sun."

I helped her undress and lay out the clothing. We lay next to each other, holding hands and listening to the lapping of the waves on the shore. She turned on her side, sighing, her breathing changing. I rolled over to hold her and let my mind wander over the twisted paths in and out of a hell that included a records room with file cabinets. Exhaustion overtook my mind and I slept.

****

I strolled up the beach to a house with a wraparound porch. Bare as the day she was born, Jessica was sitting on the railing, staring at the sands. I was naked as well and couldn't hide my interest. Sometimes it's not so much fun being male.

"Eve's on the beach," I said, "Why don't you go to her."

"I can't. I can't leave this house; he has me trapped. Please, for me, tell her to find the mirror and smash it."

"Smash it?"

"Yes, she must smash the mirror before the end of the vernal equinox."

"I'll tell her, but I don't think she'll be happy about it."

"Tell her my soul is trapped in that mirror. She must use one of the shards to draw blood."

"What must she draw with the blood?" I know, I know, but this is what my dream self asked.

"Her true name."

****

I woke with my climax.

Sobbing, I held Eve who pulled my arm around her tighter. I was tired of a dream life where I woke from a dream of doing one thing to find that my body had been raping Eve all along. No matter how often she consented, it felt like rape to me, and I couldn't stop it.

Eve rolled over to face me. "Was the dream that bad?"

"No, but waking up to find I've assaulted you in the night is driving me batty. I'm not like this, I don't do this, and I'm sick at heart about it."

"Look, listen to me. I give you permission to take me any way you want, any time you want. You want to slap me around some during sex? Go for it. You want to be aggressive? Be aggressive. Do you know what you brought me from your dreams? That necklace you told me about."

"That reminds me, if we find the mirror, you must smash it."

"You dreamed of Jessica?"

"Yes, and she told me we must find and smash the mirror before the vernal equinox. That's the object that has her soul. You must smash it, and you must use one of the shards to draw blood. You must write your true name in blood. Only then will you free her."

I didn't ask her what her true name was. I'd long suspected that she'd only told me her stripper name, and for now that was all I needed. She pulled my face to hers and kissed me with a passion that surprised me. I returned the kisses, the caresses, and soon found myself on top of her, her pulling my ass to thrust deeply within her. We slept again after we both climaxed, my arm around her like a blanket. That time there were no dreams.

While I wasn't sobbing in guilt-wracked tears when next I woke, I was none too pleased to find myself staring at a cop who had been poking me with his night-stick.

"Heh, how about you two love birds come with me to the station? There are laws against this sort of thing."

"What, sleeping on a beach?"

"No, you idiot. Now are you both going to come quietly, or am I going to have to cuff you?"

Eve must have been awake as she rose to sit. "And

exactly what are the charges?"

"Public nudity, of course."

"Look, do you see our clothing?" I joined the cop in looking around. Eve's wet ninja outfit was gone.

"No, that's why I'm taking you in."

"Officer, we're victims of a theft," said Eve. "Our clothing was stolen from us, along with our wallets and ID. Instead of arresting us you should be helping us."

"Helping you?" his voice rose an octave as he looked at her face, eyebrows raised.

She put her hands on her hips. "Yes, isn't that what police do when someone is the victim of a crime? Help them?"

"I, uh, yeah."

She tilted her head and smiled. "Then please give us a lift to our place where we can get some clothing and start contacting the various authorities about our stolen IDs. If nothing else, get us out of the cold."

The cop took out his notebook and pencil. "Any idea who stole your stuff?"

"Nope, it was dark."

"Why did they take your clothing and not your jewels?"

She lifted the necklace off her chest, drawing his gaze off his notepad. "I explained to them that these were cursed. They believed me."

"I'm not certain I should. This is sounding rather far-fetched."

Eve walked over to him and closed his notebook. "Look, we're the victims here. If you take us in, I'll push for wrongful arrest. That's not going to look good on your record."

"All right, I'll take you guys home. It's not as if you

were hurting anyone. For all I know, what you are saying is the truth."

"Thank you, officer," she said as she walked back to me, accentuating her wiggle.

We followed him to his car, passing an old man who looked like Einstein with a violin tucked under his arm. He took it out and played a simple tune which seemed to blend into the pounding of the surf. Eve turned and blew him a kiss as we got to the car. He stopped playing, took off his hat, gave us a small bow, and then resumed playing. The notes wove themselves into my thoughts. I needed to look at this all differently, but it was hard to see something I was inside of. I let myself hum the song he was playing as we crossed the board walk to the parking lot, letting go of thought to focus on the notes.

When we got to the police car, the cop radioed into headquarters about us. When the officer on the other end of the radio stopped laughing, our embarrassed arresting officer turned to us and asked for our names. He then proceeded to give them to the dispatcher who told him, "They're clear, take them home and let Detective O'Neil know when you've dropped them off."

Eve squeezed my hand as we were driven to her place. The cop dropped us off at her door and drove off shaking his head. I figured he'd be sharing this story for years to come.

"Come on up Johnny."

When we got into her room, on her bed were two brown paper packages with a note from Father Donn. Eve insisted she read it before we open the packages.

"He says he's grateful that we emerged from that small slice of hell on Earth and hopes he got the sizes right. He also says that you'll find your car in front of your place."

When I opened the package, my keys and wallet were sitting on clothes that were practically a mirror of what I'd worn when I'd met Father Donn the other day at the cemetery. I knew that when I put them on, they'd fit perfectly. I turned to Eve who was holding up the fossil of the nautilus shell I'd retrieved from my dreams.

"How well do you know Father Donn?" I asked.

"Not well, though he knows me. He's been my confessor for years."

I turned to look at her face. "You go to confession?"

Her lips pulled back and she stared me in the eye. "Look, I may be a whore, but I've got a soul and would like to go to heaven when I die."

"I'm sorry, I didn't mean to judge. I'm just surprised, that's all."

"It's okay, but just because you know something is wrong doesn't mean you can stop, and I did stop, eventually. I don't know if I would have been able to if I hadn't known all along that God loved me and forgave me of everything I did before I even asked."

I swallowed the confusing rush of thoughts and feelings and focused on the practical. For someone who prided himself on his ability to use both conscious and subconscious thoughts, I kept feeling a need to anchor myself in my understanding of reality even though I knew damn well that reality was only a construct from my mind trying to make order of what it encountered even without being aware of it.

"Let's get showered; we're covered in sand. After we're dressed, we gotta get some stuff done and fast. We don't have too many more days until the equinox, and we've got a mirror to smash. One other thing: please stop saying you're a whore. You told me you stopped doing that."

"Johnny, right now, I feel like I'm paying you with sex because I have nothing else I can pay you with. That makes me a whore. I'm actually comfortable with this, but I'm being honest with myself, and what I'm doing. Whoring has always felt like I was born to it."

"Well, *I'm* not comfortable with this. I never wanted a woman to pay for anything with sex, and I wish that I could stop whatever it is that's happening at night. I'm glad of what we did on the beach, but don't for a moment think that it was payment. We made a deal, and we're sticking to it. You'll pay me when we're done with this in cash. You are not a whore."

She gave me a big hug. "That's what I like about you, Johnny, you stick to your principles. You're right, we have a mirror to find and smash, and we only have three weeks. Let's get cleaned up."

****

My car was right where he said it would be. If it hadn't been the actual Ford Torino I'd purchased, I'm not certain what I would have done. I unlocked the car and held open the passenger door for Eve.

"Near as I can figure, we can either go back to that warehouse, or try to track down the mug who attacked me," she said.

I turned the key in the ignition, and it started.

"There is another option. We could go back to that bridge which brought us to Boston."

"And once we are there?" she asked.

"I don't know. I just have a feeling that we missed something important by going back to San Francisco."

"I know what you mean, but we have no leads in

Boston."

"Eve, I told you I'd follow a whim. Trust me, this is the right thing to do." The more she squirmed out of returning to Boston, the more I became convinced we needed to go there.

"Could we please try to find Hanrahan first?"

"Suppose it wouldn't do any harm, and I do owe Drysdale for Gladys."

I drove through town to the flea-bitten neighborhood where Hanrahan was holed up. I counted myself lucky that I was able to get a spot where we could watch his front door from inside the car. Time to sit and wait, something I was very familiar with. After about an hour, Eve said, "Why are we just sitting here. I thought we were going after him?"

"We are, but we're going to do this right."

"Oh. Is this a stake-out?"

"Yep."

"Should I be getting us donuts and coffee then?"

"Not yet. We've no idea of his habits and I'd rather we were both vigilant."

She sighed and settled back into watching. Eve was many things, but patient was not one of them.

About ten minutes later she said, "Why can't we just go up there?"

"Because we're not cops and we don't have a warrant. We don't know if he's home or has company. We can afford to watch and wait."

"Shall I get that coffee yet?"

"No, I've got a feeling we're better off if we stick together on this one."

"I'm bored."

"I noticed, but you're in luck—our wait is over."

Hanrahan came out of his building and got into a car. I put mine in gear and started to follow.

I had to keep both hands on the wheel as Hanrahan started making last minute turns, as if he knew we were on his tail. He picked up speed and started weaving in and out of traffic. The chaos he was creating made it that much harder for me to follow, as I also needed to cut folks off and slip between gaps too small for my car to keep up. He took a sharp right and I had to shift over two lanes to take the same right. When I got there, I could no longer see him.

I cursed and guessed he'd made the first left and barely caught the glimpse of his car as he made a right down two blocks. I sped up, dodged a grandmother pushing a shopping cart and took that same right. I could see him, three car lengths ahead of me. I sped up, sliding between vehicles to close the distance between us, hoping there were no cops watching me drive. Hanrahan slid over three lanes to take an exit which I took as well. I hit the gas to the floor as I slung out of the acceleration ramp onto the highway and cursed. While Hanrahan's car was no longer in sight, the Prudential Center was. We were speeding towards Boston at ninety miles per hour. I slowed down to traffic speed, which was a brisk eighty, and sighed.

"Damn, looks like we're going to explore Boston after all," said Eve.

"I'm sorry, do you want me to turn around and see if we can find him?"

"I wish you could, but I don't see any place to turn around."

"Why are you loath to be in Boston anyway?"

"My parents are near, up in Vermont."

"After my dream the other night, I think the reason we're here *is* to visit your parents."

"I think you're right."

"Vermont?" If they're in Vermont, why were we on the Massachusetts Turnpike heading toward Boston?

"Yes, Vermont. When you get to I-93, head north."

We spent the next three hours driving mostly in silence except when Eve spoke to give me directions. As the sun was setting in our rear-view mirror, I pulled into the driveway of a pale blue house with dark blue shutters.

"All right, we're here," I said, stating the obvious as a way to break the silence. "So, what's the story, you and I, so I get this straight."

Eve sighed. "The truth. I don't care if they believe me or not. I honestly don't know why we're here except you're insisting this is the right thing to do. Let's start with my real name, which is Inanna, Ann for short. You were right, of course. Eve is my stripper name."

Chapter 9

Inanna

Eve—*Inanna* I tried to remember—rang the bell of
her parent's front door. After a few minutes of
impatiently waiting in the chilly night air which smelled
of fading leaves, the porch light came on and the door
opened.

"Inanna?" a man said. "Inanna? Is that really you?"

"Yes, Dad. It's me."

I could hear him undo a lock and the door swung
open to reveal an old man, skin spotted with age and only
wisps of hair remaining on his head. Inanna stepped up
through the door and gave him a tight embrace. I wanted
to go back to the car, but she straightened and said, "Dad,
I want you to meet Johnny Talon."

He extended his hand. "Husband?"

"No, sir. I don't have that honor. I'm a private
investigator she hired to help her recover some stolen
goods. The investigation's a little odd, but it took us to
your neighborhood."

"Well, come in, both of you, come in."

I followed them through a dark narrow hall. We had
no coat to hang on the rack, so I just closed the door
behind me and stepped to the right into a small parlor.

"Dad, where's Mom?"

"She's upstairs, asleep. I was about to turn in when

the two of you showed up. So, what is he investigating that brings you back here?"

"He's helping me find things that were stolen from me."

"And that brings you back to us? After the fight you and your mom had, I thought I'd never see you again."

"I'm sorry about that."

As Inanna gave her father another hug, I looked around the room. The furniture was well worn, a small basket of dried flowers rested on the coffee table, some pictures on the wall. One was of Inanna in her cheerleader outfit. That was the same outfit she'd been wearing the other day, at least some of what she'd told me might be the truth.

I looked over at the two of them as they sat on the couch, facing each other, holding each others' hands.

"Did your mom ever tell you that she had to drop out of school when she became pregnant with you?"

Inanna stiffened. "No, I never knew that."

"She was on a fast track to a Ph.D. in chemistry when she got pregnant. She dropped out of school and took a job in a medical lab to pay the bills. That was where I met her."

"You mean?"

"Yes, while I raised you, and love you, you're not mine. She was so angry at herself for getting pregnant with a guy who didn't love her, wouldn't marry her and help her, that when she thought that you were getting sexually active all that drunken anger at her own mistakes was directed at you."

"I wasn't getting sexually active; I was being harassed and was nearly raped."

The strain in her voice betrayed tears that had yet to

fall. I had no place in that room, despite how much this was helping me understand my client.

"We found out you were telling us the truth after you ran away. I don't know that she's ever forgiven herself for that fight. Especially since she was drunk at the time. She's been sober ever since."

I could slice the awkward silence with a knife, but the squeak of a stair cut it for me.

"Sven, who are you talking to? Oh, Inanna?!"

Inanna rose from the couch and ran to her mother, embracing her as they both broke down in tears. Right then I would rather have been back in that warehouse facing the demonic shapeless monster. I had no business being part of this family drama. "Mom, Dad was just telling me about how you gave up your dreams."

"I'm so sorry that I let my fears and pain drive you away."

As they hugged again, I stepped over to the dad. "I should leave and let you guys catch up without an outsider present."

"Look," said her stepfather. "I still don't understand why your investigation brought Inanna back to us, but I'm so grateful. Please, stay the night. I'll make up a bed."

"It's a bit early for that."

"We're like birds here. We turn in as the sun goes down and rise with the dawn. This is the first time in years that we've used the electric lamp."

I felt Inanna take my arm. "You are not going anywhere. You've given me back my family. Everyone sit, I want to tell you all what has been going on and how this good man has helped me."

"Inanna, you don't have to tell us anything, it is

enough that you're here with us," said her mother.

"Mom, please sit with Dad. Somehow, I think it is important that I tell you both everything. Johnny here, pay attention, you only know the recent stuff, and some of the old history may be relevant."

Inanna proceeded to tell us about hitch hiking across the country, selling sex to pay for meals, hotels, winding up living in San Francisco working as a hooker. She described the night I freed her from Drysdale, how she met Jessica and their marriage. She told of the heartbreak of the breast cancer, of how she met the boyfriend who helped her through her heartbreak only to later break her heart when he left her, stealing everything she owned and hiring a man to take her down.

During the entire narrative, her mother sat by her side with a broad grin that rose to the crows' feet around tear filled eyes. She never stopped holding Inanna's hand.

There were a few details I filed away for thought. First, the jerk who stole from her never told her what he did for a living. The whole thing stank of Drysdale playing Inanna for a fool. The problem with this is that Inanna had never come across as a fool. How did he fool her so completely?

The second was that Drysdale was the second to last trick Inanna had played. In fact, the night after the last time she played the whore, she met Jessica. The coincidences were a bit much. The third thing was the number of threes in her life. Hooker, full time spouse, stripper. The demons also came in threes. She'd also had three lovers and told her parents I was the third. I had no idea if there was a significance that she'd only been married to the one. There had even been three boys who

119

molested her.

Inanna's mother's yawn broke Inanna's narrative with us heading up route ninety-three. "Don't stop dear, I'm tired but I want to hear every word."

"I've kept you both up long enough."

"Nonsense. Show me the necklace and bracelet Jessica gave you."

Inanna held our first her arm, and then lifted up the necklace for her mother.

"Those are old jewels. The cuts were done by hand with the old mine cut, and the setting is either white gold or platinum."

"How can you tell?"

"Your grandfather was a jeweler, he taught me what to look for. Jessica must have been filthy rich to afford these pieces." Filthy rich? I'd never see a dime from Inanna if all I helped her retrieve was things like that. No way she was selling either to raise money to pay me.

Inanna's father yawned.

Inanna said, "I'm so sorry, let's turn in and we can talk more over breakfast."

"We kept your room made up, dear. Let me get some bedding for Johnny."

After the women went upstairs, her father rose and extended his hand. "Thank you for bringing Inanna home to us, even if it is for a night."

"It is an honor, sir."

"Care for a drink before you turn in?"

Her mother called down, "Send him up to the guest room Sven."

"You better go up."

"Some other time on that drink."

Her mother met me at the top of the stairs. She

handed me a small pile of bedding and a towel. "Your room is the last room on the left."

"Thanks, ma'am."

I found a switch on the wall and took stock of their guest room. Unadorned dark wood dresser, wrought iron bed, white curtains over a window cracked open.

I put the blanket, pillow, and towel on the dresser, closed the door and began laying out the sheet. A part of me was looking forward to a night alone. Despite her assurances, I felt like a rapist each time I woke up inside her, especially since I often found her in tears later. I turned off the light and climbed under the covers. My last waking thought was that I could not bear the possibility that her consent was yet another lie.

****

I walked along a platform next to railroad tracks behind a young woman with long blond hair wearing a red dress with a black belt. The place smelled of burnt coal, and in the distance, I could hear a train whistle blow. I followed the girl past a box car. The tracks curved to the right, and I followed them around the bend to find myself strolling through a desert, though still next to the tracks. I looked back: no sight of the buildings or the box car. The young woman was still in front of me, though she now wore only the black belt. I must be getting old as my only thought was that she was going to have one nasty sunburn. I followed her up a hill but stopped briefly when I got to the top.

The city that I beheld would have made ancient Greece proud. I saw a temple with a gold roof which was nearly blinding in the hot sun. The naked woman was following a cypress-lined road to the city. I hurried to follow her.

Not soon after I was on the cypress-lined lane, I saw a skeleton step onto the path. She stopped to talk with it. I held back, neither wanting to intrude nor be noticed. The skeleton turned its skull towards me and I felt disoriented, as if I were falling.

****

Again, I woke with my orgasm's push into Inanna. I rolled off her and began to cry. She wrapped an arm around me and put her head on my chest. "I couldn't sleep, so I crawled into bed with you. I hope that's not why you're crying."

"Each time I wake inside you, and realize I'd been forcing you down, it bothers me to my core."

"Johnny, please stop worrying. I like being dominated in sex."

"Still, it's not who I am."

"Pity, your sleep self is good."

"Aren't you worried about your parents?"

"Yes, but not that way. I already told them we were lovers." She kissed me. "Tell me Johnny, what is one percent of a family?"

I answered by returning her kiss. As we kissed, while my body stayed with her, my mind was sent hurling through the stars, rushing through clouds of dust that sparkled with the light of a thousand stars, past planets and through the unimaginable dark. I flew over the moon and as I split the earth's atmosphere a winged angel took my hand and we glided back to that room in that small house in New Hampshire to find myself. Whole and impassioned I gave into the passion her kiss had inspired. When we were done, her on top of me, us both letting our breathing slow, I pulled her to me for another kiss.

Inanna was still asleep in my bed when I woke, sunlight streaming through the curtains. I grabbed the towel, wrapped it around my waist and sought the bathroom. After I'd showered, I returned to my room. Inanna was no longer in bed. I dressed and headed downstairs. Her mother was sitting at the table, naked, sipping a cup of coffee.

I blushed, and turned around, "Pardon me, ma'am, I didn't know."

"Oh, don't be silly. Turn around and sit at the table. I'll fix breakfast."

"But you're naked. What if your husband should… what will he think?"

"That you're over-dressed," came his voice from behind me.

"You mean you're naked too?" My voice must have gone up three octaves.

"Yes, young man. Now, you're free to join us at the table. Clothed or naked, your choice."

I turned back around and sat myself at the table, trying not to look at Inanna's mother as she brought me a cup of coffee, but I kept my clothing on.

"Mom! Dad! What are you both doing naked in the kitchen?"

"Making breakfast, dear. Come on in, don't worry, your private investigator isn't naked."

Inanna sat at the table. "What are you two up to?"

"Your mother's hot flashes are sometimes so bad that she's only comfortable naked. When she's like that, I get naked too, so she doesn't feel odd about it."

"Mom, would you like me to get undressed?"

"No, that's just fine, dear. I'm starting to cool off. Let me put my bathrobe back on."

The couple dressed, then her mother put a coffee cup in front of Inanna.

"Inanna, tell us the truth: is Johnny really just a private investigator you hired? If you ask me, he's very in love with you, and you two had quite the active night. Shush, you must have known we'd hear."

I'm in love with Inanna? The reality of what she said came crashing down on me.

"You're right on both accounts, Mom. Johnny loves me, and we're having sex, but he really is a private investigator I hired to help me recover everything that was stolen from me."

Inanna knows I love her? How did she know something about me I didn't? For how long?

"Well, if you ask me, I'd hold onto a guy who loved me and was so good in the sack."

"Mom!"

"Unless you're faking it, you had six orgasms last night. Lovers that good are hard to find."

"Dad, make her stop."

"Should I leave?" I asked.

"It's okay, Johnny, we both know she climbed into your bed," said her father.

"You two are impossible," said Inanna.

"How do you want your eggs?" asked her mom.

"Look, mom, we haven't seen each other in about twelve years because of an argument we had over my sex life, do you think that you could stop?"

"Twelve years? But dear, it's only been five. I thought you were exaggerating the dates last night."

"Five?" Inanna's voice went up three octaves. "Dad, what year is this?"

"1995, why?"

"Johnny and I have traveled back in time again. I'm horribly afraid that in my today that you're both—" Inanna broke down in tears. Her mother put down her spatula and gave her a hug.

"Has it really been twelve years for you?"

Inanna nodded.

"I'm so, so very sorry I hurt you that much. Johnny, you have no idea how grateful I—" her words dissolved into tears.

Her father rose and rescued the eggs. "I'm grateful too, Johnny. Time travel? So, the bit she told yesterday about battling demons wasn't a metaphor for getting over a drug addiction?"

"No. We really fought demons." I was glad that he didn't ask for details. My ego was bruised enough from the reality that I'd not made a dent in any of those demons, no matter how hard I'd fought.

I took Inanna's hand. "Inanna, why would you worry that your parents are dead simply because we're in the past? You were pretty convinced they were alive before we drove here."

"Don't you see, Johnny," she said, biting her lip, "maybe the only reason we had to travel back in time is that we can't visit them in our today."

****

We ate our eggs in silence, Inanna and her mother holding hands. Once the meal was over, Inanna's mother gave Inanna's hand a squeeze, stood up, and poured us each some coffee. She sat herself down and said, "When you get back to your time, please give us a call."

"You're not angry at me that I became the whore you told me I was?"

"I'm angry that I called you a whore. If you can

125

forgive me for that, I may forgive myself one day."

"What will I do if I get back and I can't reach you by phone?"

Her dad said, "I'll get an answering service. And if we're in a home or a hospital, I'll make certain that they tell you how to reach us."

"I mean, what if you're dead?"

"Don't worry about that. Only the good die young."

"Dad!"

"Okay, I know, but we do have to die sometime, but twelve years isn't so long and we both are healthy. Just keep us in your prayers. It's more than I ever thought we could ask for."

Her mom gave her a kiss on the top of her head. "You have to get back. I don't know if time spent with us in the past is free time, or if for each day you spend with us, you spend one or more days in the future. Jessica's soul must be set free. Now that you've come back to us, you've set us free. Do the same for her."

"I'll try, but it's all so confusing. How does a soul get trapped in a thing? How is it her ghost was able to talk to us?"

"I'd ask Father Donn about that if I were you," said her father.

"I don't want to go, but Jessica needs me."

Her father put down his coffee, a wry grin on his face. "Dear, you can't stay, that would be living in the past."

I nearly choked on my coffee. Inanna kicked him under the table as her voice rose both in volume and pitch. "Dad, please stop. I know I have to go, and bad puns won't help."

He reached out across the table and took her hand,

his expression softening to sorrow. "Sorry, they're my way of handling the fact that I may never see you again."

Inanna rose and her mom embraced her. "Don't return love with sex for too much longer. If you can't love him, find another private investigator. The longer you stay with him, the worse his heartbreak will be."

"I know. There is no one else who can help me, and I don't know that I can't love him, but right now I don't, and I'm sad about that. He is a good man. Perhaps I can only love women."

I rose and her father offered me his hand. I took it. "She's a good egg, my Inanna, but she has no idea how she's setting herself up for a hurt of her own. Forgive her, if you can, for how she's treating you."

I didn't want to think about it, not now, so I changed the subject. "If you don't mind, her name is a bit odd. What is the story behind it?"

"It means Queen of Heaven, from an old Sumerian myth. I studied archaeology in my youth."

"Thank you, that helps."

I had nothing else to say to him, and looking back on it, I think there was nothing to be said. I certainly didn't want to discuss the dream sex that was borderline rape. This was not an issue of forgiveness, but I wasn't certain I could explain that to anyone.

We walked to the front door, Inanna and her mom behind me. Her dad opened the front door and stepped outside, holding it open for the rest of us. "Nice ride. Being a private investigator must pay well."

Instead of my old Ford, an Ashton Martin sat in the driveway, gleaming in the sun. "It changes each time I drive it," I said. "What I purchased was a used Ford Torino."

He winced. "That's an old car, even today. I can't imagine what that looks like in fifteen years' time. Not exactly your ride of choice?"

"It gets me where I need to be, and right now, it seems to be having an identity crisis."

"So I see."

I opened the passenger door for Inanna, who now wore a long jean skirt with a white blouse.

"That wasn't what she wore…" Words failed him as Inanna gave him a hug.

"Don't worry, Dad. My clothing is having the same identity crisis as his car."

Her father laughed heartily. "Makes sense. Cars are for the man what clothes are for the woman."

She got into the car. I closed her door and walked to the driver's side. "It was a pleasure meeting both of you," I said to her parents.

"If we're dead in the future, don't let her grieve too much," said her mother, her voice broken with the tears that were at the corners of her eyes.

I nodded to acknowledge her concern, knowing that we both knew there was nothing I'd be able to do in that event. I closed the door, turned the key, and drove away to the sounds of Inanna's crying. Somewhere on that long lonely highway, the car entered California and I found myself following Hanrahan's car. Out of the corner of my eye I could see Inanna pull open her purse.

"Mom?"

She must have called her folks.

"Yeah, we're back in San Francisco, and must be back in our future as we're following the creep who attacked me again."

I had to take a sudden right to keep her words the

128

truth, but we were still tailing him.

"Yes, the moment we've got that mirror smashed, I'll catch the first plane out. Love you both. Bye."

I couldn't take my gaze off the road, but she sounded happy, and that put a smile on my heart. "They're okay?"

"Yes, thank you."

The weaving in and out of traffic became a joy filled challenge. I might as well enjoy being in love with her now that I knew I was. I never knew how much joy I could find in someone else's relief.

Chapter 10

The Pacific Palisades

Hanrahan parked on the same block as that surreal theater I'd been sitting in looking for Jack the Fish. I circled the block and then parked further down so I could see his car.

"Now what? Do we look for him, or do we wait for him to emerge?" asked Inanna.

"We wait."

"Why?"

"We don't know which door he went in."

"Well, you wait, I'm going into that theater. I just know he's in there."

"And if you're wrong and he comes out of another door while you're in there?"

She opened the car door letting in the damp sea-tinged air.

"Then you're just going to have to handle him until I get back."

She slipped out and slammed the door behind her. I watched her walk, annoyed at her because I'd also rather be going after him instead of sitting and waiting.

Suddenly she was naked, and that meant demons. I pushed open the car door with just enough time to shout out, "Inanna, look out!" when three demons materialized behind her. I ran at them, pulling my revolver from my holster knowing full well it would be useless but hoping to get one angry enough it would come after me when Hanrahan emerged from the theater behind Inanna who had wheeled to face the demons.

Not having a clean shot, I had to risk one. She couldn't face him as well as the three hell-spawn. I stopped, planted, aimed, and fired. Hanrahan fell like a forgotten doll. I raced towards the three demons and Inanna in her fury. None of the demons paid my shot any mind as they circled Inanna, who slashed at any that dared to move on her with her comb. They seemed hesitant, as if unwilling to all leap on her at once and overwhelm her. This made me think better of those demons, afraid to face a woman in her fury. I knew many a man who would say the same. I was a fool, and despite my prior encounters had no such reluctance to face the demons. I leapt onto the back of one, my momentum carrying it and myself into a roll, my arm wrapped around its neck.

It tried clawing at me, but its arms wouldn't reach around. It then threw itself backwards, crushing me under its weight which kept increasing.

"I can keep getting heavier and heavier," it taunted.

My breathing labored. As my vision blurred, I saw Inanna thrust her comb into the demon.

The scream was horrible, I had to pull my hands to my ears to stop it, but the weight was gone with only the foul stench of sulfur left hanging heavy in the growing fog.

I turned over, pushed myself onto my hands and knees and struggled to rise, lightheaded, I fell and tried again. Inanna lay on the pavement a few steps away, bleeding and unconscious. I hobbled over. Facial wounds bleed badly, even the shallow ones, so I refused to panic. I felt her pulse: steady. I pulled off my shirt, tore off the sleeve, and wrapped her head with it to make a bandage. I picked her up and started to carry her to the car when I heard a voice call out, "Heh, what about me?"

Hanrahan, the scum, lived.

"I'll be back for you," I called back.

Inanna woke while I carried her to the car. "What happened?"

"Don't know, but you saved my life. You've got a nasty head wound, and who knows what else. I'm taking you to a hospital."

I was very glad that the car had changed into a sixty's convertible, with the top down. I lay her in the back seat and headed back to get Hanrahan. I saw at once why he couldn't move, the bullet had entered his leg, which was bleeding badly. He had a hand on it to stem the flow. "You want to live; you're going to tell me everything about why your gang stole everything from Eve and what you all intend to do with it."

"Deal."

"That came rather fast."

"I don't want to die, and I wanted no part of the demons."

I picked him up and carried him. "Let's say I believe you about the demons. What was your role in this, besides trying to kill my client?"

"I wasn't trying to kill her, just to kidnap her, but had no idea she was so good at the martial arts."

"Why kidnap her? You already had all her stuff."

"Not that comb. Drysdale wants that comb, and he wants her. Don't know why, but he was insane when it wasn't with the rest of it. He also wants her, alive."

"What's so important about the comb?" I asked as I tore off the other sleeve from my shirt.

"Don't fucking know. You don't ask questions from someone like Drysdale. You just do what you're told if you know what is good for you."

"Where is he keeping the rest of the stuff?" I asked as I tied the sleeve around his leg. As much as I wanted to ask about the mirror, I didn't want to tip our hand.

"He has a warehouse on San Pedro street."

"Yeah, know the place. Does he keep everything there? Nothing at hand?" I asked as I helped him to his feet.

"He was very strict that everything go there, but what was done after it was delivered, I've no idea."

"So, you were to take Eve there, after you kidnapped her?"

"No, she was to go to his house, but the comb was to be taken to the warehouse."

I helped him limp to the car. "If all he wanted was the comb, why keep her after you had it?"

"Apparently, he paid for services some years ago that weren't fully delivered. He wanted her to finish her job. Nice car."

"I know. Don't bleed on it."

I put him in the front passenger seat, keeping an eye on him as I scooted around and got into the driver's seat. I was not looking forward to explaining my passengers to the emergency room nurse.

****

The triage nurse didn't ask any questions about Hanrahan's gun wound nor Inanna's facial wound; he just processed them. They took Hanrahan first, and Inanna an hour later. She'd insisted on a plastic surgeon, and it took another two hours for one to become available. During that time, Inanna poured over every magazine in the place, even ones I'd never had thought she'd be interested in.

I just sat and thought, mulling over every fact, every lead. It all came back to I didn't know squat. From the questions Inanna never answered, to the dead leads, to the bizarre warehouse and Drysdale's private gate to hell, and the fact that we found the paperwork on which crate contained Inanna's stuff very easily. The only place we could look was the last place I wanted to get back to, that city of demons, or take another crack at the crate.

If we were going demon hunting, I needed to know more about demons and how to handle them. The only thing that has gotten rid of them consistently has been her comb. For the first time in years, I wanted to talk to a priest. The triage nurse called Inanna and she waved as she followed the nurse into the office. I looked about me at the magazines thinking I needed to give my mind a rest when Father Donn walked into the waiting room.

"Tough day, Johnny?"

"How did you—?" I couldn't even finish the sentence. There were so many questions that started with those words right there.

"Know you were here? I'm doing my daily hospital visit and ran into Eve in the hall just now. She told me you were out here."

While priests do visit hospitals, the coincidences in this case were crazy, even for me. "I'm just a little freaked out because I was thinking but moments ago about needing to talk to a priest *and here you are*."

"How can I help you, son? Do you want to go someplace private?"

"Actually, let's go to the cafeteria and grab a coffee. It has been a long day."

Once we were seated with our coffees, I asked, "So, what do you know about demons?"

The priest's smile faded to that of concern. "A life of good deeds and prayer is the surest way to keep them at a distance."

I took a sip of the coffee, and smiled; I needed this. "Look, I have good reason to believe that Drysdale is summoning demons from a room in his house and setting them on Eve, and that he has a portal to hell in his warehouse and his house. I need to know how to deal with those things while we look for a mirror that was stolen from Eve. We have to smash it before the equinox."

Father Donn patted my hand. "Johnny, you need a specialist. I know of a man who hunted demons and put a stop to just such an operation in Paris before the war."

"Which war?"

He took a tall sip of his coffee before answering. "World War II."

I took out my rather underused notebook and a pen. It had been a while since this case had offered something I could sanely write down. "What's his name?"

"Henry Miller."

I practically choked on my coffee, and my voice rose three octaves. So much for sanity. "What, the author?"

"Yes, that's him."

"Didn't he write smut?"

Father Donn leaned back in his chair, and took another sip of coffee. "He once told me that in removing the sense of sin that is wrongfully felt about sex, he did more to remove the grip of demons on the world than a thousand churchmen. They can't torment you about what you don't feel wrong about, and there is nothing wrong about sex. It is a gift from God himself."

I put down the notebook. "So, the church's teachings don't say sex is a sin?"

"Never did, or at least not the church as a whole, though some within the church have made that mistake. We teach sex should be ideally confined to marriage, and the couple having sex should be open to children as a result, while recognizing that people can't live up to those ideals in all times and places. Folks have overreacted to the Church upholding an ideal to strive for as the Church asking the impossible of people. May come from the fact that we publish our documents in Latin, and translation is always a lie."

"So, sex outside of marriage is not a sin?"

"If that sex isn't adultery and doesn't come between either person and God, then how could it be? However, it is far from the ideal. That doesn't make it wrong, but certainly doesn't justify it as a good way to live and act. Do you see the difference?"

I felt a weight being lifted. I had no idea how guilty I'd been about how Inanna and I'd been acting. "Yes, I think I do."

I owed Henry Miller a debt and I hadn't met him yet, but I must find him, as I had other questions to put to him. "Do you know where I can find Miller?"

"Yes, last I knew he had moved from his place in the Big Sur to a house in Pacific Palisades. Hand me your notebook and I'll jot down the address."

I handed him the notebook and pen. He wrote in it, closed it, and handed it back to me. *Pacific Palisades?*

I'd have to look up where that was.

I pushed back my chair and stood up.

Father Donn looked up at me. "Going back to the waiting room?"

"Yes. Do me a favor, drop by the room of Sean Hanrahan. He was admitted today from a gunshot wound. I suspect he'd like to make a confession."

His eyebrows rose. "Is there a risk of death?"

"Isn't there always?"

Father Donn chuckled and pushed his chair back from the table. "I like that! I may use that in a homily one day."

"Heaven forbid."

His chuckle deepened as he stood and pushed his chair in. "Oh, I rather doubt that, Johnny. I doubt that indeed."

****

I didn't wait long before Inanna came out of the treatment room with a large bandage on her forehead. "You'll live?" I asked.

She rolled her eyes. "No, the wound is fatal. The surgeon told me when all is done, there won't even be a scar."

"Nice work. I've got a new lead for us to follow before we take on Drysdale and his demons again."

"What's that?"

"Henry Miller."

"The author?"

"Yes, and I'm as surprised as you, but Father Donn highly recommended him as an authority on combating demons." I stood up and we started walking to the hotel exit.

"Father Donn recommended Henry Miller as an

137

authority on combating demons?" she sounded rather puzzled. "In that case, let's go."

****

Some six hours of driving later with only stops for gas and to use a rest room, we got off the highway. I was surprised that all the cars I was seeing were older, vintage 1970s vehicles before the oil crisis. I passed by an Esso station and realized that we'd traveled in time again. I wondered what the past me was doing at this time as I drove past lovely homes with green lawns.

I found the house and came to a stop in front of it. Inanna said, "You helped me recover my name, but for now please help me keep Inanna as my secret identity. Let's use Eve when we're not alone."

I found a sign on the door which I read: "When a man has reached old age and has fulfilled his mission, he has a right to confront the idea of death in peace. He has no need of other men, he knows them already and has seen enough of them. What he needs is peace. It is not seemingly to seek out such a man, plague him with chatter, and make him suffer banalities. One should pass by the door of his house as if no one lived there." I liked him already. Never the less, I rang the bell.

The door opened to my relief. "Is Mr. Miller at home?" asked Eve.

The young woman said, "I'm his wife, Hoki. Please come in."

****

Hoki led us into a room where Mr. Miller sat in a wheelchair looking out a large window at the sea. In the distance we could see whales passing by. I wondered if the sperm whale I'd seen while falling was with that pod.

"Henry, you have guests."

He turned his wheelchair and lit up with a smile that was filled with the delight of the universe. "To whom do I owe the pleasure?"

"I'm Johnny Talon, detective, and this is Eve."

"I'm honored to meet you. Eve, while that lingerie is lovely, you are probably making Hoki upset. Don't you have any clothing?"

"We've long since lost control over what we wear. We put on one set of clothing and find ourselves wearing something else. My car does similar things."

"This is colorful, and all, but why are you disturbing an old man's meditations?"

"Old man my ass," said Hoki. "Henry you were disturbed before they arrived. Be polite for a change."

"Wasn't I polite when Miss Jong was here last week?"

"Yes, you can talk sex with other writers for hours and be the kindest soul imaginable. I'll have to do it for you. Feel free to have a seat. Can I get either of you something to drink, or some weed?"

"No, thanks."

"I'll take a joint," said Inanna.

I glared at her; weren't things wild enough without getting drugs involved?

Hoki opened a case sitting on a table and offered her one of many pre-rolled joints. She took it and it lit itself as she put it to her lips. Eve took a drag, and when she blew out the smoke, it took shape as a small, diminutive man dressed in woman's clothes with a feather boa wrapped around his neck. The miniature drag queen danced away on the smoke to fade into air.

"Well, that was interesting. Exactly how did you do that?" asked Henry.

"I've no idea. It is as if Johnny and I are on a long strange and not a very good trip. Demons keep attacking me, and we'd like some pointers on how to handle demons. A mutual friend told us that in your youth you hunted demons."

Hoki sat down. "Henry, is this true?"

"Father Donn. It was Father Donn wasn't it? He is too kind. When I lived in Paris, I knew a dame who got herself involved with a bunch of Satanists. She started to attend the Black Mass and came to me one day with this tale of having sex on the altar with a demon, begging me to come with her. Can I get a drag off that joint?"

"Isn't that why they're called joints?" Inanna asked as she passed him the joint. Henry took a long inhale. The drag queen that came from his exhale had a red boa and a green dress.

"I went with her. She was careful to try to hide the route, but by then I knew Paris pretty well. Everyone there wore a mask and nothing else. The dame I was with put on her mask, stripped, and encouraged me to join her. I let her know that I intended to keep my clothing on, and I found a hidden place from which to watch the show. While they performed the abomination, no demons appeared, to the great disappointment of my date who sought me out to take her home. The Satanists later learned of my presence and blamed me for the lack of demonic attention, but I have reason to know that from that point forward they could never again summon a demon."

He passed the joint to me, but I handed it to Eve without a second glance while he continued the narrative.

"Over the next few weeks various Satanists would

140

try to kill me, but their attacks were always foiled, often in the most ridiculous way. My favorite was the Satanist who got a bucket of shit dumped on his head from a balcony. While the demons stopped showing up at their Black Mass, if I was walking the streets of Paris alone a demon would attack me. After the third attack, I found a priest and talked to him about what was going on. He encouraged me to come to church and carry a crucifix, which I refused. It would have been hypocritical of me. I may not have been a Satanist, but I was certainly no saint. Instead, I followed a different part of the priest's advice, I sought out those aspects of me for which I was ashamed or felt guilty about and did something about it.

"You see, I'd noticed the various places where the demonic attacks would happen, Pistorums, whore houses, etcetera. From that point on, I worked on being an unashamed man. I let myself become more truly free, and each time a demon came, I heaped upon it insults related to that shame, pummeling it with my words and my fists. I sought out the places and the activities to purge myself of shame.

"I reveled in pissing in public. I reveled in whoring. I reveled in taking another man's wife. Take that, ten commandments, she wanted to be taken and her husband wasn't filling her needs. I reveled in eating on another man's dime, sleeping in a room paid for by someone else. When I had no shame, when I became the happiest man alive, I wrote! No longer was I writing literature, I wrote a song for the ages of fucking, of beauty, of the god-awful truth of existence not some flower-strewn-fantasy. And it was glorious.

"From then on, I was only plagued by one demon; that my then wife, June, was a lesbian."

141

"Excuse me, but may I ask a question?" asked Inanna.

"You just did."

"These demons of yours, none of them seem to have attacked you physically. The last one that attacked me put me in the hospital. How do you get rid of demons like that."

"Stay off the drugs."

"Huh?"

"Stay off the drugs. I know that this hashish we're sharing is wonderful, but the opiates, LSD, etcetera—just stop."

"Mister Miller," I said, "I don't know that drugs are involved here. I see them too. I put a bullet through one."

"So, the demons that are attacking you are more like what the Satanists had summoned with their Black Mass. Simple, disrupt their ritual, mock it so the sincerity of the Satanists is questioned."

"So, don't stop them?" I asked.

"No, that would be honoring the ritual as valid. Demons can't abide being laughed at."

Inanna stood up and offered Henry Miller her hand. "Thank you, Mister Miller. You've given me a lot to think about."

He rose, took her hand, and kissed it with undeniable sincerity. "You are very welcome. I hope you are able to overcome your demons."

Her smile didn't reach her eyes. "Me too."

Chapter 11

Murphy

We left the Miller's to find that the car was the kind of old car that you always saw in movies about Eliot Ness. I held open the door for Eve and got in the other side. I was mildly surprised that the key fit, but as always, my key worked and the car started.

I asked, "Was that at all useful to you?" I had my own ideas about how useful Henry Miller's ideas were, but I wanted to hear Inanna's take.

"Oddly enough, yes. I've always been a bit ashamed that I became a whore, and then an exotic dancer. I also used to do drugs, but until that joint, I'd not touched anything for a few years, and it didn't make me high, just relaxed and open to ideas. What is interesting is that ever since our visit to my parents, I've no longer felt ashamed that I am a whore and a stripper. I may even start calling myself the more politically correct sex worker. Shall we go back to the warehouse, or to Drysdale's home?"

"The mirror could be in either, but I think we'd be better off taking a second shot at that warehouse. I do have one more thought, about the demons. You're always attacked by three demons. Are there two other things you were ashamed of besides having been a prostitute? Were you ever ashamed of your drug use?"

"I might have been, at the time, but I stopped using

years ago. I also have no idea what third thing has ever filled me with shame. As for the mirror, I wonder if the bastard doesn't keep it on himself."

"Good point," I said. "Finding him in the present may be difficult. Both times we've gone after him, we've wound up in the past, and we have no control over our movement through time."

Inanna patted my hand. "Just now, when we needed to visit Henry Miller, the car brought us to both where and when. Perhaps we just need to be focused on our objective."

"In car we trust?" I chuckled.

"Hasn't steered us wrong yet."

I ignored the pun and started driving towards Drysdale's house, so I was more than a little surprised when I found myself parking in front of the warehouse. "Well, that is unexpected."

"This is where you wanted to go; I guess the car listened to your wants."

I put my hands on the top of my head and pulled my hair back. "Yeah, but how did I get here? We just got off the freeway, at Drysdale's exit, and here we are without driving on any of the streets we needed to get here."

"I thought you used surrealism as a method. You've got to stop wondering how. Why is the more important question. I hired you because I know you're the guy who can help me. If the reason why is that this is what you wanted, then that's good enough. Let's go."

I let go of my hair. She was right. How was the least important question. I was becoming overwhelmed. "You're right, *but,* let's wait until sundown. I want everyone out of there, at least, everyone human. It will also be interesting to watch who enters and leaves that place."

"So, how shall we pass the time?" she asked while unzipping me.

I put my hand on hers to stop her. "Nothing that will draw the attention of the cops."

She pushed my hand aside. "Johnny, this *is* the warehouse district. They're less likely to bother us parked here if I give you oral sex than if I don't. You'll look like just another John, and I'll look like just another whore."

Sure enough, five minutes after she began a cop walked past and gave me the thumbs up. One thing was for certain, she knew the rules of the underside of San Francisco better than me.

Keeping alert and keeping my composure under the circumstances was difficult, but I was glad I did when I saw Drysdale himself come out of the building. "Stop, that's Drysdale. I want to follow him."

"I'm keeping my head down. Follow him, but I don't want him to see me."

A black limo stopped in front of the warehouse and Drysdale got in. I started up the car and put it into gear. Once the limo was three blocks away, I pulled out of the parking spot and started to follow it down the road. It slowed as it neared a group of working girls and came to a stop. I drove past, pulling into the next cross street. I quickly make a K turn and waited for his limo to drive past. It took about five minutes, but the limo drove by us. I waited a moment and then took the corner to follow it. It had the same license, so unless he got out with the crowd of hookers, I hadn't lost the tail.

Drysdale's driver made no further stops until the car pulled into the driveway of a house I'd not known about.

From down the block, I watched as first what must be one of the hookers, now naked and on a leash, get out of the limo. The other end was held by Drysdale who also got out. We stayed in my car until the limo had driven away and the happy couple had entered the house.

"Okay, Inanna, time to get up. He's taken a hooker into a house on a leash, so I'm guessing he's got designs on her much like what I took you from."

She stopped long enough to say, "How exciting."

I pulled her head up. "I mean it. Stop. We've got to go in there."

"I know that, but it would be best to wait two hours for him to finish with her and go to sleep. Besides, I'm running a personal record here and I don't want to stop."

"Record?"

"This is the longest I've ever given oral without the guy coming. I want to see how long we can keep this up." She licked me. "You're delicious."

I pushed her back to her side of the car. "You don't want to stop him from whipping that girl?"

She grabbed me with her hand and started stroking me. "It's what she's being paid for, and likely paid well. It might be the best trick she's pulled, and she agreed to whatever is being done."

"I seem to recall that once he had you bound and gagged he started going beyond your agreement."

"Yes, and no. In agreeing to be bound and to be dominated in sex, which I'd done, I hadn't thought through much of what he was going to do. I'd not agreed to the specifics, but when I think back on it, I'd agreed to him doing whatever it was he wanted."

I forced myself to keep my anger out of my voice by speaking slowly and evenly. "So, I should have left you there and let him finish what he'd started?"

"Please don't be hurt. I'm glad you got me out. I was in over my head and if I'd understood what I was agreeing to, I'd never have agreed. However, before we rush in and pull this woman out of whatever it is she has gotten herself into, we should remember that she agreed to get into his car. Perhaps, unlike me, she knows what she's getting into.

"Oh, look what you've done. You've lost your erection. I'll have to start all over again."

****

We went around to the back door, which I found easy to pick. We had left our shoes in the car, and our bare feet made no noise as we crept through the ground floor of the house. We found nothing on the ground floor. Inanna insisted we go down to the basement, and sure enough, the door to the basement was sound proofed. As we opened it, we heard the crack of a whip and a scream. Inanna whispered into my ear to go slowly and quietly, but to put my piece into my hand. I drew it out of my shoulder holster, and we proceeded down the stairs. Gun in my hand and up, I peered around the corner at the bottom of the stairs. Drysdale was naked, as was the girl who hung from her hands manacled and chained to a thick wooden beam. Her legs were pulled apart by ropes. Drysdale was circling her, whipping her with something I could only describe as a flogger.

I waited until his back was to me, stepped around the corner, leveled the gun and said, "Drop the whip Drysdale."

"Not Johnny Talon again." He dropped the flogger and raised his hands, but as he turned to me I saw only a wide grin on his face.

147

"The same."

"Do you have the whore with you?"

Inanna stepped into the open room. "I'm here. What of it?"

He snarled, "Strip, whore, and give me what you owe me."

She spat at him. "I owe you nothing, thief."

"Thief! That's rich. I stole nothing from you."

"Fred took everything he stole from me and gave it to you."

"Take up your complaint with Fred, but in the meantime, you owe me sex, bitch."

She took a step towards him, pointing her finger accusingly. "You killed Fred in one of your demonic summonings after taking from him everything he stole from me."

Drysdale shrugged his shoulders, but his smile returned. I preferred the snarl. "What of it? He owed me much more, which is why I had his life torn from his worthless hide. Now, strip and honor your agreement. I paid you richly for six months of sexual slavery. I own you."

"Here's what you're going to do, Drysdale," I said. "You're going to untie the girl behind you and remove her gag. If she still wants to stay with you, then she can stay, but you're going to return to Eve everything you took from Fred that's hers. Once she has that, she can return the money you gave for using her. That contracts been canceled."

He started doing something with his hands that I couldn't follow. "Oh, don't worry, Talon. She still has all the cash I gave her. Fred never found her hidden bank accounts. All I got was some worthless clothing and

148

trinkets. I'm so big hearted that I gave it all away to good will."

Inanna shook her fist at him. "Fuck you, Drysdale. You voided our agreement when you tried to have me serve Murphy and there was nothing in our contract about using me to summon demons. Also, I have things you didn't give to good will. Things of mine you wanted. You didn't give this away." She held up the bracelet. "And I've got the necklace, the stone, and my purse back. I want the mirror that goes with them. Hand it over. As for the money, you'll have it back before the day is done. Even though I served you for three of those six months, I'll refund every dime."

Drysdale chuckled but didn't look at her, his hands never ceased moving, his smile was now a snarl. "Talon, what have you done to her? The whore is suddenly free with money? You've ruined a perfectly good whore, and you're going to pay for that. Let's start with putting you both in your place."

He stopped moving his hands and snapped his fingers. I felt myself falling through time and space to land and roll, coming to my feet, pistol in hand. I felt a breeze. Wherever I was, I was outside in the starless night. I breathed in deeply the clean smell of pine.

"Johnny, are you there?" Inanna sounded frightened.

"Yeah, I'm here."

"It's so dark. I can't see anything."

"I've got some matches. Let me see if I can light one in this breeze."

I pulled out a pack. With the long practice of a smoker, I lit a match. I could see Inanna, about ten feet away, and some trees in the distance. Wherever we were,

149

we weren't going anywhere until morning. I could see tears on her cheeks.

"Aren't you going to ask me about the hidden bank accounts?"

"No." I shook the match out, as it had gotten too hot for my fingers.

"No?"

I got on my knees and started collecting some sticks I'd noticed when the match had been lit. It was cold, and likely to get colder before morning. "Inanna, you've been keeping things from me from day one, sometimes outright lying to me, like when you told me you'd lost your house key in the fight only to produce it out of your comb. You didn't hire me to pry into your affairs, but to get things back that were stolen from you."

I could hear she was holding back tears as she said, "I wasn't lying to you about what was stolen from me, I just didn't tell you about what wasn't stolen. The bracelet, the necklace, the mirror, the clothing, the wallet and purse, the money gone from my regular bank account: all those were really stolen. I hadn't included the hidden accounts because even then I intended to return the funds to Drysdale. As far as I was concerned, the money wasn't mine. I just hadn't figured out how to do it safely."

I kept my gaze on the pile of wood I was stacking for a fire. "And getting the clothing, the gems, the purse, etcetera, back was worth hiring me?"

"Yes."

"I'd have a better chance of getting things back to you if I knew more."

"Perhaps."

"What do you mean?" I lit another match and held

it against the leaves I'd loosely packed between the sticks. It caught quickly and the flame spread.

"I'm missing the mirror, the money from my personal bank account, some clothing, and a few small things of no import. You've gotten everything else despite my lies. You've not needed the truth to do what I hired you to do. Besides, I've told you the truth about the important things."

"Like Jessica?"

"Yes, and my family." She was sobbing.

"I could use the truth about Drysdale. Who he is. How he can summon demons and manipulate time."

Once I got a constant blaze with the flames licking the wood as the sparks reached to meet the hidden stars, Inanna sat next to me and put her head into my lap.

"I don't know much about Drysdale," she said. "He runs a small syndicate which distributes specially crafted drugs, the kind of porn that you still have to purchase underground, and runs some small-scale protection rackets."

I stroked her head as if she was a girl I could comfort. She wasn't the only person lying; I kept lying to myself about her. "What kind of porn?"

She poked the fire with a stick. "Kiddie porn, snuff films, real sadism, things like that. Drysdale has a reputation on the street for being a sadist, but he pays very well. When he hires a private gal, which he does every so often, he pays them often a hundred thousand for being his plaything for six months. The girls need another six months to recover, but none have had permanent damage. When he approached me, I was very depressed and the offer seemed a way out. Not out of prostitution, mind you, out of *life*. I was hoping that I'd die and I arranged for the money to go to my parents should I die."

She poked the fire some more as she fell silent, and I waited, staring at the flames. She'd continue when she was ready.

She sat up, brushed her hair back off her face and looked at me for the first time since I lit the fire. "Every so often, he'd take me into one of those rooms, like the one in the basement you refused to enter. He summoned demons there, binding me to the altar, cutting me and drawing the words on my back with my own blood. Each time they came, it felt as if I was burning alive, from the inside. Ironically being bound to the altar, cut and bleeding, made me want to live, made me want to get out of there and find a new life for myself. For the first time since I'd left home, I thought that perhaps I could be more than a whore. The day you came was the first time he'd shown me to anyone else. He told me he was going to let him do to me whatever he wanted, even though our contract was for him alone. I could do nothing about it. So, when you asked me if what was happening was consensual, I didn't lie, I just didn't tell the whole truth. I couldn't until you had that gag off of me, and then me in the now was talking to me in the then, and I never had a chance to fully explain things. You showed up just as things were beginning to get bad, and you gave me the way out I needed." She shifted to face me, her face fading into the shadows of the night behind her.

"After I got home, I cleared out and started looking for a new way to earn a living. I never wanted to touch the money and would have gladly given it all back if I knew a way to do that without risking him finding where I was."

I could see the tears glistening on her cheeks even in the dim light of the fire. "That was when you met Jessica?"

"Yes. She was a frequent customer at the club where I was dancing. She loved watching me dance, and we fell to talking on a slow night during a long lap dance that wound up with me going home with her. I moved into her place the next day. We had about two years before she found the lump, which was months too late for a treatment to work.

"Those demons are me. All I was, all that is wrong within me, became real. This is why only I can deal with them. I've been thinking about Miller's approach to demons. While he's right that if you don't let what you do come between you and God, if what you do hurts no one and takes no one from God then there is no sin, and no demons. What I had been doing took me from God, family, friends, in fact most of humanity. Perhaps someone else can be the divine whore, but that is not me."

She took my hands in hers. "I've no idea how Drysdale is using the demons, but I think it stems from his sadism. That which was wrong within me has become his slave to do his bidding. The worst thing is he's doing this to other people. My poor deluded ex-boyfriend." She let go of my hands and turned back to the fire, poking the wood. I listened to the sound of the flames, the occasional pop as an insect burst, and her breathing.

"Johnny, somehow you're the key to stopping him. I don't care that the now me told this to the past me. I trust all of that. Being with you, we've restored my relationship with my family, recovered much of what was stolen. I've been confronting my past, no matter how painful it's been."

She stood up, walked around the fire, and came back to where I sat. She squatted in front of me and took my hand. "Yet, you've been doing this through mixed motives. While I've every intention of paying you, you're also doing this because you have feelings for me. Have I been using you? Have I turned into a whore again to keep you on this case, using sex's strong links to love to wrap you around me so that you'll stay with me?"

She collapsed to her knees in open tears. I let her cry, holding just her hand as her grip on me tightened with grief while I wrestled with her question.

"No, I don't think you've turned into a whore again. You've been honest with me about how you feel. The sex has never felt like a payment, in fact you're flirting every chance you get as if you can't get enough. No whore does that, except perhaps that divine whore you mention. You've given me every opportunity to walk away; I've chosen to stay."

"Thank you." Her sobbing changed, deeper, shaking her entire body.

Chapter 12

The Right Use For Drugs

Once the tears stopped, the noises of the night
brought to mind something she'd never mentioned
before we met Miller. Drugs. In the two weeks she'd
been my client, I'd not seen evidence that she was a
junkie, but for that matter, I'd not had so much of a
cigarette in days either. It had nothing to do with
Drysdale, or did it?

"What were you taking?" I ventured.

"Taking?" her voice cracked. She needed a drink I
didn't have. So did I.

"The drugs."

"Oh, those," She stood up and threw a log onto the
fire. "Mostly heroin, some marijuana. I did speed and
Quaaludes when I could. I'd do one drug to get me
through a john, and a different drug to get me through
the times when there weren't any. I don't like thinking
about it. In some ways it was worse than doing tricks to
stay alive."

Well that answered the question about why this
hadn't come up before. "You didn't seem to be on
anything when I took you out of Drysdale's. Either you
hide it well, or he kept you off the stuff while you worked
for him."

"The latter. That was part of his sadism. He'd lay

155

out trays of the stuff just out of reach, fuck me and whip me until I bled while I was bound. I wanted the drugs to take myself away from what was being done to me, and he knew it. Ironically, the time I spent in his employ started me on my journey to get clean. I went through the DTs while ropes held me down. If I didn't hate him so much, I suppose I should be grateful that he didn't keep me on the stuff. He certainly had enough of it. Come to think of it, the joint I had at Miller's place is the first time I've done drugs since you got me out of there."

This time the silence was punctuated by a yawn.

"We did it all wrong just now," I said through my yawn.

"How's that?" She returned the yawn.

I lay down on my back, twisting a little to move off a rock I'd not seen. "We went in guns blazing. We took him seriously. Let's get some sleep."

"Here? In the middle of who knows where?"

"Yes."

"I don't know. I'm kind of afraid." Still, she lay down next to me.

I rolled over and held her. "We slept naked on a city beach, and you're afraid to sleep in the woods by a fire?"

She took my hand and placed it on her hip. "Yes. Part of it is that I don't know where we are, or when."

"I know but staying awake isn't going to change that. I think fear is why we got it wrong at Drysdale's—fear of him bringing more demons into the world. You kept away from your parents out of fear intertwined with anger. We need better motives."

She wiped the tears away from her eyes with her hands. I couldn't read her expression in the shadows, but I think I recognized the same eager determination that I first saw in the warehouse.

"The fear that is driving me is that we only have three weeks to find and smash that mirror, and I have no idea where it is."

Certainly her voice sounded more in control.

"Understood," I said and turned my head to see the stars. "Look up."

"Okay, I see stars. Now what?"

I lifted myself onto my elbow and pointed with my other hand. "Over there is Polaris. I've marked the direction on the ground. From the stars I'm seeing, we're still in the northern hemisphere, and about the same latitude as San Francisco, perhaps a bit south. We're probably in Yellowstone. Yes, there are wolves and bears, but with the fire they're likely to leave us alone. I need to think on some things, and sleep will help."

"Are you hoping to dream?"

"Yes."

Dream I did, of a temple aflame in the desert.

I woke. The sky was lightening. I slipped my arm from under Inanna's head, stood and stretched. At the edge of the clearing was my Torino, on a dirt road we never would have seen at night. I stirred the fire, wishing for food and drink we didn't have. I can't imagine Drysdale intended the car to follow us, so I began to hope that whatever he was trying to do to us, he failed, and that we were not where he intended for us to wind up.

Eve stirred, groaned, and sat up. "I slept better than I thought. You look good without your shirt on. You've lost some weight." She tossed me my shirt, which I'd placed on the ground to keep her face from getting filthy. "Is that your car?"

"I'm pretty certain it is, but there is only one way to

157

find out." I put my shirt on and helped her up. "Let's see if the key works." I put out the fire, using my hands to smother it with dirt. I stepped back from the smoking ashes to make certain it was out when Inanna took my arm, put a finger on my lips and turned me. A doe with two fawns were at the far edge of the clearing. She was obviously watching us while the fauns nursed from her. We just stood there and watched, Inanna letting her hand slide down my arm to take my hand.

Once the fawns were done, they pranced around the clearing, even cautiously approaching us. One let Inanna scratch its head, and then scampered off. Finally, the mother barked, the two fawns went to her and they disappeared into the wood.

"That may be the sweetest thing that ever happened to me," said Inanna.

"It's a wonder the fire didn't scare them off."

The car started, and we drove along the narrow dirt road for about an hour before it opened up and we saw we were near tall mountains. The road we were following led the other away, down through pastures where sheep grazed. We finally came to a paved road, but no markers to show where we were or what road it was. I looked at where the sun was and chose to go south west. Soon I discovered I was on Forest Road 117 heading to Salt Lake City.

****

I'd just driven past Mill City when we came upon a car with its hood up, steam rising from the engine. I pulled over and got out. There were two young women sitting on the side of the road smoking in the heat.

"Need a lift?" Inanna called to them.

"Yes! Is there any way you can get us to Burning

Man?

"Where is that?" I asked.

"Black Rock Desert."

I looked at Inanna. "It's out of the way, but I hate to leave anyone stranded. Are you okay with the detour?"

"One of your hunches?" she asked.

"Yes, I think it is essential that we help them."

"Let's do it then."

We got out and helped the women load their things into my trunk, which now had plenty of room as the car had changed to a Volkswagen Jetta.

I started to drive. "Car overheated?" I asked.

"The water pump died; serpentine belt must have broken somewhere back along the highway. Unfortunately, we couldn't get a cell phone signal to call for help. We're so grateful to you."

"I'm Inanna, and this is Johnny Talon."

"I'm Jane and this is Louisa. I'm surprised you're not going to Burning Man, practically everyone on the road is heading there."

"We're headed to San Francisco," said Inanna. "You both live in Salt Lake City?"

"No, Denver. We're students at the university."

"How can you afford Burning Man?" I asked. "Summer job?"

"Sort of. We work there during the school year too, putting ourselves through college."

"What kind of job gives you that kind of dough?" asked Inanna.

"Legal weed," said Jane.

"Yeah, best job in the universe. Care for a smoke?" said Louisa.

Not at all what I'd been thinking. "No thanks, I need

to make certain that I get you ladies where you're going."

"I'll take one," said Inanna.

"Open the windows," I said. "I don't want any secondhand highs while I'm driving." I'd deal with the hot highway air.

I heard the flicks of fingers on lighters, the skunk-like smell of weed, and then screams. In my rear-view mirror I saw two demons materializing from the smoke. I hit the brakes, skidded to a stop and everyone got out of the car. Inanna stood, naked with her comb at ready, as the two smoky demons became solid mockeries of men that charged at her. I leaped on the closer of the two, pinning it down so it couldn't swipe at me with its claws. Good thing too, as I looked up I could see scrapes across Inanna's stomach, and one of her arms hanging oddly. In my best Latin, I wrote IESVS on the back of the demon I sat on. The demon screamed in agony as it writhed and began to burn. I leapt off its back and hit the other, knocking it away from Inanna who landed a blow on it with her comb as it went down howling in anger and pain.

"You okay?" I asked, knowing the answer before I heard it.

"I think my arm is broken, and I need to get these scrapes clean."

"Okay, girls, put out the magic cigarettes and get in the car. We've got to get her to the nearest hospital. You'll have to hitch a ride with someone else the rest of the way."

"What the hell was that?" asked Louisa.

"Demons," groaned Inanna. "Johnny, there were only two this time."

"Yeah, I noticed that too."

"Demons? You guys are in some crazy kind of trouble," said Jane.

"You could say that," said Inanna. "I wonder why smoking weed summoned them. The joint I smoked at Miller's place was fine."

"I doubt demons would dare to show themselves there. These caught you unawares. Those scrapes look bad. I'm going to look in the trunk and see if the first aid kit has survived the transitions. I'll rig a sling if I can."

I popped open the trunk, looking to see if we had anything I could use for bandages. The first aid kit was there, so I put some ointment and bandages on the scratches. I grabbed an old shirt, tore it into strips which I wrapped around Inanna's arm and shoulder as an improvised sling. Once Inanna was in the car, seat belt on, I ran around to the other side and slid behind the wheel. I started driving as I closed the door, fastening my seat belt as I accelerated.

The women talked about the demons. I did my best to focus on the drive, pushing my old car faster than was good for it. Somehow, I knew that time was of the essence. I barely registered when Louisa and Jane said their farewells.

****

The hospital took a better part of the day, but the break wasn't bad, just a light fracture. They put a soft cast on her and dismissed her around midnight. The only hotel in town was full, likely other pilgrims to Burning Man, so I figured we'd have to sleep in the car. I drove until I was too tired to continue and then pulled over.

"I'm too tired to stay on the road, let's catch a few winks here."

"Johnny, I know you're not going to like this, but

before we go to sleep, I want to try something."

"We're in the middle of nowhere, what are you going to try?"

"Louisa and Jane felt horrible about the weed and gave me some acid to make up for it. I think I need to go on a trip, and I'd like you to come with me."

"You want me to drop acid in the middle of the desert?"

"Exactly, but not for fun. I've been thinking of some of the things that have been happening, and I need to figure it out, but I don't think I should do this alone. Are you willing?"

"This could bring more demons."

"Yes, it could. I'm ready for them."

"Well, we've already been to hell together once, what could be worse than that?"

"Johnny, thank you! Thank you!"

We got out of the car, stripped, and sat facing each other. She handed me a pill and put another one in her mouth. I took mine and the world opened to me.

It was as if I'd never seen the stars before. Their light was diamonds glittering against a dark felt cloth. They sang to me. Light shone through, I could feel it on the back of my head. I felt Inanna's hand grip mine with an urgency and turned from the silver luster of a half-moon whose shadow pulsed with the hidden mysteries of the faces we never show to Inanna who had tears flowing from her eyes.

"Don't speak. Hold me."

I pulled her to me; she cuddled like a child in my lap. Her scent in the crisp night air filled me with unbridled joy while her sobs into my shoulder mixed sorrow in. I could smell the salt of her tears, tiny wet stars that caressed her cheek. She soon burrowed into me.

Suddenly, Inanna pulled away from me, her eyes wide and fully dilated. "Get them off me!" she screamed, brushing her legs. "Get them off!"

"What? Get what off?"

"Don't speak to me! The words hurt! Get them off!"

I reached to brush her leg and she started frantically hitting herself. She started to claw at her legs with her nails, raising angry red stripes that crawled up her body to wrap around her neck. I moved to grab her arms to prevent her from making the scratches worse, but she snarled, pulling her comb from her hair and readied herself to attack me, and then screamed, dropping the comb and pulling back from it, pointing.

A man walked into the clearing. Naked, and paler than the moon. Impossibly handsome. I felt like a shapeless old piece of trash. Inanna backed away from him, holding herself, shaking her head, muttering something I could not understand. Whoever he was, he was unwelcome to her. I could not hear what he was saying to her. Something in his tone filled me with rage. I ran to her comb, grabbed it, and swung at him.

Without looking at me, his dismissive kick sent me sprawling, but I'd thrown the comb which glistened in the starlight until it sank into the base of his neck. Smoke spewed forth as he writhed, shrinking until nothing was left as a cold breeze blew away the smoke. Inanna collapsed, holding herself while she rocked back and forth. I sat next to her. She leaned over and set her head in my lap, falling asleep with me stroking her hair.

With her asleep, I stepped outside of my body and looked at myself holding Inanna, stroking her hair as she slept. I was soft. Soft of gut, soft of will, soft of heart. I'd not pushed on unanswered questions, inconsistencies in her story, even in our payment arrangements. I'd treated her as a friend in need of comfort, therapy, and support, not as a client who needed my help in tracking down stolen goods. She needed me for both, but only as long as the stolen goods were missing. I followed the trail back and realized that I had no proof that I'd brought her the bracelet, and only circumstantial evidence that I'd returned the necklace. I had been believing what she'd told me again and again despite knowing how often she'd lied to me.

I was again within my body, holding Inanna. The stars were merely stars, the moon just the moon, and the heavens were beautiful but held no clue to the mystery. I only hoped that when Inanna and I discussed the trip after she awoke, there would be some insight on her part. As for me, I knew that I needed to treat her more like a client, but right then and there she was a woman who had reached out to me for comfort. I shifted gently, moving so that her head slipped from my lap to my leg so that I could lie down. I watched the sky for a while and saw a meteor fly across, star-bright in its death throes through the atmosphere.

"Were we having the same trip?" asked Inanna, her voice small and soft.

"Did you see an impossibly handsome man?"

"Yes, did you see the things crawling all over me?"

"No. All I saw was you."

"Not quite the same then. Sorry I yelled. You'd turned into a giant cockroach."

"Sounds like me."

Inanna sat up. "Don't say that. You're a man, and a good one."

"Thank you. I'm too soft. I've been too soft on you for that matter."

"I know." She lay back down, head against me.

I asked, "Do you remember the words that were burning on you?"

"Karkid. Any idea what that means? I've noticed something. Last night, when we slept in the clearing, we didn't have even unintentional sex. I think it was our first night without sex since I climbed in your apartment window."

"We didn't have sex that night either."

"Actually, we did. You don't remember?"

"No. I don't remember any of the times we had sex while I dreamt."

"Does that still bother you?"

"No. You were right, having some sex while awake made me feel better about the whole thing."

"Would you be okay with just holding me? I don't want to put on my clothes just yet, but I want to sleep under the stars."

"Sure thing. What if my unconscious has other ideas?"

"I'll worry about that if and when that happens."

I rolled up my clothing as a pillow and she curled up to my side, her head on my chest.

****

To my dying day, I'll never know if the stars actually sung to us as we slept or I dreamed it, but in my dream, as the stars sang, four mountain lions came from different directions. They walked around us in a circle three times before each lay down, one by our feet, one by our heads, one to either side. I woke as the sun rose. If the cougars had been there, they were gone. Inanna still slept, and I let her as long as I could, but eventually the urge to urinate became too strong, and I shifted, hoping to remove her head from my lap so I could go.

My shifting woke Inanna who groaned. "The earth is already clothed under the sun's rays, the grasses and trees adorn her," she moaned.

I looked at Inanna and said, "That may be, but your skin is as fair as the winter snows which melt when the sun's rays are high and will redden and blister."

She stood and stretched. "I will clad myself then, gladly, content to momentarily let the cool morning air flow next to me like a lover's caress."

The song the sun sang to me as I stretched was deeper than that of the stars, but with the same exuberance. I went off to the side, dug a small hole, and filled it. She was dressed when I returned, and I put my own clothing on.

"Did you find the path away from demons as you slept?" I asked.

"They and I are of one being split asunder through shame and sorrow," said Inanna. "So, while the stars sung me to sleep and I dance within and breathe the same air as all, the only path is within, without which life is unmoving."

"Yes, the demons you face are but you attacking you. As you love yourself more, their number may diminish but their desperation to do you harm increases."

"Did you dream last night?" asked Inanna.

I told her of the lions and the song the stars sung to me. "I think it's time we hit the road. Let's go."

In dawn's rosy rays I saw a red corvette, the old kind with the white panel doors when it was still a sports car, not the muscle car it would become. I held open the door for Inanna who slid in and looked around.

"There are no seat belts."

"This car was made before those were standard equipment. The car has a trunk, so it must have been made before 1962. I wonder if it has the faster engine. Just like your dress has always been the right thing, so has the car. I've no idea why we need a fancy sports car, but I'll drive carefully."

"It's not you I worry about."

Sure enough, my key started it. I found myself driving faster than I'd ever driven, taking the corners tightly. Later, as the stars rose, their music seemed to urge me to go yet faster, and soon I was at the maximum speed the car could handle. During the drive, Inanna said nothing, and I couldn't spare her a glance to see if her knuckles were white. I was driven as much as I was driving, and the stars urged me on.

Chapter 13

Advice

In the fourteen-hour drive to San Francisco, I only stopped for food, gas, and to use the bathroom. Inanna and I spoke no words the entire drive, and I drove faster than was wise but with the stars singing me on. In all those miles, we didn't pass a single police officer, nor for that matter, and much odder, were there any cars in front of us. Bleary eyed, I drove the final miles to San Francisco as the sun set and the fog started to gather. Inanna and I stumbled a bit as we walked into the hotel, our rears sore from all the sitting, but as I put my name on the registration form, I realized we only had five days before the equinox. When we were sent to Colorado, we were also sent weeks into the future.

"We're running out of time," Inanna said, gripping my hand tightly.

"Explains why I felt so pressed to get back here. Let's go get some rest. Neither of us will be in any shape without some sleep."

The room was small, not much more than a bed, but that was all we needed. I no longer needed her invitation; we slept together naked. As I lay holding her, I let my mind wander to the song the stars had been singing which became softer until my thoughts and the music became snores.

****

Different music than that of the stars filled my dream. It made me want to dance. The music was played on flute and reed, with something like an oboe, and drums that tapped in a lively cadence. The density of the woods I found myself in put that desire to dance aside a little. I followed the sound, hoping to catch a glimpse of the players. The brush of leaves against my bare skin felt good, but I worked hard to avoid the solid thwack of a branch or stepping on a root. These things slowed me down until I found what seemed to be a well-traveled narrow path through the undergrowth. I caught the scent of honey and wine from the direction I was heading.

I followed the path up a steep hill, wishing for a stick of some kind to add some balance up the slope. As I crested the summit, the music became suddenly louder, and below me was a crowd of people, most of them as naked as I, but a few were dressed in lab coats. These appeared to be lost in the contemplation of objects they held close to their faces, as if the merry dancing around them didn't exist.

I could make no sense of the pattern of the dance, if there was one. Most of the dancers were in a group, though I couldn't see any uniformity to their movements despite all being in rhythm. Those who danced separately may well have been dancing to a melody I could not hear. One had her arms wrapped around a tree and was slowly dancing for it, swaying to a slower tune than the one I could hear.

As I watched her, one of the men dressed in a lab coat tapped me on the shoulder. "The nautilus shell is a magnificent thing, no?"

I took a closer look at the shell he was holding out

for my inspection. He handed it to me, and I put it to my ear. Instead of the sea, I heard a slow gentle melody with the same rhythm of the surf. "Indeed, this is a magnificent specimen."

I made to hand it back to him, but he shook his head. "No, you must look within the chambers for the music. It is a deep reflection of the waters before they were parted. In its presence, all language is poetry, all movement dance, as long as words and movements are true."

"I will look within."

"Not you, Her. *Tell her to be careful, there are notes within that will shatter. They must be sung in reflection of the inner manifestations of cosmic truths."*

"You know of Inanna and what she seeks? Can't you give more straightforward instructions?"

"The problem is and has always been the limitations of what will survive translation. Think, Johnny, think! Why are you here and not her? What would be plain to her is impossible for you, so we must translate."

"Who are you?"

"Who we are."

"Why is it every time I have a dream, I wake up having had sex with her?"

"Time is a tricky thing, and hard to understand when you're inside it. You know of three places where you can step outside of time. Do it again when you've need, for time and place are tricky things and the paths don't always lead where you think they do. Sex also allows you a path to step outside of time, especially with her being who she is."

****

I felt a hand on my arm and turned. "Inanna?"

Someone was pounding on the door. I rolled away

from Inanna and grabbed my pistol from under my pillow. I waved Inanna to the side of the door. I leveled my piece and she pulled open the door. A rather large man stood there, a scowl on his face, a baseball bat in his hands. I could smell the whiskey on him from where I stood.

"My Stella in there?"

Inanna stepped around the door; I lowered my piece.

"Is Stella your wife or daughter?" Inanna asked.

"Wife. I know she's sleeping around, and the clerk told me you were the only couple who checked in without luggage."

"What makes you think she's at this hotel?" I asked.

"A private dick I hired called to tell me she'd checked in."

"And what did you plan to do with that bat, exactly?" asked Inanna.

The man lowered his head but didn't respond.

"I thought so. Go home, get rid of the bat. If she comes home, talk to her, learn what is missing, start giving it to her," said Inanna.

"She's my wife!"

"You want to be her husband? Or a jerk?" I asked.

"But she's betrayed me!"

"When was the last time you made her feel loved?" Inanna asked.

"We have sex all the time."

Inanna laughed a single harsh laugh. "When was the last time you did the dishes, the laundry, or vacuumed. When was the last time you told her you loved her, held her hand, or took her someplace she wanted to go? When was the last time you listened to what she had to say?"

He pointed his bat at me. "You, with the gun, is this

how a man should treat his woman?"

"Yes, if the man is a real man, and not a coward," I said.

He raised the bat to threaten me. "Are you calling me a coward?"

I kept the gun at my side. I was not at all worried about him actually trying to hit me. "If you are worried about what your buddies will think, then you are a coward," I said.

"What can I do?" He let the bat fall to his side again.

"Go home. If she goes home to you, listen to her," said Inanna.

"What if she doesn't come?" I heard tears hiding in his words.

"Then she is gone, and you have only yourself to blame," said Inanna.

"It goes against the Bible—" he raised his voice, but I didn't let him finish.

"Nonsense," I interrupted him. "The bible says, 'he who would lead must serve.' It also says that you are to please your wife."

"It says that?" The tears almost broke through his words.

"Yes, in Exodus, a man is commanded that if he takes a second wife, he's not to diminish his relations with his first, implying his duty to delight her. Now, go home," I said.

He lowered his face and his shoulders slumped. His voice not much more than a whisper, he said, "Thank you."

Inanna closed the door and looked at me with her eyebrows raised. "I didn't know the bible tells a husband to please his wife sexually."

"Yeah, most people don't read it the way it was written."

We turned the lights back off, got back into bed, with Inanna snuggling into me when I heard another knocking, gentler but still persistent. I groaned, but we both got back out of bed. Again, Inanna stood to the side of the door as I pointed my piece at it. She threw open the door. This time I saw a woman standing there.

"I'm so sorry to disturb you, but I overheard you talking to my husband."

"You must be Stella," I said, lowering the gun.

"Yes. Can I come in?"

"What is it?" asked Inanna.

"Do you think I should go back to him?"

"That depends on you," said Inanna. "Do you want to?"

"I think so. Part of me still loves him, or who he was. He's changed over the last few months."

"Any idea as to why?" asked Inanna.

"Until tonight I thought that perhaps he was gay. Lately Frank seems to prefer the company of men to me."

Inanna went to Stella and took her hands. "What about before those months?"

"His love making was passionate, until he found out I was faking my orgasms."

"Why did you tell him?" asked Inanna.

Stella looked down at her feet. "My girl friends told me that if I continue to fake them, I'd never have a real one."

"It was half of good advice," said Inanna.

She looked at Inanna, tears at the corners of her eyes. "I don't understand."

"Men are absurdly fragile regarding their sexual egos. What he heard from you was that he's a bad lover."

"Oh." Her shoulders slumped and she looked at the floor.

"Is the rest of your life good with him? Does he beat you? Is he drunk all the time?" asked Inanna.

She spoke through tears. "He is a good man. He never lifted a finger to me."

"Go to him, what have you got to lose?"

She threw herself around Inanna. "Thank you! You're the best!"

After Inanna closed the door, I said, "You've found a new career in marriage counseling."

"Hardly. All I did was ask questions."

"You knew which questions to ask."

She shook her head. "Let's get some sleep."

Perhaps we got an hour's sleep before another banging on our door woke us. Without a word, but with groans in chorus, Inanna hit the light as I grabbed my piece, and she threw open the door. Stella and Frank were there, together, holding hands.

"Can we come in?"

I waved them in, putting the useless pistol under my underused pillow.

"How can we help you?"

Frank looked at the floor. "Stella told you about her faking it. We talked and decided no more lies in bed to pretend anything. The trick is I don't know what to do to please a woman." He looked up again, tears in his eyes.

"Your turn," Inanna said to me.

We spent the next hour discussing everything from oral sex to role playing, toys, games, and safety. When they finally left, Inanna got back into bed and stretched.

"I feel strangely good about what we just did," she said.

I lay down next to her. "Me too," I said before rolling over to caress her thigh. "Shame we need to get going, all that talk about sex has got me very interested."

She turned over to look at me. "Do you know, that this is the first time you've told me you *want* to have sex with me."

I kissed her on the tip of her nose. "Is it really?"

"Yes, it is. Think we have time for a quickie?" She rolled me on my back and climbed on me.

I shook my head. "I want to be gone before those two return looking for a demonstration."

"Right." Inanna rolled back off me and we both got out of bed.

We got dressed and left as quickly as we could.

I found a Shelby Mustang parked where I'd left the car.

"I think your car is giving you a hint."

I fished in my pocket for my key. "Might be. Get in. Let's see what this thing can do."

The key turned in the ignition, and we set off for the highway. The sun was just rising, so the road wasn't busy. I hit the accelerator.

****

I parked a block away from the warehouse. Waited and watched as folks left. After an hour of quietly watching, I realized Inanna had fallen asleep. I smiled, wishing I could join her. I looked back up at the warehouse, watching as Drysdale drove away, followed quickly by us back then. It was weird watching yourself.

"Heh, Inanna, wake up."

"What is it?" She stretched.

"We just left, following Drysdale to his house. It's the perfect time to go into the warehouse."

She yawned. "We didn't lose any time. It's as if the car gave us a second chance."

We got out of the car. I gave it a pat as I locked it. "We owe this car a lot."

Chapter 14

Addictions

The lock had been changed, but not to anything harder to pick. I opened the door slowly, but no alarm sounded, at least not one we could hear. Unlike last time, our outfits had not changed, so we had no way to illuminate the room, nor see where a light switch might be. The light through the door I held open revealed nothing of what that room held.

Inanna stepped into the darkness, and her necklace blazed brightly to illuminate a cave with stalactites dripping a putrid-smelling fluid. I opened my mouth to tell her not to step in the puddles, but roses came out instead of words, filling the air with their scent. The room started to shake as I crossed it behind Inanna, speaking roses as fast as I could. As Inanna reached the door on the far wall, I leveled my pistol, ready for whatever might come through.

"Even for this place, that's weird," she said.

My roses agreed. Instead of the dismal hall we remembered, we were faced with a fur lined corridor heading straight. My warning to leave her shoes on came out as petunias, so I grabbed her hand as it reached for a raised shoe.

"Ow! What? Oh! You're using flowery language. Let me guess, you want me to leave my shoes on?"

I nodded.

She put a foot forward but pulled it back quickly. "I don't know how you knew, but the fur burns the bare skin of my ankles. Anyway you could carry me?"

I nodded and picked her up. Suddenly she was in the same wedding dress she'd worn in the thrift store. My words had turned into lilies, whose petals lay upon the fur like a fragrant carpet that I had no problem walking on. Soon, this opened into another cavern. This one had stalagmites that broadened at their tips, some into flat table-like tops, others more phallus shaped.

"Johnny, please run through here as fast as you can!"

The panicked desperation alone urged me on, as Inanna curled into my arms, eyes shut. The faster I ran, the larger the room became, so I came to a stop. So did the room. I stepped out of it, and we started falling up, past a potted plant and a large whale. I followed a butterfly that was smoking from a hookah it carried, past a large pig with a door in its belly, and a giant using its leg as a table to play cards with a walrus and a girl with dark hair and sunglasses. I was able to put my feet down next to the pair, but my words were marigolds.

"You don't have to shout," said the Walrus. "We've been waiting for you."

"I need to find Jessica's mirror," said Inanna.

"And you will find it in the possession of the demon summoner, as you well know."

"But how will I overcome him so that I may get the mirror back?" she asked.

"First you must overcome your two remaining addictions."

"But I'm not addicted to anything."

"Is that truly how you understand yourself? Even after the acid? Didn't that burn away your ignorance at least?"

"I don't, oh, sex, drugs, rock-and-roll, but I don't understand. I'm not a junkie. I've not done drugs for five years?"

"But you've not stopped wanting it. Yes, you turn away from your desire, but it is still your desire. You never chose to stop, you were forced. Because you were forced, you lost the physical dependency. You need to lose the emotional and mental dependencies. You need to choose."

"So, I should start doing drugs again so I can go through the withdrawal all over again by choice?"

"This is not what is needed, and you know it."

"And how can I be addicted to rock-and-roll?"

"What about that inner soundtrack? Can you fight without 'Fast As You Can,' can you have sex without 'This is Love' running through your head?" asked the Walrus.

"That is an addiction?" she asked.

"Can you?"

"I don't know. I didn't know I'd overcome an addiction to sex."

The girl with the sunglasses turned to Inanna and took off her sunglasses, light blazing from her eyes. "Johnny knows."

I did? My brain started spinning thoughts at a thousand miles per second and I came to one conclusion. Something about her had changed, and that something was sex. How I knew that without knowing I knew that I didn't know, but that was the part of my job I was used to.

"Johnny?"

"Yes, something about you and your need for sex changed. I don't know what or when, but she's right. You no longer need it the same way." Thankfully my words were words again.

"Oh," said Inanna. She looked glum and I wanted to hug her and tell her it would be all right, but I was not her man, I was her employee.

The girl put back on her sunglasses and everything went dark. I felt Inanna grab my hand, felt her pull hard and realized she was falling. So was I. I saw nothing under us, just a black void. Last time we fell up, this time, we had no bearing to tell direction from, neither up nor down, no substance, until I spoke. My words came out as white letters against the dark.

"I know when things changed."

The letters illuminated our surroundings. We floated about three feet over a bleak landscape, no color, no shape.

Her word came out green. "When?"

"At your parents."

"But we had sex there."

"Since then, you've stopped flirting. Before then, you flirted constantly, as if you craved my attention."

"You are right, that is a change. Up to then, if I was around a guy, I needed him to want me. I think that was part of why I stripped for a living. I was so insecure that I needed the sex as validation. The sex we had at my parents felt different."

By then, I saw a soft glow about the landscape as the words spread out.

"I wonder why I can healthily want sex, but not drugs. Yet the walrus was right, I do still want the drugs."

The green in her words was soothing, like the green of the forest in summer.

"Perhaps, it is because sex is healthy, but those drugs aren't?" This time, my words were so bright it hurt to look at them.

"Yet, the LSD was okay, as was the first time we did weed."

"So, maybe it isn't the drugs themselves, but how they're used."

"Could be," she whispered, but her words grew vines.

"Damn, that is odd. What do you think that is?" I pointed to an odd-looking thing on a bicycle with no pedals meandering through the words.

"It's right out of a Gorey," she said.

"A what?"

"Exactly, from a Gorey."

"What is a Gorey?" My words this time were gray and shadowed.

"Gorey was an artist who drew absurd and creepy things. Let's follow it!"

Inanna was off at a trot, and I ran to catch up with her. Whatever that thing was, it was keeping an even pace.

****

As I reached the end of our words, the landscape became more defined. Though I felt nothing underfoot, I passed floating rocks and large shapeless bodies of water just hanging in thin air. I passed things that looked like bushes chasing each other and gray ooze that dripped to become one with the grayness that was beneath me, though my feet and the thing's bicycle never seemed to touch it.

Nothing I saw, except Inanna, had any color to it, and nothing was white enough to be called white. The air had no smell, no taste. The best you could expect to see was a light shade of gray. It reminded me of a stake out, the necessary tedium of doing what must be done devoid of interest. The thing on the bicycle had taken a more deliberate course, heading straight, so following it was a bit easier until I caught a glimpse of what might be its intended destination. In the far distance, but distinct, a black mass oozed. I shivered cold at the sight of it yet could not easily pull my gaze from it. I glanced at Inanna, who looked strained.

"You still want to follow that thing?" I asked.

She shook her head. "Want to? Those would be the wrong words. I'm repulsed by that thing, yet I am drawn to it, like I must go there."

"We can choose not to follow this thing." I was glad at the growing distance.

"I don't know that I can."

Suddenly my heart was filled with the song the stars had sung. "Then let's go with a song on our lips."

"Song? Johnny, is this place getting to you?"

"No, I just have a hunch it will make things better."

"Okay, I'm game. What song do you have in mind?"

As an answer, I started singing the song the stars had been singing to me. The bushes, the ooze, the water, the rocks all started to vibrate. Inanna added her voice to mine, and I had to fight to keep singing, her voice was so beautiful and vibrant. The looming black mass began to pulse differently, and the thing fell off the bicycle. It scampered away, not looking back at what we'd thought was its destination, nor the bicycle.

I could feel Inanna straining to follow the thing, but

our course continued straight for the fallen bicycle, straight for that black mass. I ignored my pun, deepened my voice in the song, putting more force into my baritone, and the vibrations increased. I heard Inanna's alto rise an octave, as her singing also became louder, more intense. That vile thing we were hurtling towards at an increasing speed began to pulse in time to our singing. I heard a loud crack and light broke through from above, bringing color where before all had been gray. That sickening black thing began to smoke and then burst into black flames that writhed and smoke which made me cough until I tumbled down onto brown fields among fallen rocks and pools, next to the fallen bicycle. Inanna landed next to me.

I shielded my eyes as flames shot down from above, rich in colors and fragrance, consuming the black flames and the foul stench. Inanna rose and began to dance to the rhythm of my singing, arms uplifted, leaping, twirling, blending the sensuousness of the strip with the beauty of ballet as I sang my heart out. The brown around her feet turned green, as grass sprung and spread a green flame across fields where the sky was turning a rich blue. As the flames from above became embers that shimmered every color of the rainbow, Inanna brought her dance to a close, to sit cross legged, palms open on her knees, thumbs pressed against her pinkies. I stopped singing and took a closer look at where we found ourselves. Green bushes, tall trees, and hills with the green of both mixed with the rich colors of many flowers.

I picked up the bicycle, which now had two seats, but still no pedals. "Inanna, it is time to move on."

She opened her eyes. I saw an intensity in her gaze

I'd not seen before, though she quickly shielded it, almost as if I'd caught a glimpse of who she truly was. Each time I turned around I learned more than I knew was possible. People were like that, but the best part of my job was unraveling the mystery, exploring the depths. I offered my hand and she took it.

We both got on the bicycle, which started to move the moment we were mounted. Speeding past trees that were visibly growing in front of us felt like we were racing through time at a snail's pace, with years passing as we crept through the landscape on the perpetually moving cycle. It felt odd to have no place for my feet, but as we crested a hill and picked up speed on the way down, wind I'd not noticed before in my face, I held out my legs straight like every eight-year-old in the world, in delight of speed. I heard Inanna's laughter behind me as we sped past rabbits.

At the bottom of the hill, next to a meandering brook, I saw a tall and broad stone building. Unlike the buildings we had last faced, the architecture was Euclidean, though grotesque. The towers looked like the barbed teeth of a half-opened maw. The bicycle came to a stop at an arch that loomed with a black door studded with spikes.

We dismounted the bicycle and lay it on it's side on the grass that halted at the building's shadow. I found no handle on the door. I felt Inanna's hand take mine, and I clasped hers firmly. We walked around the edifice; this was the only door.

****

I let go of Inanna and walked to one of the walls. The stones were set too close together for my fingers to find any gaps. However, the wall above the door looked like it might be scalable. I tested the spikes. They were only sharp at the point, so I started to carefully climb up the door. One spike moved under my foot as I was about half-way up, and the door swung open. The smell that came from the darkness turned my stomach. All was rot in there.

I jumped off and grabbed the door to keep it from swinging closed. "Found the doorknob. Shall we?"

"Good thing I'm not afraid of the dark. It is pitch in there. Let's hold hands again so we don't get separated."

"First let's see if the metal on these spikes can help us have some light."

I placed my foot on one of the lowest rungs of spikes and pushed down as hard as I could. The spike bent, must be wrought iron. I kept pushing until it scraped the floor. I then bent other spikes near the open edge of the door outward, and the spikes closest to the hinge in the direction of the hinge. With any luck, this would keep the door open, or at least prevent it from locking behind us. It worked. As we stepped away from the door, it started to close until the spikes on the bottom got caught on a stone, holding the door open. This provided a little bit of light for us as we entered the edifice.

Even with the light from the door, all I saw were shadows. After about a minute we were walking in almost total darkness—my one hand in front of me, the other holding Inanna. I heard a hiss and light erupted from five points around us. Five hands of glory on pedestals at the corner of the pentagram we'd just stepped into the center of. The smell of rot grew worse, as if the flames burned grease.

"Are those human hands?" asked Inanna, her whisper a sinister echo in that place.

I nodded and took a look at the pentagram. The markings were in cuneiform, much like those I remembered from the door to that demon infested non-Euclidean hell. "Inanna, can you read this?"

Inanna took a look. "I can, but I'd rather not. I don't know if this needs to be read out loud, but it summons a demon."

"I thought as much. Let's go further in."

I took two of the candles off of a hand of glory and handed one to Inanna. With that gray light to keep us from walking into walls, we crossed out of the pentagram and all candles except those we held went out. The light the remaining candles gave us was barely enough to show each other, but it was enough to help us find a door. The door was heavy, and would not open more than an inch. I handed my candle to Inanna and heaved at it with both hands. Using the strength of my legs, I dragged it open enough for us to pass through.

I noticed a torch on the wall next to the door and put my candle to it to light it. It erupted in flame, as did torch after torch. The room was some sort of library, with three tables surrounded by stone shelves filled with scrolls and large books. I saw a scroll open on the table which was otherwise bare. Inanna went over to a rope I'd not noticed until she untied it, letting down a large chandelier. I lit one of the candles from mine, and all the candles burst into flame.

"Well, whatever this place is, the lighting is enchanted," she said as she pulled the rope to raise the chandelier, retying it to its hook.

"Inanna, the scroll is in cuneiform. Want to take a look?"

"It is the seventh tablet of the story of Gilgamesh,

the part where Enkidu tells Gilgamesh of a horrible dream he's had of Ereshkigal's realm. Damn lies, all of it."

"Lies?"

"Yes, lies. Enkidu was arrogant and careless and did not die quietly in bed. Enkidu entered Ereshkigal's realm to seek out the drumsticks that Gilgamesh dropped there. He ignored Gilgamesh's advice, wore red, carried arms, and thus offended the dead. When Ereshkigal met him, she embraced him, forcing him to stay in her domain."

I asked, "How do you know that all those things are wrong or didn't happen that way. You make it sound like it actually happened."

"I don't know how I know. I just know I do."

"Inanna, is there something you're not telling me?"

"Probably, but I really don't know why I know these things. Please forgive me, but it is not deliberate."

"Forgive you? There's nothing to forgive."

I'd never thought that she was as ignorant of the truth as I was. Perhaps she was not aware that she was more than she appeared to be, even after the acid.

The building started to shake violently. Inanna and I looked at each other and ran for the door, over the now-smoking pentagram and through the still propped-open door to open air. We were not long past the threshold, still panting from our sprint, when we heard behind us a noise like a thunderclap. I turned. The building was gone, and my nose caught the faint odor of ozone.

Inanna took my hand, and I felt her shiver.

"You okay?" I asked.

"I wonder if that place is where the demons come from, or if that is how he gets into this place without having to come to the warehouse."

"Could be. I'm more worried if the building came down because he knows we're here and that was an attempted take-down. That place was solid. Whatever took it down was some sort of combination earthquake and lightning strike."

"Gula and Marduk," she said.

"Huh?"

Inanna looked thoughtful. "What I don't get is why would Gula be working with Marduk? She's quite happy with her husband last I knew."

I stared at her. "Inanna, are you okay? Ever since we got off the bicycle you've been acting as if the ancient myths have an element of truth to them."

"Speaking of the bicycle, any sign of it?" She looked around.

Either it had gone off on its own, or some*thing* had taken it. I went over to the rubble, but the building had imploded. I saw no rubble beyond its foundation. "Wherever it is, the bicycle wasn't crushed by the building's collapse. Do you want to try to backtrack, or just pick a direction?"

"This place seems to have no directions, no place where the sun rises nor sets. The light or darkness seems to be tied to other things than the rising of the sun." She picked a blade of grass and let it fall. "Let's head that way," she pointed in the direction the thin part of the blade pointed.

I shrugged. "It's as good a direction as any."

We found a path of sorts, but it had a stench to it, and the ground along the path glistened with a sickening pale slime.

"Something about that slime reminds me of that creature you slew in the warped city," said Inanna.

188

"However, the environment is so very different it may not be the same creature. Do you think we should follow this path? You no longer have that magic sword."

"I don't know if there is any way to make an informed choice in this place. In my detective work, I'm used to the surreal, but this place is beyond my experience. However, I firmly believe in letting the subconscious rule when it comes to things like this where rationality doesn't help. Besides, choosing to follow the path is not enough. We have to also choose which direction to follow it."

"Subconscious, eh? How do we do this in this context?"

"Simple, we came upon this path from an angle. Let's just follow that angle's direction."

This time she shrugged. "Okay, why not?"

The direction I'd chosen soon turned hilly, and the first wind we faced was against us, as if something didn't want us going that way, but what that something was and if its goals were the same as ours was up for debate. I needed a clearer sign than a wind against us to change direction.

****

We crested yet another hill and stopped. Before us, as far as I could see, were mirrors: large, small, oddly shaped, square, round, fun house mirrors, and flat mirrors.

Inanna's hand squeezed mine. "Do you think Jessica's mirror might be in that field?"

"I hope not."

"Why?" she asked.

"What makes you think we can look at every mirror we see before the equinox? I'm reminded of Horton

189

looking for a dust speck in a field of clover."

"I'm disappointed in you, Johnny."

"Oh, how so?"

"Shouldn't your subconscious guide us to the right mirror?"

"Yes, but we can also fall into a trap. We need to be careful; this strikes me as a trap."

It took longer to reach the field of mirrors than I'd have thought. They were larger than I expected, which had made them appear closer than they were. I found myself longing for a grease marker as we wandered through reflections of our appearances. Every now and then I could swear that I caught a glimpse of something else in one of the mirrors, but when I tried to focus on it, I could never find it. When Inanna finally collapsed, claiming to need a short rest, I knew I was right; this entire field was a trap.

I took out my revolver, holding it by its business end, and smashed the closest mirror.

"What the hell, Johnny?"

"Exactly," I said as I smashed another. "We're lost in this field"—*smash*—"and have no idea"—*smash*—"what we've seen nor how to get out."—*Smash!*—"It's a trap, unless we find a way to mark our progress." I smashed two more for good measure.

Inanna rose. "Got anything else we can use to smash mirrors?"

"Sorry, my gun's the only thing I got that's hard enough."

"I don't know about that."

"Thanks for the compliment, but that would hurt."

"You're a fourteen-year-old boy. Your shoe should work."

"Yeah, but I'd rather keep them on my feet."

She walked in front of a tall straight mirror, sized up her reflection and said, "I wonder…" swung herself around bringing her leg up in a wheelhouse kick right out of Kung Fu, but instead of smashing the mirror, she fell into it. Without more than a moment of thinking "What the—" I dove in after her.

A black sun hung in a white sky over a street that looked familiar despite being all colors leached into shades of gray. Inanna lay prone on the ground by my feet, not moving. I felt her pulse, alive, but nonresponsive. I put my revolver into my holster and bent over her. Sliding my arms under her, I rolled her onto her back. I saw a small trickle of blood coming out of her nose. I took out a handkerchief and held it against her nose until I thought the bleeding would stop.

I then lifted her in my arms and looked to backtrack through the mirror. Nothing. A trap indeed, and Inanna and I were well caught. Seeing no discernible features, I figured I'd try singing while walking. It worked last time. Nada, though Inanna stirred. After I'd grown tired, I lay her on the gray ground and sat myself next to her. I shook her good arm gently, but no response. I felt her scalp, no bump. Whatever had knocked her out didn't seem to be a head wound. Her pulse was solid, and her breathing regular. On a whim, I leaned over to kiss her on the lips, after all, for the moment she seemed to be a sleeping beauty.

I kissed her and stood. I felt something hot behind me and turned.

Dragon?!

I'm holding a sword and shield?!

Fire?!

I brought up my shield to protect my eyes. Thankfully, the blaze hit the shield square on. I held my ground, though it required bending my knees and placing one leg behind the other, presenting a side to the dragon.

Once the blaze stopped, like a ten-year-old fool, I shouted, "By the grace of St. George!" ran to the beast and swung the sword. It lunged to swallow me, but I leapt aside and brought the sword down on the head that snapped at where I'd been.

I collapsed in the middle of a field of mirrors, Inanna beside me. As I fell to my haunches, she sat up.

"Was that a dragon?" she asked.

"Certainly looked like it." It took a lot out of me to speak, and my heart was pounding.

"You looked good in the armor."

I smiled, which revived me a bit. "I prefer my raincoat."

"That's my Johnny, knight in shining raincoat."

I rolled my eyes. "What happened to you when you went through the mirror?"

She shrugged. "I don't know. Let's resume our search."

We rose and I returned to smashing mirrors with the butt of my revolver. I don't know if time passed in that place, but we never tired. We did, however, run out of mirrors, without finding Jessica's. When I smashed the last one, it fell over to reveal a cave.

"Shall we?" asked Inanna.

"Maybe. I don't know why it was hidden, but that seems important somehow. Trouble is we have no way of bringing light into that cave, and no idea how deep it goes. We may need ropes to get back out, ropes we don't have. Then again, we don't know how to get out of where we are, so the only issue is being able to see."

Inanna leaned over the hole and gave it a sniff. "I don't like the smell of the air down there, let's avoid it for now. We can always come back."

****

As we walked from the field of mirrors, I told her of my dream of the nautilus shell and the song. "It may be that the song it has within it will help you with your addiction to rock-and-roll. I'm curious about the story in that building. That was from the ancient Sumerian epic Gilgamesh, but you acted as if it was real."

"What I told you is what happened. Besides, you're wrong, that was the Assyrian version of Gilgamesh, what I told you is the Sumerian. The true version of the events."

"I don't understand. How can you know this?" I asked.

"I don't know, I just know it to be the truth of what happened."

"Yet you go to church. You're a Catholic."

Inanna shrugged her shoulders. "Yes, so?"

I took a deep breath. "How can you believe in the Holy Trinity and an ancient Sumerian myth?"

"Just because God is God doesn't mean there aren't other spirits who haven't done great things, to be mistaken for gods by people."

"Thank you. I don't know when, but it will be important for me to know this." I may not agree with her beliefs, but the more I understood her, the better.

We walked in silence for a while, hand in hand. While pathless, the ground was springy under foot. We came to a grass covered hill and began to climb. The hill was steep, so our climb meandered. We rested at the top, gazing down on a valley filled with red flowers.

"Johnny, I'm worried about those flowers."

"Poppies?"

"I think so."

"It's not as if they've been turned into anything."

"Still, I'm frightened."

"Worried about flying monkeys?"

"Huh? Oh, that. No. It's just…. How can I say this without appearing silly? Ever since I got off heroin, I've even avoided poppy seed bagels."

I smiled. "Gateway drug?"

"You're making fun of me."

"No. Well, maybe a little."

She stamped her foot. "It's not fair."

"Look, you didn't get over unhealthy sex by avoiding healthy sex. Enjoying the flowers should be healthy. Come, let's walk through the flowers."

She reached out her hand. "Hold my hand?"

"Of course."

Her hand gripped mine tightly as we descended into the field. I found the scent of the flowers pleasing. After walking a bit, I glanced at Inanna. Her outfit had changed. She had a turban on her head. She wore a dress that did not cover her breasts and a necklace which had egg-shaped light blue beads with diamonds under each bead. For the first time since we met, she had make-up on. In one hand she held a rod, the other sported a gold ring.

Her bearing was also altered; she was walking taller. Something about the poppies was doing her good. Her dress, her jewels were all clues to the mystery of her being. If the scent of those red blossoms did anything for me, I was only aware of a growing apprehension that we were wandering aimlessly in that unknown place; and had no sense of time. I caught a glimpse of another building, like a two-story house with a porch. Quite the wholesome sight in that odd place.

"Do you think we should go there?" I said, pointing out the place to Inanna.

"Why not?"

Indeed. We headed for the dwelling, which seemed to recede from us instead of getting closer. Inanna picked up her pace, causing me to stumble at first until my pace met hers, but the building moved even faster away from us. We stopped and turned around to find the building right in front of us. With a shrug of my shoulders, I stepped onto the porch, as did Inanna. With no bell to ring, and no door knocker, I used my knuckles.

"Who is there and what do you want?" The voice was raspy, as if it was mechanical and needed oil.

"I am Inanna, and I seek entrance."

"If you enter, you may never return. If you are to enter, you must undress, putting aside everything you carry," said the rust.

"I am Inanna, and shall do no such thing, and I shall return as I please."

"You must not challenge the ways of the underworld, Inanna."

"If you do not permit entry, I will tear down this door, its posts, and its lintel."

"You are not queen here, Inanna."

Queen? What did her name mean again? Queen of heaven?

Inanna took her staff and started beating on the door. The door shattered inward with the eighth swing. She then grabbed the doorposts, one with each hand, and pulled. I had to cover my ears, the scream was not of stressed wood; but of a thousand demons in agony.

"Our halls are empty. Why do you destroy my last abode?"

An old woman with wrinkled brown skin and wisps of gray hair stood at the doorway.

"Was it you who told me I'd have to disrobe, and forfeit my right to leave if I entered?"

"No, that was my door warden, who is now hiding in terror. He remembered my instructions from the second-to-last visitor I ever had, before you destroyed my last door."

"Have you forgotten the laws of hospitality?" demanded Inanna.

"Let us say I have. What of it?"

"Fair Sodom and lovely Gomorrah lie in ash, burnt from within to their very foundations from their violation of those laws. You must honor your guest; and treat them as if they were the Most High Himself, come to spend the night."

The old woman sighed. "That was my last guest. It is because of Him that I am alone."

"You still have your door warden," said Inanna.

"Yes, I suppose I do, for all the good it did me. Now, I've not even a door."

"Take your door warden and go. Become doors that open."

"Go into that shapeless void?" asked the old woman.

"Look again." Inanna stepped aside and the old woman took a step back, bringing a withered hand to parched lips.

"Poppies? Here?"

"Yes, one for each of the dead you harbored until

they were ready," said Inanna.

"Is that what I did? Is this what I deserve?"

"What is it you think you deserve?"

****

I heard a tapping, turned, and saw a cop rapping on the window of my car. Inanna, asleep in the seat next to me stirred and awoke. I lowered the window. "Yes, officer? Can we help you?"

"Was worried the two of you were ill, that's all."

"No, we're fine. We just needed a nap after a long drive."

The cop walked away which gave me a moment to take in our surroundings. The car hadn't changed, but that was no surprise. We were still parked across the street from Drysdale's warehouse, but fog had come with the night so we couldn't see more than a block from where we sat.

Chapter 15

Opium

After the cop had walked away, Inanna asked through a yawn, "Was all that a dream then?"

I rubbed my face with my hands. "You mean the discussion with the walrus and the library with the manuscript?"

"The one that collapsed and the field of poppies?" she asked.

"Don't forget the bicycle and how you tore down that door."

"I've never had a shared dream." She snuggled into my shoulder. "Thanks for slaying the dragon."

"You're welcome, that was a first for me too," I said, stretching my arms forward to the windshield. One of the good things about the Torino was how much space it had inside.

"Did you find Jessica's mirror?" she asked.

"Do you have it on you? Each time I found something in a dream, you woke with that object."

"Let me look about me." She checked her arms, legs, and then began to rummage in her purse. "Nothing. Then again, sleeping in the front seat of your car, I doubt we had the necessary sex."

"Shall we give that warehouse another try?" I asked, looking out the window to the door I'd unlocked in our dream.

"Why not?"

We got out of the car and made our way to the door. I found the lock quick to pick, and we entered the darkened room. Inanna flipped the light on. Everything was the opposite of how we remembered it, including that the door on the far wall opened on the other side— into whatever lay on the other side.

Remembering the demons from our first foray, I said, "Ready?"

Inanna moved to the side of the door. "Ready."

I readied my revolver, knowing full well it would likely do me no good. She threw the door open. Nothing came through. Gun ready, I looked through the door: an empty, non-descript hall heading either left or right. "It's clear. Your guess is as good as mine if we'll find the destinations are also reversed or not."

"Let's see if going right brings us to his files."

We started to head right. The door slammed shut behind us, the floor tipped, and we found ourselves sliding down a ramp, which just as suddenly became a deep pit into which we fell, either incredibly slowly, or down into a very deep pit. Inanna was right behind me. As the bottom came into view, I saw spikes waiting for me. I also saw some light to one side.

"Do you see the light?"

"Yes!"

"Try to bounce off the other wall into it!"

"How?"

"Somersault!"

I pulled my legs in, grabbed my knees, and spun until closer to the wall and then kicked, flying in the direction of the light. I landed and rolled to my feet, hearing the thud of Inanna landing behind me.

"That was almost fun," she said as I helped her up. "But now what?"

"The only exit is how we came in." I peered down. "Too far to jump and not get impaled."

"Could you lower me down?" she asked.

"It would still be a long drop."

"Do it."

"It may mean your death."

"To save Jessica, I'll take that chance."

"I'll go first." I said, more out of male pride than anything.

I lay myself along the edge. Without something to hold on to, I was just as likely to fall to my death as well. I swung my legs off, then let my torso drop until I hung by my hands. Inanna climbed down next to me.

"Now, climb onto me, and then climb down as far as you can, quickly, I'm not certain how long I can hold on."

I felt her hand on my shoulder, then my hands started to slide. "Hurry!" I strained but my hands kept sliding until I felt her hands let go of my feet.

"They're not spikes!"

I fell and landed on my haunches. What had looked so much like spikes were just dots on the floor. We were no better than before, though. No exit. "If this is not a trap, the dots may be the key. Let's see if we can find a pattern."

Inanna and I searched for what felt like hours, trying combination after combination. Tired, we both sat. Then she rose and drew on the wall in front of us a vertical line and then a horizontal line from the middle of this, with a v shape crossing it point down, and one more vertical line at the end. The wall in front of us silently rose to reveal yet another darkness. Inanna's hand took mine and we stepped into the void. After a few minutes, I became cold and could feel Inanna's hand shaking, so she must have been even colder.

"Should we turn around?"

My words echoed until my ears hurt from it, but neither of us let go of each other. I began to hear a beating heart, then a second. They were not in sync with each other. From the tightness of Inanna's hand, I imagined she might also be hearing the heart beats, but after the last echo of my former question had died down, I didn't want to say anything else.

Inanna pulled on my hand and I felt her arm grow stiff. She'd stopped. I stopped as well, to feel her let go of my hand, slipping her hand up my arm to my elbow, pulling me closer. I felt her arms moving but couldn't see a thing. From the loud rustling, she might be looking in her pocketbook.

I heard a grinding and then something hot and my eyes hurt from the blaze that I turned to. Now I could focus, Inanna was holding up a lighter, which in that darkness was as bright to my strained eyes as the noon day sun. I could even smell the lighter fluid. I blinked a few times and looked away to see what could be seen.

A black lava field with a smooth path cut through it.

I only had a few feet of visibility, so for all I knew there was a wall before us or a ceiling above us. By that faint light, we started moving again, following the smooth black soundless path through the desolate landscape.

We soon came upon a black wall, with a black door set at the edge of the path. While Inanna held up the light,

I looked for any way to open the door. I found no handle, and no hinge, so the door must open inward. I tried pushing, but it didn't budge. Feeling along the surface, I came across little indentations. Thankfully, after a few tries at the combination, I tried one that produced a loud click, and the door opened.

While not as dark as the path we'd just trod, through the open door I saw a dark and smoky room. I could see some wooden platforms on which reclined figures half-hidden in the smoke emerging from long pipes.

"Opium," said Inanna, her voice a bare whisper.

"So it would seem."

She started to back away, tears in her words. "I can't go in there."

I was a bit surprised that the smokers on the other side of the door didn't hear her, as her voice had risen three octaves, and echoed.

I kept my own voice low. "You know we can't go back."

"No, we're only presuming that because when we left, we saw no way back. Perhaps there is now. We could go back and check."

"Are you that afraid of the opium?"

"Yes," she said, her voice barely a whisper.

"Was opium one of the drugs you used to do?"

"No, I did heroin, which is an opioid, and I was hooked. I'm terrified."

"You're going to have to confront that smell, and that fear. You know that the only way is forward, and that the only way through the addiction is to transform what these things are to you. Simply avoiding them is not breaking the addiction, its much like an alcoholic counting how many days sober knowing full well they never can stop saying no because they're still addicted."

I saw tears in the corners of her eyes. "I always thought that being able to stop the craving, and never using it again was enough."

I took her hands in mine. "Have you truly stopped craving it? Or are you just always avoiding it, always saying no, like now."

She looked at her feet. "I don't want to confront that question."

I let go of her hand to lift up her chin so her eyes faced mine. "I know. You have to do more than that."

"I know."

"To really kill an addiction, you need to be able to change how your mind works when exposed to the substance. That is damned hard, in fact it can be impossible for some people."

She took my hand and gave it a squeeze. "Is that what happened with me and sex?"

I smiled. "Yes, and as you did that, your life stopped revolving around when you were going to get more. You stopped flirting with me, flashing me, putting your hands on me while I drove. You did all of that without avoiding sex. That is harder to do with drugs because of the way drugs work, but the endorphins that sex produces are similar to how the brain responds to a drug."

She looked back into the room and in a small voice asked, "Sex was a drug? I was addicted to the endorphins?"

"Yes," I said. "Now, you're not. You have to do the same thing with opioids."

Her shoulders fell and she looked back at me, eyes wide open in visible fear. In almost a whisper, she said, "Damn, this is not going to be easy."

"In a way, yes. Haven't you noticed that this place is a little like hell?"

She smiled, the fear fading just a tad, but I could still hear it in her voice. She was holding back tears. "Yes, now that you mention it, although I've not abandoned hope."

I smiled back. "Nor me. I was never much for following instructions in any event."

She let go of my hand and turned to the open door. Her voice a bit more assertive, as if steeling herself for a struggle, she said, "All right, let's go."

If the second-hand smoke is anything like taking it directly, I can well understand why opium was so popular. I was instantly at peace and without any pain the moment we crossed that threshold. An elderly woman approached us with two pipes and said something I didn't understand.

"No thank you," said Inanna.

As we passed the last beds on our way to the stairs that lead up and hopefully out, a man reached out to Inanna, grabbed her, and said, "Tammuz, the lover of your earliest youth, for him you have ordained lamentations year after year!"

"What did you say to me?" she asked.

"And you loved the stallion, famed in battle, yet doomed him to the whip, the goad, the lash, what would you do with me?"

"Get the fuck away from me." She tried to pull away, but his grip was too strong.

"No, I will not marry you," he said with a growl.

"I did not ask you to marry me. Now let go of me." Her voice was terse, but he didn't let go.

I stepped between the man and Inanna and said, "Let

go of her."

I immediately regretted it. He let go of her, all right, but stood up. He was a good two feet taller than me, broad with muscle and thick curly black hair. "Who are you to tell me what to do."

"I am Johnny Talon."

"Oh." His face collapsed from a glare to sorrow.

I had been expecting a fist in response.

He stood aside and we climbed up the stairs.

****

While downstairs I hadn't noticed how people were dressed, I certainly did as we emerged from a door that on the other side looked like a wooden panel along the back side of a warehouse. On the other side of the fake wall were rack after rack of ceramics, mostly of Chinese styling with straw layered between the pieces like you'd see in an old movie warehouse.

Inanna and I were ignored by the young men with shaved heads and black loose-fitting garments as we made our way to the front of the building. I opened a well-worn wooden door at the far side to reveal a store front containing more of the Chinese style pottery. A short older man with gray hair to match his wrinkles turned to us.

"Did you dream well?" he asked.

"Yes, thank you," I lied. *Or did I.* I thought back to the shared dream in my car.

"Good. Come again, any time."

Inanna opened the painted wooden door of the shop and we stepped outside to find a wooden sidewalk and a road paved in stone. She took a deep breath, and I realized she'd been holding her breath. "I think we've time traveled again."

"Agreed, or we're on a movie set. We need to figure out how to get back to our time." I looked down the block in both directions hoping to get a sense of which way to go.

"Each time we've deliberately traveled in time, we've been driving your car. I think Drysdale's used our break-in to his warehouse to trap us in the past, since his spell failed."

"Well, either we'll find my car near where I parked, even though I parked it about a hundred years from now, or we'll find another way to get back to where we belong. If I'm right, we should go that way." I pointed to the right. "Once we know exactly where we are, we can see if we can find my car."

The sunlight felt good after the gloom of our latest visit to hell. We started walking towards the end of the block, hoping for at least a street sign. Some of the folks we passed stared at us. I suppose I can't blame them, especially since Inanna was the only woman not wearing a long flowing skirt, jacket, and hat. With the hills we were climbing, we must have stepped back in time to the early twentieth century. San Francisco before the quake. When I came upon what had to be Market Street with the trolley, I knew this was San Francisco before the quake from photographs I'd seen. It took us another half hour before we stood at the corner where the warehouse would one day stand. Curiously, right where I'd parked my car was a horseless carriage, the kind that was steered by a handle, not a wheel.

"Do you think?" asked Inanna.

"Only one way to find out." We climbed up, and the engine started on its own. "It is as if the car knows it's ours."

"Shall we let it drive?" she asked.

She asked a good question, as the car made its way onto the road, quite obviously steering itself. "Why not? Seems to know where it is going. I wonder, is it haunted, or possessed?"

We drove south for a bit, until the buildings faded into fields as we left the city. At the zephyric pace of about ten miles per hour, wherever we were going was going to take us a while. Inanna cuddled in as the air cooled while the sun sank on the horizon.

The sun sank and I found myself speeding along the interstate in my Ford.

"I am never selling this car," I muttered as I took the first exit and looped around to head back on the highway in the other direction. "I've no idea what day it is, so I think the best we can do for the night at this point is to get some rest and see what tomorrow brings us."

"I can help with that." I heard her rustle in her bag, "According to my phone, it is the same day as when we woke this morning, if that makes any sense to you."

"It does. Now, let's find a place to park and a hotel."

We finally found that the Hotel Vertigo had a room up on the top floor. We found a parking garage nearby where I left the car and then climbed the hill up to the hotel. Inanna was waiting for me at the top of the stairs, looking down the famous stairwell.

"I love the movie. Part of me wants to go down to the lobby and watch it," she said.

"As for me, I'm just hoping that tonight we get a better night's sleep, without interruptions from an unhappy couple."

"I wonder if they're okay," she said.

"I wonder if we're going about trying to find the

mirror the wrong way. Drysdale obviously knows we know about the warehouse and has put protections on it to keep us from getting at where he's storing things. Each time we've gone in, we've gone in through the front door. Tomorrow, I suggest we try the back door, or the loading dock."

"I'd like you to try my back door," said a voice I didn't recognize.

Inanna and I turned to see a thin young man in lacy lingerie.

"I'm sorry, but I don't swing that way," I said.

"I was afraid of that, but no harm in trying. I thought maybe you two love birds would like a threesome."

"Thank you, for the kind offer, but tonight we're just going to get some sleep," I said.

He blew me a kiss. "You are quite the gentleman. Well, toodles."

"Good night." After he closed the door, I asked, "Which is our room?"

"Follow me."

We entered a small room with a bed that could be folded up into the wall during the day, a chair, and a small desk. We undressed and fell asleep practically right away without even turning off the light.

****

I was walking through San Francisco, without touching the ground, though neither was anyone else I saw. We were all in various stages of undress, with some of the men in obvious states of arousal. I climbed the hills into Chinatown, to the same block where Inanna and I emerged from the warehouse in pre-quake San Francisco. I found a procession of people wearing black hooded cloaks heading into a storefront. I followed them, hoping no one would notice naked me. I saw the last of the cloaked people head down a stair in the back of the establishment that sold Chinese style porcelain.

The black cloaks were gathered in a circle around something. I couldn't see what it was, so I looked for a place to climb up and see over the group when I found myself floating higher. In the center was a red-cloaked figure standing next to an altar upon which lay a naked woman. He had a cup, a plate, and a pipe with thick white smoke willowing up from one end. He handed the woman the pipe, and she began to smoke. Unable to control myself, I rushed over the group, knocking over the cup as I faded into the smoke.

I was in a cool small, whitewashed room with walls of dried mud, sitting at a worn wooden table, with color still visible in the carved pattern cut into the side and edge of the top. A tall golden metal cup was the only thing on the table. I tipped it slightly to see the cup was empty. Beautiful, but lighter than the golden color made me expect it to be. The smells of mud, manure and poppies mingled in the cool air. A woman came in, dressed in a white cloth wrapped around herself with the end thrown over her shoulder to hide one of her two lovely breasts.

"You're early," she said. She poured a steaming liquid into my cup. "I've made some tea for you."

I tried to speak, but no words came out. I picked up the cup and breathed in the hot bitter smelling steam to find myself walking in a field of red flowers, Inanna by my side.

"Another shared dream?" I asked.

She didn't reply, but we walked together for a while. In the distance, I smelled smoke and could hear the sounds of men fighting. Inanna started to trot, and I had to run at first to catch up with her. As she ran, her garments shimmered, changing so she was bare from the waist up. I saw a pointed leather helm on her head, and a bronze sword in her hand.

The terrain dipped and from the height I'd not known I was at, I could see two armies of men hacking at each other with bronze swords. Inanna cried out something I couldn't understand. The army that had the device of an eight-pointed star raised their voices in a cheer, as the other broke and began to run.

****

I woke in bed, sweating and panting. Inanna, asleep by my side, still peacefully sleeping. I swung my legs out of the bed, rose, and sought the bathroom in the dark. What I'd dreamed was important, but I'd need research to understand it. I washed my face and ran a quick shower to cool myself off. Once dry, I crept back into the room, but sought the chair not the bed. I didn't want to lay back down on sweat soaked sheets, and frankly right then I was a little frightened by some of the things my dream was pointing to. I couldn't believe that the Inanna in the bed was the Sumerian goddess Inanna, but my dreams indicated otherwise. I knew nothing of Sumerian myth. If I was to understand that dream, I needed to know more.

Bronze swords, poppies, tea that smelled like poppies, an army that fled at the sight of her. I knew Sumer was a bronze age civilization, so that made sense. Did they make tea from the poppy flower? Or was that just symbolism of Inanna's addiction? There was always more to a woman than met the eye, but there was even more to a goddess. If I took my dream to the illogical conclusion, she wasn't named after the ancient goddess of love and war, she *was* the ancient goddess of love and war. The addictions to sex and opium made more sense if she was, but why an addiction to rock-and-roll and not to war? She certainly came alive in battle. Do I dare tell her? Did I dare not? I sat there and watched her breathe until I was too tired to hold my head up any longer.

****

Her kiss on my cheek awoke me. "Why are you on the chair?"

"I woke in the night, sweaty and panting from a bad dream. I washed and didn't want to lie back on sweat-soaked sheets."

"You brought me back something from your dreams. Look."

She handed me a golden thin tall, fluted cup, with crescents connecting the point of each flute. On the bottom was an eight-pointed star.

"This is lovely, and quite heavy, as if it were real gold," I said, handing it back to her.

She turned it over and over in her hands, looking at it from all sides. "I've never seen anything like it before. Unlike everything else you've brought back to me, I've no recollection of ever owning something like this."

"The eight-pointed star is linked to some of the events of my dream. The shields of the one army had this same symbol emblazoned on them, as did you. They cheered when you arrived, and the other army fled at the sight of you."

She looked at me, her eyebrows wrinkled in confusion. "Me? I was in this dream?"

"Yes. Look, I'm telling it all wrong. Let me start at the beginning."

I told her all I could remember. The cup I'd drunk from in the woman's house had looked nothing like the golden cup she'd woken with. "Not only were you in this dream, but this is the first time you've woken with something I'd brought back from a dream without me having forced myself on you."

"Actually, that must have happened before you woke. I'm pleasantly sore from a most vigorous night."

"Oh." I looked down at my feet. "I wish I'd stopped doing that."

"Johnny, do we have to go through all of that again? I'm going to take a shower. Why don't you dress and get us some breakfast?"

I rose and stretched. Sleeping in the chair had left me stiff and sore. We'd left our clothes hanging in the closet, so I had to confront my reflection from the full-length mirror in the door. I'd lost weight. This case was good for me in that way at least. Pulling open the door, I groaned. Instead of my suit I found a pair of worn blue jeans and a flannel shirt. Inanna's outfit had also been replaced by jeans and a flannel shirt, though hers was a green flannel, and mine was blue. My wallet was where I'd left it, with everything it should have. I went through her purse as well. Only the clothing had been changed.

I dressed. At least everything was clean and fit nicely. I'd not worn jeans since I'd been a teen. They were stiffer than I remembered, as if they were brand new or freshly laundered. I put my wallet into my pocket and looked for the menu. The name of the hotel was odd, not the Hotel Vertigo at all, but a Marriott in Philadelphia. I called down to the kitchen and ordered us some breakfast.

Inanna shrugged when I handed her the clothing.

"Plaid?"

"Yep, not fond of it myself. By the way, we're not in San Francisco; we're in Philadelphia."

"Odd. I wonder if Drysdale did this, or someone else."

"Don't know. What I do know is that I want to get to a library, preferably a university library. I want to do some research on some of the things in my dream."

A knock on the door. "Room service."

I looked for my gun under my pillow. Gone. Of all the things to go missing... Then again, without a jacket, I had no way to conceal the weapon. I cautiously opened the door. Room service had left a tray with two covered dishes on the floor of the hall. I picked up the tray and brought it into the room, placing it on the desk.

I gave Inanna a mock bow. "Breakfast is served."

She responded with a fake curtsy, which was delightful to watch as she was still naked. "Why thank you. Why so courteous this morning?"

I had to take the chance, as it might be the key to freeing Jessica. "Know how you're named after the Sumerian goddess Inanna?"

She sat on the bed, plate on her lap. "Yeah, so?"

"In my dream last night, you *were* the goddess Inanna."

Inanna laughed. "Is that why you stopped sleeping with me? I was afraid I had gas."

I grabbed my own plate and sat next to her. Damn, the eggs were runny. "Nah, I told you, I didn't want to lie back down on sweat soaked sheets."

"I know that, silly. I'm just yanking your chain. Any idea why this is important?"

I'd known her long enough where I could

understand her even with a mouth full of food. Unfortunately, she'd not understood where I was going.

"No, but I trust it is. Since we're in Philadelphia, after breakfast, let's see if we can get anyone at the University of Pennsylvania to help us," I said.

"Sounds like a plan. Do I really have to wear a flannel shirt?"

"It's all we have, unless some of the clothing we bought for you at the thrift store is in my trunk. What's the deal, don't like plaid?"

"I'm about to get my period. When I'm on the rag, my nipples get very sensitive and my breasts heavy. If I'm to be braless, which is my preference, I'd rather be wearing silk. If I've got to wear cotton, I'll want a bra. Also, we're going to have to drop by a drug store and pick up some tampons."

"Gotcha. Need me to go down and check out the trunk?"

"After breakfast. I'm not due until tomorrow, but I want to be prepared just in case its early."

Chapter 16

An Unexpected Cup

I sighed. All the clothing in the trunk had changed to flannel shirts and blue jeans. Inanna wasn't going to be happy. We'd have to find a store and pick her up a bra and hope it didn't change into a flannel shirt. At least she still had her comb. I worried not having my revolver at hand, though I'd only used it effectively against the mug who'd attacked her. It had been worse than useless against the demons.

I headed back to the cool air-conditioned inside and up the elevator to our floor. When the elevator doors opened, I saw a forest with tall trees. I poked my head out and looked around. I couldn't see any walls in which the doors were set, so I was pretty certain that if I stepped through, I'd never find my way back. I called for Inanna. No answer. I stepped all the way back in and pressed the button for the first floor. The elevator descended; the doors opened. Mountains, with a wintry storm in progress. Again, no response from Inanna. A little frustrated, I pressed every button. On the sixth floor, a tall man in a tuxedo stepped into the elevator from a desert. His black hair was slicked back, mustache and beard impeccably groomed. If I'd been a betting man, I'd have said the tux was an Armani. The hairs on the back of my neck stood up as he pulled the stop button right after the door closed.

"Johnny Talon, surreal detective. Pleased to make your acquaintance."

He extended a hand, which I took. Colder than ice.

"And you are?" I asked.

"I think you know who I am."

"Let's presume I'm dumber than you think. Your name is?"

"Immaterial for this discussion. I have a vested interest in your failing to help your client and will reward you handsomely for just walking away from the case."

"I don't break faith with my clients."

"I can give you anything you want. You'd never need to work another day in your life."

"You mean I'd be dead." Might as well say what was on my mind, if he was who I thought he was.

"That is more likely if you stay on the case."

"The carrot and the stick, I'll take the stick. I don't walk away from a client."

"I can prevent you from ever getting back to her, give you no choice but to break faith."

"No, you can't. I'd go through hell itself to get back to her, and I'd never stop trying." That I meant it surprised me a little.

"You're a fool, Johnny."

"Perhaps. But I'm an honest and honorable fool."

"I could kill you right now. You know this to be true."

"No, you can only destroy this body's ability to function. That isn't death, and you know it. You also know that if you slay this body, I'll be much more dangerous to you." I had a feeling I wasn't wrong.

"I can cripple you, trap you in a living corpse."

"I seem to recall that I've done as much good for her asleep as I've done awake. Leave me. Your threats are empty, and you know it." When bluffing the devil, it's best to raise the stakes.

"And who are you to order the likes of me? Do you really not know to whom you're talking?"

"Actually, I know very well what you are. As you said, the name is immaterial. Speaking of names, in the name of Yeshua ben Yoseph, I tell you to be gone."

I stood alone in the elevator. I pushed back in the stop button and the elevator jerked back into motion. The doors opened, this time to my floor of the hotel. Not really trusting it, I stepped out of the elevator and walked to our door. My key unlocked it and I opened the door. Inanna sat on the corner of the bed, still naked.

"Nothing?"

I saw no need to tell her of my meeting, at least not yet. "All the clothing in the trunk had turned to flannel shirts and jeans."

"Even the wedding dress?"

"Yes, even the wedding dress."

"Damn. Okay, give me a moment and I'll get dressed."

"Do you want to do the drug store or the lingerie store first?"

****

Turned out the university was just down the road from where I'd parked to shop for tampons, so we walked to the campus. The first hurdle was to figure out which department to talk to, or if we should go straight to the museum. Inanna won out; we went to the museum and asked to speak with one of the curators of Sumerian artifacts. An older man, with long gray hair and thick glasses sitting on top of his head, brought us to a small office cluttered with papers and books piled haphazardly on gray steel shelves and a small metal desk. The chair creaked under his thin light frame.

"Please, sit."

The hard plastic chairs were cold and provided no support for our backs. I took my notepad out of my pocket, flipped it open, and grabbed a pen.

"I am Dr. Fayad. How can I help you?"

"This object came into my possession. I was wondering if you could tell us about it."

Inanna handed him the cup, which he took with two hands. He muttered something and pulled his glasses down to rest them on his nose.

"This is either a brilliant fake or an original electrum cup from the end of the Sumerian era before the Assyrians conquered Ur. The markings all indicate it is hand-made with the same tools the Sumerians used. How did this actually come into your possession?"

"You won't believe us," I said.

He put the cup down and stared at me over his glasses. "Try me."

"I had a dream where I was served poppy tea in this cup by a woman. When I woke, Inanna had the cup in her hands." I left out a few details, but I wasn't certain they were pertinent.

"Your name is Inanna?" asked Dr. Fayad.

"Yes."

"That's whose cup this is."

"I don't understand," said Inanna.

He picked up the cup and pointed to the bottom. "Look at the star. That star is the emblem of the goddess Inanna. This cup would have belonged to her cult, and

218

they would have told you that it belonged to the goddess. You say you were served poppy tea in it? Can you describe the woman's dress better than she was dressed oddly?"

I told him about the white cloth wrapped around the woman below the breasts, with one end thrown over the woman's shoulder.

Dr. Fayad stroked his chin. "You said poppy tea. Did you know that poppy tea was supposedly one of the gifts of Inanna to the people of Sumer?"

"No," we said in unison.

"Yes. Poppy tea was brewed throughout the ancient and classical era in many cultures. It was considered to be the goddess's greatest gift to humanity, removing suffering."

Inanna leaned forward in her chair. "Can you tell us more?"

He stood up and began to pace as he talked. "Inanna was the goddess of love and war. She is thought to be associated with the planet Venus, and the story of her descent into the underworld is to explain why Venus disappears for three days on the horizon to reappear on the other side of the sky. The eight-pointed star and the poppy were both associated with her cult."

"Do you have any idea what they drank from these cups?" I asked.

He walked back to his desk, picked the cup up, admiring it. "Not many such cups have been found. Thankfully, the electrum they're made from is very durable and rather inert, but we've not been able to identify what they drank. Are you serious about waking up with this cup in your hand?" He glared at me over his glasses.

I kept my best poker face. "Yes, I'm serious. Could you tell me a bit more about Inanna?"

He resumed pacing the room, tapping his chin as he walked. "She is likely a Semitic addition to the Sumerian pantheon, made popular by no less than Enheduanna, daughter of Sargon of Akkad. Inanna possessed the holy Me, given to her by the god of wisdom after she got him drunk."

"Sorry to interrupt Professor, but what is a holy Me?" I asked.

"No worries, I wish my students would ask more questions. The Me were powers of godhood. Some of the Me she took were related to her role as a goddess of war, such as the standard and the quiver, others related to her as the goddess of love, such as the art of love making, kissing the phallus, and prostitution. She had cult prostitutes, and both the tavern and the shrine were holy to her."

I'd written all of this into my notebook as he spoke. I glanced at Inanna. She kept fidgeting, probably uncomfortable due to the mention of cult prostitutes. Perhaps she just hated sitting on these damned chairs.

The professor continued, and I resumed my note taking. "The most famous myth has her demanding to be let into the underworld, threatening to tear open the gates and let everyone out if they don't let her in, so that she can attend the memorial of her sister's husband who had been killed by Enkidu. Once in, her sister has her stripped and killed. Inanna had expected something like that to happen, so she had arranged for her servant to plead with the different gods for help, and the chief of the gods sends two creatures he creates from the dirt under his fingernails to restore Inanna with the water of life. They find her sister, who treats them with respect, not knowing if they're god or man. She offers them many things, but they insist on Inanna. They take her corpse down from a hook and sprinkle the water of life on it. Inanna comes alive and prepares to leave her sister's domain. The judges of the underworld demand she send a proxy, a replacement. Inanna searches through the kingdom and finds that her husband alone has not mourned her loss. She orders him taken as her proxy, but he's able to escape."

Inanna asked, "So, she escapes from the underworld without harm?"

"Yes. Unlike the Persephone myth, there is no sense that she has to return. There are variations where her sister takes her place in the world above for the three days."

"Three days?" Inanna asked.

"Yes, the same period between when Venus disappears in the west to reappear in the east. Many scholars think that the myth is simply to explain the planet's disappearance."

"But you don't?" I asked.

"No. The fact that the myth is not cyclic speaks against it. I think the form of the myth as it has come down to us is a retelling of an older story, where her city is overcome in battle and liberated by an allied force. Notice the words, take back your city? I suspect civil strife, thus her husband is implicated. Symbolists, however, think that the story tells of the young goddess risking all to become transcendent, sort of a divine coming of age myth, and believe that her cult practiced sadistic rituals to bring about their own transcendence. I don't give it much credence myself, considering that many Sumerians ascribed the tavern as her most important temple."

"Are there other myths with Inanna that have survived?" I asked.

"Yes. She is featured in both the Sumerian and Assyrian versions of Gilgamesh, and there are a few minor myths that have survived, one of her stealing the boat of heaven, one of her destroying a mountain, one of her being raped while she slept."

"Raped?" asked Inanna.

I glanced over at her, and she looked coiled and ready to lash out. I'd never seen her so tense. I just hoped the professor didn't notice and went on lecturing; this was exactly the information I needed, and I continued to write everything down.

"Yes, she went to sleep under a tree, and woke to find herself violated. She searched high and wide for the man who did this to her, destroying the land in the process, until, turning into a rainbow, she found him in the mountains. He confessed to his deeds, and she told him that his name was to be praised and would make songs sweet."

"She didn't punish him?" Her tone was so sharp you could cut with it.

"Not in the fragment that is left of the story. She told him that he was to die, and that meant nothing to her, but that his name would be remembered in song, and it would make the song sweet. It is likely this story was told to explain a rather destructive storm, and the peace that followed, sort of like the story of the great flood but smaller, more intimate. Her search matches the journey of Venus in the horizon of the area, so the entire thing is possibly a metaphor to explain the planet's journey, but

I'm not certain of that. Again, it is not cyclic, so there is no reason to think that the story is told to explain cyclic events, such as the journey of a planet."

I asked hoping to diffuse her tension, "Why would a goddess get so angry, destroy things in storms, and then relent when he confesses?"

"In his confession, he tells her that after he had intercourse with her, he kissed her on her genitals. I think we're supposed to understand that his action was not aggressive destructive, but of love and desire, and she, the goddess of love, is pleased when she inspires love and desire in men. It is hard to analyze the myths of a society from over five thousand years ago when so little has survived. There is a school of thought that has her become a mature goddess who is able to put aside her own anger and deal with him justly, and frankly, there are those who believe that she kills him herself, but that doesn't survive in the tablets we have."

I decided that I needed to bring the conversation back to more pressing concerns. "You mentioned the poppy was associated with Inanna. How so?"

He continued to pace, talking to an entire class that wasn't there. "It is a puzzle, as none of the myths that have survived associate Inanna with the poppy, but images of her in Sumerian art show her with the poppy, so we know that her cult is associated with that flower. Poppy tea was known to ancient societies as a bringer of peace, tranquility, and relief from both physical and emotional pain. We know so little, it's amazing that any of the myths survived at all."

"Thank you," said Inanna. "Professor, what was the name of the man who raped her, this man whose name was to be sung, whose name would make the song sweet?"

"Cukaletuda."

I didn't know about Inanna, but the name was not sweet to my ears. I just wish she had let this drop; it wasn't pertinent to the cup nor the case—or was it? Either way, she was very upset by this story.

Unfortunately, she didn't let it drop and asked, "You said that Inanna was able to find this Shukaletuda after she took the form of a rainbow. Was there a rainbow in the Sumerian flood myth?"

The aged scholar looked sharply at her. Did Inanna just correct his pronunciation? What was going on here?

"In early Sumerian mythology, the rainbow was the bow of the goddess; a weapon of war. After they were conquered by the Akkadians, the symbolism may have changed. The Akkadians were a Semitic people. They retained many of the Sumerian gods and myths, though some names were changed. However, since much of what we have of the Sumerian myths was what was written down by the Akkadians, we don't know to what extent they changed the stories."

"So, you think the goddess forgave him after using the most destructive of her powers, war, to find him?" she asked. She was baiting him. I needed to get us out of there.

"It is hard to gauge the age of the myth. If this is one of the stories added to the cannon after the Assyrians came to Sumer, the rainbow could be a sign of forgiveness, not war. The Assyrians were a Semitic people, whose symbolic language came to become the symbolic language of our own Bible."

I touched her arm. "We should really get going and let the professor get back to his work."

She shrugged my hand off and was at the edge of her seat. "You really believe that she'd forgive him? She called him dog, pig, ass; she was livid."

He stared at her and spoke in slow measured words. "How do you know what she called him? I didn't say that. Who are you two? Is this some kind of joke on an old man?"

"We are not joking," I said, trying to sound calming. "Please, could you explain your thinking? It doesn't make sense to me either."

It worked, he slipped back into lecture mode, and resumed his pacing. "The tablet is fragmentary. After he confessed to her, told her what he'd done, we know something changed, but not what. When she speaks to him, her words are dismissive of even his death, as if it has no meaning for her, not even a way to seek revenge for his transgression. She says, 'So! You shall die! What is that to me? Your name, however, shall not be forgotten. Your name shall exist in songs and make the songs sweet. A young singer shall perform them most pleasingly in the king's palace. A shepherd shall sing them sweetly as he tumbles his butter-churn. A young shepherd shall carry your name to where he grazes the sheep. The palace of the desert shall be your home.' Inanna is reassuring him, something she need not do, but chooses to do, because as a goddess, she is bigger than the events and no matter how horrible, he can do her no harm. In the kiss he'd given her, something she'd not known, he'd let her know that he didn't intend rape. He'd simply given into her overwhelming sensuality as the goddess of love. He was to be punished and immortalized in a sweet song, with his name making the song sweet. She showed him a measure of divine mercy."

Inanna stood up and pointed her finger at him, "You guess at much but ignore the truth though it sits in front of your eyes. Sweet his name in song, but only to shepherds. Gardeners would grind their teeth at the mention of his name. Gardeners would groan in the hearing of this song. This wasn't divine mercy. She was letting him know that those who despise gardeners more than any would rejoice to hear of his punishment. A gardener condemned to the desert where nothing blooms? No gardener could imagine a worse fate. Gardeners would know the perils of crossing Inanna." She put her hand on my arm. "Let's get out of here."

"I don't know who the hell you think you are coming here and speaking to me like this. Five minutes ago, you didn't even know of this story, and now you tell me I'm wrong with how it is understood? Young lady, if you were my student—"

She took a step to him, but I held her back. "If I was your student, I'd point out that you must understand the divine stories as they were understood to the people of the age. Shepherds and gardeners hated each other, and the king was a shepherd."

He was shaking. "Inanna's husband was a god."

"No," she said, "he was a shepherd."

"I don't know what this is all about, but I'm starting to think that you two are here to try and deliberately humiliate me. Get out of my office before I call security and have you thrown out."

I reached for the cup on his desk, but he snatched it up before I could grab it. "May I please have our cup back?" I asked, trying to restore some manners to our visit.

"I'll be turning this over to the police," he said, his face flushed. "It must have been stolen from a museum or smuggled into the country illegally."

I walked around the desk and took the cup from him. "Call the cops if you want. We got the cup exactly the way I said we did."

The professor picked up the phone and started to dial. I handed the cup back to Inanna. The professor put down the phone, staring at her. "How did you do that?"

"Easy. I reached out and gave her the cup."

"Not that, you dimwit. Her clothing. How did you change your outfit, and where did you get an authentic Sumerian dress?"

Inanna was wearing the same dress the woman in my dream had been wearing, complete with one bare breast, but instead of the blue beads, the diamond necklace resting above her bare boddice glistened in the dim lighting of his office. Remembering the effort we'd put into getting her the bra she'd been wearing just a few minutes ago, I figured this would just add to her bad mood.

She grabbed my arm and pulled me in the direction of the door. "I don't know, and I don't care. Come on, Johnny, let's get out of here."

Chapter 17

Poppy Tea

Thankfully her clothing changed back into the flannel shirt and jeans by the time we left the museum, so I wasn't worried about the police arresting her for indecent exposure. I had to walk quickly to keep up with her, as she was obviously walking off her anger. A pink Cadillac convertible was waiting for us where I'd parked. "Where can we get some poppy tea?" asked Inanna as we got into what I hoped was my car.

"It's illegal," I said as I got in on my side.

"I know that," she said. "You're the detective. Where can we get some?"

I turned the key and let the engine rev up. "I imagine the best chance would be in a flower shop."

She hit my shoulder. "They don't serve tea in a flower shop."

"No, but they sell poppy seed pods. We'll have to make the tea ourselves. However, first I want to get on the highway and drive us back to San Francisco as quickly as possible. We've got a good three days of driving ahead of us, and I want to start it with us both awake and alert."

I should have expected her to plead to get her way. "Please, let's go to a florist first. I can't think of any other reason we'd be in Philadelphia than to learn about poppy tea. Nothing else he told us was of any value."

"Not quite true," I pointed out as I made a left turn.

"How so?"

"He told us about the star at the bottom of the cup, and known facts about the goddess. Where did you learn all that stuff about ancient Sumerian myth?"

"I grew up with her name. I wanted to learn more about my namesake. I taught myself to read cuneiform and read all I could about her, way back when I was about ten. I'd forgotten most of it, but it came back to me while we were talking."

She was lying again; except I think that this time she was more lying to herself than to me. Something about the cup brought it all back to her and I figured she didn't want to talk about it.

The light turned and I made a right, following a sign for the highway. "I'm concerned about you drinking poppy tea. Perhaps the girl with the sunglasses is right, you may still be addicted to heroin. Drinking poppy tea could be the worst thing you could do."

"Or the best," she said. "If I am still addicted, I need to overcome it myself."

The light ahead turned red so I slowed down. "Choosing not to drink the tea would be a better way to overcome the addiction."

She began to caress my leg. "I've been making that choice daily for years. Apparently, I'm still addicted."

"Yes, that is why you need to keep making that choice. For the rest of your life you need to choose not to have opioids. Every moment, every day."

She put her hand on mine. "Normally, I'd agree with you. We took LSD and it opened both of us. One of the things it did for me was convince me that I had to change my approach to opioids. I'd forgotten the poppy was associated with my namesake. Besides I didn't get over my addiction to sex by avoiding it. It was changing what sex meant. I know this will be harder, but I must try."

The light turned and I accelerated. "Okay, okay, you're turning my words against me, but that doesn't mean you're right. I'll help you do this, but I think you've got one thing wrong."

"What?"

Time to be more direct. "You are Inanna," I said, squeezing her hand.

"What, of course I am."

"No, not like that. You are the ancient Sumerian goddess."

"The goddess of love and war?" I could see from the corner of my eye that she was shaking her head.

"The same." I knew I was right, and it frightened me a little.

"Johnny, you have quite the sense of humor or you've gone mad."

"Actually, if you think on it, it makes sense. Think of all the strange things that have happened, that I'm able to pull things away from Drysdale while having dream sex with you, that ever since you showed up, my car and your clothing changes to what we need at that moment, not only do you read and write cuneiform, but when you do, it counter acts Drysdale's spells. Your addictions were the things associated with her—"

"Not music," she said.

"Damn, I'd forgotten about that." I slowed down for another red light.

"Look, Johnny, I know this case is odd but I am only a woman."

I glanced at her, keeping an eye on the light. "So, I should ignore all the evidence just because of one fact?"

She gave my hand a squeeze. "Please do. Even if you are right, I just want to be a woman. The last thing I want is to be an incarnation of a goddess, especially not one who introduced both opium and prostitution into the world. I'm hoping, praying that you're wrong."

The light turned and I continued to follow the signs for the highway. "Understood, but if I am right, you may need to deal with this before you face Drysdale again."

"You think so? He is just a man, after all."

I had to take my hand out of hers to make a left. "He is a sorcerer with demons, *your* demons at his control."

"Johnny, like every other person on this planet, what I need to do is to control my own demons. With your help, I've got one down. Please help me with the opium. Help me brew some poppy tea."

Just then I caught sight of a flower shop on the next block on my side of the road with a parking spot right in front. Never ignore a coincidence is my motto. I pulled over. "Hopefully we can get enough seed pods here," I said. "We'll need to purchase more than poppies, however, so as to not raise suspicions."

"Got it. Shall I pretend to be your girlfriend, wife, or mistress?"

"I doubt much we'll need to pretend anything."

"Suit yourself. I was hoping you'd say mistress, it sounds so much more fun, and is more than kind of true."

I hoped she didn't notice my eyes rolling. "Let's just keep it to I'm your client."

"A client, buying his employer flowers? How inappropriate, but all right, if you must."

I held open the door to the shop for her. The bell on

the door rang as I let the door close behind me.

A woman, who had been reading, looked up from her magazine. "Can I help you?"

Inanna started to speak before I could begin. "I need a large assortment of flowers for a still life I'm painting.

Her face brightened. "Do you have a list?"

"No, but I can show you what I need."

I stood back and watched as Inanna and the salesclerk pulled flowers and other florals from various tubs around the store. Thankfully, they had five poppy seed pods, and she chose all of them. The entire thing came to about two hundred and fifty dollars, which I paid for with a credit card. Carefully folding the receipt, I couldn't help but smile when Inanna kissed me for a demonstrative thank you.

An Alpha Romero waited for us when we got to where I'd parked the Cadillac. She put the flowers in the back seat.

"Thank you, Johnny. I know you have reservations, but this really is the right thing."

I was not in the mood for her kisses, which I found odd. This was the first time that I found her attention irritating. "Let's go. We have a long drive."

We didn't get far out of Philadelphia when I found myself driving north on California 101 just outside of San Jose. Not certain of what day it was this time, I got off the highway looking for a hotel.

Inanna said, "Johnny, I just saw a sign for the Winchester mansion. Any chance we could go there?"

"The heat of the car would wreck the flowers and may damage the seed pods." I didn't want to waste all of that money. At the rate this case was costing me, she better have a lot of funds yet to be retrieved.

"If we can get there before they close," she said while I pulled into the parking lot. "I'd like to brew and drink the tea right away, and then tour that house."

"While on the drugs? Okay, we'll try." I pulled into a parking spot and turned off the car.

"Yes, I want to explore that place under the influence. I'm trying to change everything about what taking an opioid means to me."

****

My college roommate had taught me how to make opium from the seed pods. It turned out poppy tea was similar, and easy to make in the hotel room. I poured it into Inanna's electrum cup and handed it to her. From the smell, it would be bitter, and the expression her face made when she sipped it told the truth of that.

"Aren't you going to have any?" she asked. "It's so yummy."

"No thanks. I think one of us should have our head on straight." I had seen too many junkies to want any part of that. I was not looking forward to when she crashed.

"You're more worried about this than you were with the LSD."

"Damn straight. This stuff is addictive."

"Well, it's bitter, but it is helping me relax, filling me with a sense of peace. Can we go? I really want to tour the Winchester house while the poppy tea is still active."

"Finish it first. Last thing we need would be to be pulled over by a cop with you sipping from that cup."

"Okay." Inanna drained the cup down, making a sour face as she did so.

I put the "Do Not Disturb" sign on the hotel room door and made certain I had the room key. Inanna hummed a tune that pulled on my memory as we walked the halls and took the elevator down. This time the car had changed to be a van painted with large flowers on its sides.

"How appropriate for our destination."

"Just as long as there's no dog poop, I'm cool with this."

Sure enough, the key started the van. The hotel was only a few miles away from the mansion, but by the time I parked, I was a little sick of the tune which I couldn't quite remember.

We were the only two in the gift shop which was also where you purchase the tickets for the tour, so I had a small hope that we'd be the only people on the tour. As luck would have it, the tour would be the last they'd run that day, and there were no others waiting with us in the courtyard. Inanna sat under a tree, a soft smile on her face. I walked around a little, looking at the flowers and the outside of the house, keeping an eye on the time. I returned to the courtyard and sat next to Inanna just in time for someone to come out of the house looking for the people on the tour. No one had joined us. We rose, took each other's hands, and followed the tour guide into the carriage entrance to the house.

I found the house itself amusing, with the low riser stairs, doors and windows that led nowhere and all the beautiful Tiffany glass doors which had never been installed. Inanna pointed out the one that appeared to be two-star maps and said, "That is a window to heaven for those who know how to open it."

We entered a room where the guide showed us a cabinet door that had no cabinet, just air. Inanna gripped my hand. "There was a horrible battle here, a long time ago. Two men strove to take what had been hidden behind that door."

The final room was the most finished, as if they'd done the tour in such a way as to show you what might have been in that strange and beautiful house if Mrs. Winchester had ever let anything be finished. We thanked the tour guide and left, heading to the car, now a recent model Ford T-bird. "Did you get anything out of that tour that is helping us?" I asked as I opened the door for her.

"That battle, I'd not known about it. Two magicians battled over an Egyptian papyrus."

"Magicians?"

"Yes," she said. "Like Crowley and Yeats, only one of them was Swiss, the other French."

"Wait a minute, Yeats was a poet, not a magician," I said.

"Shows you how much you know. Yeats defeated Crowley in the famous magical battle of Blythe Road, and openly mocked Crowley in his poem; The Second Coming, referred to him as a rough beast."

I laughed, remembering the poem from high school. "Okay, okay, tell me more about the magicians and the papyrus."

"I didn't pick up much, more a residue of the battle. The Swiss magician was the stronger, and the spells he cast to try to steal the papyrus from the Frenchman caused the ground to shake horribly, toppling the tower on the grounds."

"You do realize you're describing the 1906 earthquake," I said.

"Of course I do. I'm not ignorant. I had no idea it was caused by a magical battle."

"Any idea of who won?" I asked.

She shook her head. "None. Hopefully it's not important."

****

I didn't sleep much that night. Shortly after Inanna lay down, she started to shake. Her temperature rose, so I wet a washcloth and lay it on her forehead to help keep her comfortable. Then suddenly she was out of bed, leaning over the toilet and vomiting. She started shaking violently, so I knelt next to her, holding her so she wouldn't bang her head. She started begging for more tea. Thankfully she'd drunk the last of it. I'd emptied and washed out the pot and cup before we'd left on our tour.

I'd dealt with junkies before, so I let the insults she flung at me that night roll right off me like water off of a duck. The vomiting and shakes weakened her so the one time she attacked me violently, I was able to avoid harm to either of us, wrapping her in a blanket to stop the shakes.

She fell into a quiet sleep at about four in the morning. I sat in the chair and watched her sleep. She'd gone willingly into the nightmare of opium and with the morning I'd see if she had the steel to leave it behind. While I sat, I went over every aspect of the case. Nothing added up, but I was fine with that. Life rarely added up. What was bothering me was three things: what Drysdale wanted with her comb, what Drysdale wanted with the mirror, and how addiction to a song was a bad thing. At least I finally knew what Drysdale wanted with her: demons summoned through holding a Black Mass with a goddess would be powerful indeed. He wanted her power.

With the dawn, I checked what day it was. We were

still in the past. I let her sleep until she woke, around ten that morning.

"Johnny?" Her voice was like chalk on a blackboard.

"Morning."

"Ugh, don't talk to me about morning. Can you please get me something to drink, my head is splitting."

I brought her a glass of water, which she downed.

"Sorry about last night," she said.

"Think nothing of it."

"I treated you horribly. I'm never touching opium again."

"You think it will be that easy?" I asked.

"No, it won't be easy, but I've done it before. I can do it again. At least Drysdale deserved the insults I threw at him."

"Come, you'll feel better after a hot shower and some breakfast."

"Do we still have time?"

"Unless we time traveled during the night, we're still in our past."

While she showered, I debated which of the two options we should try, the house or the warehouse, or if there was some aspect of her case we'd not explored properly. We'd been to the warehouse a number of times, including once in a rather lucid dream. We'd been to his house more than once as well. However, we'd recently learned he kept more than one house. I remembered the dream where I was told he'd have the mirror with him.

Inanna stepped out of the bath with a towel wrapped around her hair, but otherwise bare. "You know what is odd?"

"Many things, but I've no idea what you've got in

mind."

"I don't have my period. I certainly felt like it two days ago in Philadelphia. I had all the typical PMS symptoms I always get, and I'm never late."

"We should pick up a pregnancy test."

She frowned. "But I can't get pregnant. Doctor told me that years ago."

"Doctor may have been wrong."

"I can't believe it. I've had unprotected sex my whole life without getting pregnant. I have the perfect body for a whore, and don't you dare tell me that this is because I'm some Sumerian goddess."

"You can believe that we've traveled in time, that we've fought demons, that your lover's soul is trapped in a mirror, that my car changes shape, but you won't believe you can get pregnant?" I said, trying to keep the irony out of my voice.

"I know, absurd, isn't it? It might just be late." She took off the towel and combed her hair. I was almost used to seeing her naked but the joy of it hadn't diminished. As I watched her groom I wondered about fatherhood. Was that something I was willing to step into? Was I willing to walk away from that?

"Let's hope." I had no idea if she wanted a kid, but it was obvious that she had lived a life never considering the possibility.

She put her brush down, walked over to me, and climbed into my lap, putting her head on my shoulder. "What if I am pregnant?"

I hugged her and kissed her on top of her head, but I was not ready to answer that question. "We'll cross that bridge when we come to it. Get dressed, we've got a mirror to crack. Right now, however, I want you to listen to the music in the nautilus shell."

She sneered slightly and clicked her tongue as she leaned over to kiss me on the cheek. "I know it is a shell, but Johnny, it is a fossil, it won't have any sound." She got off my lap and walked back to the bathroom where I could see her hang up her towel. I tore my gaze away from her; she wasn't the only one who needed to be refocused on what we needed to do.

"I forgot to tell you about my last dream." I told her about the man with the shell. "Practically the last thing he told me was that you must look within the chambers for the music. It is a deep reflection of the waters before they were parted. In its presence, all language is poetry, all movement dance, as long as words and movements are true."

"Let me get it out of my purse." She rustled in her purse and pulled out the shell. She put it to her ear and closed her eyes. "As I expected, nothing."

"Perhaps you need to meditate on it."

"Perhaps, but not now. There is no way I can concentrate on this right now. Let's go hunt Drysdale."

I went to the couch where we had laid out our clothing before turning in the night before. Her clothing had returned to the gray yoga outfit, and mine to my slacks and shirt. Even my revolver hung in its shoulder holster. My wallet still had the bills I'd grabbed from my place. I cracked open the revolver. It had three bullets left in the chamber. I'd not waste another on a demon, I didn't care much if it got me put into the slammer, one of those slugs was going to kiss Drysdale. I owed Gladys that much.

Inanna opened the door to the room. "Ready?"

"Yeah."

"Can we grab some food before we hit the road?"

"Of course."

We found a bagel place that still had some stock. Inanna devoured it all as if she'd not eaten for days while chatting about the mystery house. I'd not known her long enough to know if that was typical for her when she was on the rag. After she'd finished, she grabbed a paper and started to flip through the pages while I sipped my coffee.

"I can't believe I've not checked our horoscopes since that first morning. Mine gives me a lot of hope that today's going to be excellent. It says, 'The table is set, the food is ready, feast on what you've long prepared.' Yours is a bit more troublesome. 'What lurks under stones today is not the same as yesterday nor tomorrow, yet you must turn them all over if you want to find what you're looking for.'"

"There is one stone we've never turned over," I said.

"What stone is that?" She took a forkful of my hash browns.

"Remember that bloke I shot when I pulled you out of Drysdale's?"

"What of him?"

"Drysdale had a reason to share you with him. I think it's important. When you're done eating my breakfast, I'm going to pick up that particular stone."

She put down her fork. "Oh, sorry about that."

"No issue. I'm not fond of hash browns. Eat as much as you need."

"I've never been so hungry, Johnny. I'm starting to really believe I'm pregnant."

"We'll pick up a test later, but this is more likely you are replenishing what you lost last night. You threw up most of what you ate yesterday." I finished my coffee. "Let's get a move on."

Sure enough, the car's sense of humor was a kick in the pants. A Honda Odyssey was waiting where I'd parked. The quintessential family van.

"Looks like the car agrees with you," I said.

"You've no idea how happy I'll be if I am pregnant!"

She had no idea how many reservations I had both at the prospect of fatherhood, and of her as a mother.

Chapter 18

Pulling A Favor

Tracking a guy when you only know one name is not the easiest thing to do in the world. However, tracking someone who is a business associate with someone like Drysdale is much harder, as neither have good reasons to bring much notice to themselves. This is where having some contacts in the underworld could be helpful, and I'd done some favors for a major mob boss a few years back, the kind he promised me I could collect on if I needed help. It was time to collect. I drove to Japan town and parked in front of his townhouse.

"You know Hiromichi Fuyuki?" she asked.

"Yes, and obviously, so do you. I imagine professionally."

"Yes, he was a good customer."

"Same. He owes me one," I said. "It is time to collect."

"I'm impressed."

"Don't be," I said. "Let's go."

I rang the bell. After a moment or two, an old Japanese man opened the door and bowed deeply. "Mr. Talon! Mr. Fuyuki will be honored with your visit. Please come in."

I returned the bow. "Thank you, Akito. It is an honor to be admitted as a guest in this house."

We removed our shoes, and he took us to a room with a tatami mat on the floor, white walls, and a single pedestal where an incense burner held a stick of smoking incense that filled the room with the scent of a sexually aroused woman. We both sat on the mat and waited.

After a few minutes, one of the walls opened and Hiromichi stepped into the room and bowed deeply. "Johnny Talon, it is good to see you again."

I rose and returned the bow. "I delight in being in your presence."

"I have had tea prepared in my study. Shall we take it there while your woman awaits our return?"

"While I have no desire to correct you, Eve is my client. I am here on her behalf. She needs to hear what I'm here to learn more than me."

He bowed to her. "It is an honor to meet you, Eve."

Eve rose and continued the polite fiction, bowing deeply. "It is an honor to meet you."

We followed him into his studio where two women wearing only aprons stood to either side of an ornate antique wooden table and cushions. We sat ourselves on the cushions. The women poured tea into cups of delicate bone white porcelain and then left the room, closing the door behind them.

"To what do I owe the honor of this unexpected visit, Johnny?"

"Hiromichi-san, my client had some very valuable things stolen from her. She's hired me to track down the thief and retrieve the stolen items. We've reason to believe the thief is Drysdale and an associate of his who goes by the name Murphy. I was hoping that someone in your organization would know this Murphy and help us by providing some information on both men."

Hiromichi hesitated. "Eve, are you willing to walk away from these men and these items? This would be the wiser course."

"Hiromichi-san, I would sooner slit my wrists," she replied.

"It may amount to the same thing."

"Even so, I will retrieve what was stolen by these men. It is more than a matter of honor to me."

"More than an issue of honor?"

"The soul of my beloved is trapped in what they stole. I have only learned of this since the theft. I would free my beloved."

He turned to me. "Johnny Talon, are you willing to die to help her?"

"As you well know, Hiromichi-san, I always put my life on the line for my clients. Besides, I don't think he wants either of us dead. He could have had us killed many times, in clean ways that are not traceable to him."

"Please forgive me, and I've not forgotten my debt to you. If you could rid the world of these two men, you will bring a smile to the weary face of the Buddha. They are both dangerous, in ways that most men are not. Now that I understand your resolve, I will help you."

He clapped his hands twice, paused, and clapped a third time. The door opened and the two women entered and bowed.

"Please find Edamame and bring her to me."

They bowed again, closing the door behind them as they backed out.

"I've asked my servants to bring me someone who has deep personal knowledge of the two men you seek information on. While we wait for them to bring her, let me tell you what I know. Drysdale is a sorcerer who traffics in drugs. Mostly his organization sells opiates, but they also sell customized drug cocktails to a high-class customer base. Murphy traffics in women. He sells women to various rich and powerful men to do with as they please. Neither is above murder. In fact, Murphy has done murder for sport. This is most likely why you are still alive; they are sporting with you. I'll let Edamame give you the details when she arrives."

The door re-opened and a woman limped in, her right foot dragging as if she couldn't lift it. Her face was badly scarred, and she wore an eye patch. She bowed to us, her face betraying the pain in the act.

"Edamame, you have heard me speak of Johnny Talon, and my life's debt to him. This is him, and his client, Eve. They are going after the man known as Murphy and are hoping that the information you have of him can help them. Would you be willing to share this?"

She ignored me, looking at Eve. "You know Murphy?"

"Drysdale introduced me at the edge of his whip."

"I see no scars, no disfigurations, no proof. How can you have been with him and escaped so easily? He always damages his toys."

"I owe that and so much more to Mr. Talon."

"It won't be enough to kill him. You must dismantle his organization."

"I understand. If it can be done, I'll do it."

"And you, Mr. Talon?"

I was not a knight in shining armor. "I'm just a private dick. However, Eve is my client and I've never been known to disappoint a client."

"I appreciate your honesty. I will tell you what I know. Murphy's full name is Seamus Murphy. He owns and operates a legitimate business that does offshore gambling here in the States. He uses this to kidnap women, who are then taken to an estate in Berlitz where they are drugged with custom cocktails purchased from Drysdale and taught to be sexually submissive to those who are sadistic. He sells these women at an annual auction at his estate. Drysdale sells the owners the cocktails. Murphy picks one woman a year to be his personal pet. He deliberately disfigures her. Most of the time she dies during the disfiguring. Once he's done with her, he throws her off of a cliff. I don't know if I'm one of the lucky ones, as I survived all of this."

"If your information helps bring him down, you will have done women all over the world a service," said Inanna.

"Besides Drysdale providing the cocktails," I asked, "do you know anything else about the relationship between the two men?"

"The year I was thrown off the cliff, I overheard Murphy swearing that one of Drysdale's bitches—his words not mine—had gotten him shot, and that he was putting the squeeze on Drysdale to produce that woman or he'd find another supplier."

"I was that bitch," said Inanna.

"Thank you," said Edamame, who bowed, her face wincing in pain.

"Thank Johnny. He was the one who plugged Murphy."

"Then thank you both. It brought me great joy to see him in pain, even though he took it out on me. I look forward to learning from you about his death. I encourage you to make it as painful as possible."

Of all the private dicks in the world, I had to find

myself in a case that had escalated from returning stolen goods to finding a mirror that contained a soul to destroying a white slavery ring. I didn't need a calculator to know that one percent of whatever Inanna had would not cover my expenses, and I didn't need a genius to know that one Shamus and his revolver were not sufficient to take down such an organization. Surreal detective methods might bring significant insight and allow for ways to resolve the otherwise unresolvable, but this was beyond me. She'd provided me with no less imprecise location as an entire nation for Murphy's operations.

"Do you have any idea where in Berlitz his mansion is located?" I asked.

"No, but I know Drysdale's phone number."

"Cell phone?" I asked.

"Yep. 413-555-1313."

I turned to our host. "May I borrow your computer?" I asked.

Hiromichi said, "It is yours to use."

I left the three of them to their tea and went back into Fuyuki's office. He'd left the computer unlocked. I opened a browser and went to a darknet site I knew that tracked smart phone locations as they traveled. I was in luck. Through the site I was able to get the GPS coordinates of where Drysdale had spent two weeks in Berlitz last year. I put them into the maps search app and put in the coordinates. I had the location of Murphy's private estate.

I went back to my friend, and the two women. "I know where his estate is located. It will be easier to deal with him after we've dealt with Drysdale, and we have a deadline."

Inanna said, "Johnny, while you were in there searching, Edamame and I came to a mutual conclusion. After you help me take down Drysdale, she and I will take down Murphy. Without you."

"Why?" I must confess, I was hurt.

"It will hurt him more if he's overcome by only women, and we want it to hurt."

"Understood. By the way, I now know exactly where Drysdale is, and can track his movements, and he doesn't know we can do that."

Inanna smiled. "An edge."

"Yes, presuming he has that mirror on him. My gut tells me he does."

Inanna rose and bowed to our host. "I have a mirror to break. Please excuse our haste."

"Before you go, you must both wear these around your necks." Edamame handed us each an *onenju*. "That will both keep the demons at bay and prevent Drysdale from using his sorcery against you."

"Thank you."

"Yes, thank you."

I took a look at my phone. While everyone had been talking, I'd been tracking Drysdale's current location. He was in his warehouse. I had no idea if the *onenju* beads would protect us from the sorcery that had greeted us the last few times we'd attempted entrance, but even if they did, they'd not protect us from the bullets of his minions. We needed to see where he went when he left the warehouse and go after him there.

"Talon, one more thing."

"Yes, Edamame."

"Drysdale has a safe house that most don't know about. It is located at 2448 Pacific Street. He's been going there a lot lately."

"This means we have him frightened," I said.

Hiromichi clapped his hands and the two mostly naked women returned. "Yes, it also means you'll need better armament." He turned to the women. "Take our guests to the armory and let them equip themselves."

****

I followed the two women into a room that had everything from authentic samurai swords and ninja throwing stars, to modern automatic pistols and rifles. I'd always preferred my revolver, a traditional six shooter, to the high-tech armaments available on his walls. The mechanism never jammed, but reloading was slower. After trying a few, I settled on a pair of Beretta M9s. I also strapped two pairs of throwing knives on my legs. I looked over at Inanna. She was testing out two swords that had the gleam of well-polished bronze.

"Are those bronze?"

"Yes, better than iron. Won't rust," she said.

"What about steel?" I asked.

"It'll rust."

"Yes, but iron and steel are supposed to be better against the fey."

"We're going against demons and sorcerers, not the fey," she said. "Iron is related to magic, especially earth magic. Bronze isn't. That is why your bullets didn't do any damage. They're lead, which is poisonous, dull, malleable, and heavy without any worth. Shooting them with lead is kind of like feeding them."

How on earth did she suddenly know this? Or was it sudden? "Are you suggesting I find bronze bullets?"

Inanna laughed. "No, silly. I'd think that even you would know about silver and gold bullets."

"That magical sword I used was good carbon steel. It cut the demons."

"Like I said, iron is related to earth magic. I'm packing a gun for Drysdale, but a blade for the demons," she said.

Out of the corner of my eye I saw a blade that I'd swear hadn't been there moments before. I walked back to the corner where I'd looked over various weapons and unsheathed the sword to take a closer look. Like hers, the sword was bronze, and I swear that it felt like an electric current was running through the blade, at a frequency that energized me. Someone had stamped words onto the blade in Hebrew. I re-sheathed the sword and buckled it onto my waist. Inanna had strapped her blade onto hers and had two knives strapped to each leg. We'd certainly draw the attention of the first cop we ran across.

"Where is he now?" Inanna asked.

"Wherever he is, I need a good night's sleep before I can go after him."

"Me too. Would you mind if we went back to my place?" she asked. "I'm tired of hotels and would love to sleep in my own bed."

"I'd offer mine, but I doubt much if that is habitable yet."

"Was it ever?"

I glanced at her face; she was serious. Good to get honesty from her, even when it hurt.

"Yes, for a single man." Well, I had to defend myself.

She took my hand, and we started walking to the front door. "Speaking of single people, would you be hurt if I choose to carry the child but not marry you?"

I felt a weight lift off my shoulders. "I know you

don't love me. I was ready to do the honorable thing, but I'm not fond of empty gestures."

"I have too much of my life to put back together before I can love again. Hopefully, nine months is enough. Otherwise, I'll put the child up for adoption."

"Understood." I was not going to offer to raise the child on my own, and I felt sick about it.

"You can help with some of that tonight," she said.

"What?" I missed something.

"Understanding. I am addicted to two songs. The walrus was right. I need to find a new song to have sex to, a new song to fight to, or to learn how to have sex and fight with no song at all."

"Tonight?"

"Yes? Are you up for it?" she asked.

"I'll see what I can do to rise to the occasion," I said, regretting the pun. "Well, I'll be—"

"What is it?"

"The car's become a black Chrysler Imperial Crown with what appears to be certain modifications."

"Johnny, what on earth are you talking about?"

I tried to keep the excitement and awe out of my voice. "Ignore me, but if I'm right, we're in for some trouble."

I went around, got in, and enjoyed the roar of the engine a bit too much. I put the car in gear and started to drive when I caught from the rear-view mirror that we had a tail. I tried some sudden last second turns, but they kept on us. Having a distinctive car didn't make it easy to lose a tail. I made yet another turn to find the road blocked by a tractor trailer. I hit the brakes and turned the wheel hard, which to my surprise worked just like in the movies, with us reversing direction to a great squeal of tires. With my tail right in front of us, I put the car into gear and drove at them, accelerating hard. Hoping it would work, I waited to almost the last second, hit the button labeled gas, and swerved to miss the oncoming car. It worked; for the moment we whizzed by them at high speed. I cut sharply to the right at the end of the block.

Two large black demons stood there, eyes glowing red, black wings spread. I hit the button for the car to open fire on them.

"This is the first set of demons we've seen since Burning Man," I said, gripping the steering wheel tightly. "I wonder why."

I accelerated at them. Whatever the car was firing seemed to be tearing at the fabric of the demons, with light breaking through each hole until each demon burst into light and dissipated as we drove through where they'd stood.

"Those were not your demons, were they?" I asked.

"No, I don't think they were." Her voice had risen like a question. "I didn't feel the rage against them that I felt with the others."

"Rage?" I asked as I took a tight left into traffic.

"Yeah, that I could have been so stupid."

"Could you check today's date on your phone?" I asked, taking a tight right.

"You think we're getting close?"

"We've been traveling in time so often; I want to know when we are. We got rid of those demons rather easily, but I'm thinking they're a warning."

"Why would either Drysdale or demons be warning us?" she asked. A good question too.

"No idea. They probably hope to frighten us away,

which means they're frightened."

"While I love the idea, why would he be frightened of us? Last time he was able to dismiss us with a wave of his hand."

I came to a stop at a red, looking impatiently in all directions while waiting for the green. "Inanna, I've told you that my method isn't logical, but I know that Drysdale is desperate just like I know you're the Sumerian goddess—wait, that's why he's nervous. He's afraid you're going to wake up and know yourself."

"Except I'm not the Sumerian goddess. There is only one God."

Green. I tried not to accelerate too quickly; the car was responsive. "Think back to Exodus, where the God of Israel cast judgment on the gods of Egypt. Perhaps things are more complicated than we know."

"And here I thought you were a Catholic," she said.

"Even there, think on your creed. God from god, light from light, true god from true god. We all say it, none of us really knows what it means. We know there are angels and demons, and for all we know, people mistook them for gods before they knew God, and some of them encouraged this. I could well imagine the fallen angels encouraging this, reveling in the worship. What if Inanna regretted what she'd done, and was trying to find a way to repent, to become again one of the Lord's angels? What if she did so by following Jesus, letting herself be born, and taking on some of the things she introduced to the human condition, to understand it experientially? Two of your addictions are both things Inanna was known for, sexual love and opium."

"And my addiction to particular songs, one for sex, one for battle?" Her voice sounded thoughtful, but I was worried about the lights in the mirror.

"Perhaps it is because for you they are your two fundamental passions, sex and war, the two domains of Inanna. What are the songs?"

"Whenever I have sex, 'This is love' runs through my head."

I took a sudden left that had us both thrown as far as the seat belt let. "Don't know that one. What about battle?"

"'Fast as you can'."

"Hmm, don't know that one either. Well, we got you over your addiction to sex by helping you change how you were having sex. While I'm not certain I understand how we got you over your addiction to opium, then again, we changed the context of how you were using it."

"It is odd. The withdrawal symptoms were much easier this time, and I've had no cravings for it since. Then again, poppy tea is so much milder than the crap I'd been taking, and I'm certain that you gave me a small dose. So, you think that if we change the context for the songs that will cure that?"

I came to a stop at the base of a hill. "Or if we get you focused on different songs. Either could work."

"How would we do that?"

"We could put headphones on you and spin a different song while you fought or had sex. Or we could play those songs while you were doing other things. Or you could just leave well enough alone. Not all addictions are harmful."

"Ignore the girl in the sunglasses?" she asked.

"No. Some addictions help. They provide the extra reinforcement that a person needs in life. The way you were approaching sex, where you weren't happy, unless you were getting constant sexual attention was not healthy. The constant craving for opium wasn't healthy, and certainly the opium wasn't healthy. What is unhealthy about having the same song in your head every time you fight?"

"Rhythm. If you know the song in my head, you know the rhythm I'm fighting in. Same with the sex, though I'm not certain how that would be a problem unless I become a boring partner. So, let's focus on the fighting. It would be easier to have a new song I could pull in when I wanted a different rhythm for fighting. Put on the radio. Let's see if your car has a suggestion."

"While I do, grab the nautilus shell and hold it. Listen to it as well as what is on the radio."

"Okay. Got it."

I turned on the radio. The overture for Carmen blasted from the speakers. Inanna reached for the knob and turned it up.

"Yes! I love it! What is this joyful song?"

"You don't know Carmen?" I asked.

"No. Who is Carmen?"

"Not who, a what. Carmen is an opera. This is the overture."

"This music is perfect!" she said. "What is Carmen about?"

"Free love and jealousy," I said, leaving out the bit about prostitution.

"Care to give details?"

"A soldier falls in love with Carmen, a gypsy who believes in free love. Eventually tormented by his jealousy over her behavior, he kills her."

"Bastard."

"It's opera, thus it has to be tragic. We're here, and

in luck. There's a parking spot." I pulled in with small regret, that had been a fun drive, and I wasn't entirely certain I'd lost our tail.

"It may sound a bit odd, but I'm looking forward to sleeping in my own bed."

"It will be a bit odder if we can. Drysdale destroyed my place. And the forensics lab. We should be careful; this may be a trap."

"Didn't think of that," she said. "How will we tell?"

"Let's start with what day is it. Can you check on your cell phone?"

"Sure thing." Inanna pulled her phone from her purse and unlocked it. "Damn. We've time traveled again."

"When are we?"

"About five years ago."

"Right when you were working for Drysdale."

"Could be. I was only at his place for a couple of months when you pulled me out of there. I wish I could remember which days I did that trick."

"Well, the place is not likely to be a trap, but we may run into you."

"Something tells me this car of yours got us to a time when we'd be safe. Shame it couldn't take us to a time after Jessica had given me her mirror."

"You know it won't be that easy," I said.

"I know. A gal can wish. Let's go to a drug store first. I want to get one of those pregnancy tests. *Then* let's get some rest."

Chapter 19

Songs For Love And War

Her apartment didn't have much in the way of things. A nightstand with a cellphone charger, a dresser with jewelry boxes on top, some stuffed animals on the bed. She gave the stuffed animals big hugs and then plugged her cell phone in.

"I'm surprised the battery held out this long. Why don't you have a seat? I'm going to take that test, then change into my exercise clothing and work through my fighting exercises to new songs."

She came out of the bathroom with a huge smile despite the tears running down her cheeks.

"May I be the first to congratulate you," I said. I stood up and embraced her.

"Clear, blue, and easy. I never knew I wanted a child until I found out I was having one." She started to sob into my shoulders. I had no desire to be a father, but sometimes you can't choose.

After a few minutes, she pulled back, wiped the tears off of her cheeks, and went back into the bathroom. She came back just minutes later with a washed face dressed in a beat-up old heart t-shirt and a pair of shorts. "Time to get to work," she said, her voice firm with resolve.

She did something with her phone and a panel opened up across from her bed exposing a speaker.

Moments later, Barracuda started blasting. She pulled her comb out of her hair and started to shadow fight as her playlist went through Heart, Patti Smith, Joan Jett, St. Vincent, Fiona Apple, and others I didn't recognize.

"It's no use. I just can't get into a good rhythm," she said, panting as she took a breather.

"You looked pretty good to me." My complement was genuine. She was good.

"What was the name of that opera again?"

"Carmen."

"Right."

Moments later, the overture to Carmen blasted from the speakers. She whirled through her exercises at Carmen's tempo. After that song, Orpheus in the Underworld came on and her movements became a blur. Finally, the song ended, and she leaned over, hands on her knees, panting a little.

"That was awesome!" I said.

"Yeah, thanks! Much faster than how I usually fight. I want to do that again."

She replayed the music, first the rock, and then the two more classical pieces as she upped the tempo of her mock battle, this time using both comb and sword. After an hour of this, she took a break, sauntering into the kitchen to grab two drinks. She handed me an iced tea.

"Thanks."

"No, thank you! That was great! Now I need to find other songs, and I need your help for that too."

I took a long drink from the bottle. "I think I know just the songs. Give me a moment to figure out how to use your phone."

She had an older version of a smart phone, but I got onto a video streaming site and found an old song list I'd created back when last I had a lover. I hit play and spun as my favorite Righteous Brothers song began. She reached for my hands. We danced to the Righteous Brothers, Roy Orbison, Marvin Gay, The Temptations, and every other romantic song in my playlist as we shed clothing and eventually wound up in bed where our dance became at first heated, then tender. I held her close, with her fingers clasped in mine, listening to her breathing until I slept.

****

I turned from a clock whose hands ran backwards to behold a bell tower. I walked the heated sands towards the tower but got no nearer no matter how fast I walked. Just behind me, something walked, matching my stride.

"The key to getting the mirror is to remember that it is not a reflection but is an instrument of reflection."

I couldn't turn to look at what followed me, but something with fur brushed against my leg and I was alone. The bell tower was no longer in front of me, but a lonely edifice shaped like a thin tall cone, was. As I neared it, I could discern the shape of a man frozen within the stone, and near the top of the cone, another clock. The hands on this clock weren't moving. I turned to look at the bell tower and saw a woman, naked, standing in the shadow of the bell, taking up that shadow as her garment.

The ground beneath me began to shake. The man within the stone was awakening. I began to run from the cone, the man, the woman when I realized that I was falling as the sands beneath my feet started to shift, with walls long hidden beneath emerging to block my flight. As I fell, I realized that shadows were the opposite of mirrors.

****

I woke with that thought pounding in my head. Shadows are the opposite of mirrors. That was important somehow. Inanna still slept, but I knew that once again my sleeping body had joined with hers. The dream was both clear and murky. Time, it would appear, was slipping away. Was Inanna taking on shadows? Or did she need to? Or was that woman Inanna? When Inanna had been in my dreams before, I'd recognized her. This was a woman I didn't know. I didn't recognize the man.

I knew better than to dismiss the dream as irrelevant. It could simply be a matter of understanding that the mirror had to be exposed to light, not to shadow to work. Whatever the case, there was one thing that was crystal clear: today was the day we had to act. Most of the dream had been about time.

I rolled over and caressed Inanna's cheek.

She smiled. "What is it?"

"It's time to take that mirror away from Drysdale."

She rolled over and stretched. "Today?"

"Yes, and soon. Another thing, shadows are the opposite of mirrors."

She reached up and caressed the stubble on my cheeks. "You must have had another dream; I'm wet with you."

"Yes, somehow you slept through this one."

"Think we have time for a shower?"

"Don't know what time the equinox is. Let's find out."

I turned on the light. All her items were gone again, except one of the stuffed animals. Thankfully, her phone had been fully charged before the charger disappeared in slipping into the present. I handed it to her. "Can you check on this thing?"

"Yes, give me a moment." She sat up, her fingers giving the phone her instructions. "The equinox is at three fifteen and twenty seconds this afternoon. Let's get cleaned up and grab some breakfast."

I paused, my head turning to follow the sound. Music. The overture to Carmen was coming from her purse. Inanna walked over to where it lay on the floor and picked up the shell. The music was emanating from the shell. She gave it a hug, put it down, and started dancing wild to the music. When finally the music stopped, she turned to me. The smile she wore was met by eyebrows lowered and closer together. If I'd not known it before, I'd have known her as the goddess of war right then. Drysdale didn't know what was coming.

****

Thankfully the clothing we came in with, and the weapons we'd picked up at Hiromichi Fuyuki's were still in the apartment. We had no towels, so we stayed naked after our shower until we were dry enough to dress. The clothing we'd purchased in the thrift store was still in the closet where we'd hung it, so Inanna was able to hide her weapons under a jacket. Mine were readily hidden in my trench coat.

"Where is Drysdale hiding out?" I asked, buttoning my cuffs.

She slipped her comb in her hair and then glanced at her cell phone. "Looks like he's in his place on Pacific. Can we grab some grub first?"

"No problem. What's good around here?"

She took me to a mom-and-pop place on Sutter that served breakfast to order, and then ordered two egg sandwiches for herself. I ordered one for myself and joined her at table. "The kid likes breakfast?"

"Yeah. I'm waking up famished. I'm just glad I don't have morning sickness. I don't know how I'd manage with how hungry I am."

"Do you care if it is a boy or girl?"

"No, both terrify me," she said while chewing. "I've not lived the most responsible life. How can I be a good mother?"

How many times was I going to cross the line between detective and friend on this case? If not for the one dream, I'd have given up trying to be professional by now. I'm glad I hadn't as that professionalism was helping me distance myself from the idea of fatherhood. "You're working on putting your demons behind you. Focus on becoming who you're called to be."

The clerk behind the counter brought our sandwiches. Inanna tore into one, speaking with her mouth full. "The trick is being a whore felt so natural to me, as if that is exactly what I am. It's why I was so angry at my mother for so many years, why I didn't reach out."

I took a sip of the coffee, nice and dark. "Yet you walked away from that years ago."

"Stripping is almost the same thing, making less money from less sex but still making money from sex. I honestly don't know what else I know how to do. What kind of mom will that make me?"

I put down my cup. "You are not what you do. If you love our kid, and raise the child in that love, you'll make a great mom."

She reached out and touched my hand. "I like the sound of that, *our* kid. Thanks, by the way."

"Thanks for what specifically?"

"Not offering to take on the responsibility of paying

for everything, the typical trap of just retire and I'll take care of the money thing that too many men offer to the women they get pregnant."

I'd been thinking about saying exactly that. Must be part of that Y chromosome or something. I let myself swallow my food while I worked out exactly what to say. "Part of me wishes I could, but I don't make enough for that, and like you, I don't know what else I can do with my life."

She pointed her fork loaded with breakfast potatoes at me. "You could do more traditional gumshoe work."

"Actually, that wouldn't pay quite so well. The PI business is dying out. Besides chasing after unfaithful spouses ain't my idea of a good life. You tend to get beaten up by a lot of faithless men."

"What kind of cases do you handle?" she said while chewing, then swallowing the coffee to wash down her question.

I put some potato on my fork but let it sit there for a moment while I thought about what I do. "I do a lot of missing persons, but I also handle investigations into suspicious deaths where the standard police methods turn up empty."

"I imagine that your methods don't produce results that stand up in court."

I wiped some ketchup from my cheek with a napkin. "I'm usually upfront with clients that I'll get them answers, but the results may not stand up in court. That didn't seem relevant in this case."

"Many clients sue you for fraud?" she asked as she stole some potatoes from my plate.

I pushed my plate towards her so she could reach it more easily. "No. Not one." I was proud of that.

"I'm surprised." Her eyebrows echoed the surprise. "Unhappy with my results?"

"No, but our society is littered with litigation, and your methods are unorthodox." She pushed away my now empty plate.

I sipped my coffee. There were limits to what I would share. "Your case is odd. Ignoring the demons and the things retrieved in dreams, there hasn't been a lot of tangible evidence, and our relationship hasn't been terribly professional. However, what tangible evidence we did have led to both those who stole from you and the people who hired them. The intangible evidence has helped us both to identify motive and locate many of the stolen items, especially those which have had some value. That's often what happens in my cases, and mostly what my customers are truly interested in is the motive. Why has person X disappeared; why did person Y kill person Z."

"So, what is Drysdale's motive?" she said, wiping her mouth on her napkin. "I'm not buying that he's done all of this to get his money back. Speaking of tangible evidence, are you ever going to try looking at that piece of paper you found on Fred?"

"As near as I can figure, Drysdale's trying to get a very powerful goddess under his control because you give him access to power. Between the fact that historically you've been involved with poppy tea and human sexuality, you're perfect for his business operations. What I rescued you from five years ago was his program to have you voluntarily place yourself as his slave, dependent upon him and him alone for everything. He miscalculated when he brought in Murphy, as that gave you back some fight."

I took a break to down some more Joe. "Then, when I showed up, instead of submissively staying, you fled, which didn't devastate his plans, but certainly derailed them. That somehow at least part of Jessica's soul is trapped in that mirror is his last hope. He's been using that to try to draw you back to him. That spell he cast at us was to put us both into our place, but it didn't work. Instead, it started you on the road to healing and revelation. What he forgot about you is that war is as important to you as sex, and when I showed up, that part of you began to waken. He gave you something worth fighting for."

She rested her chin on her clasped hands in a triangle ending with her elbows on the table and batted her eyes at me. "All of that is nice, except I'm just a woman with the same name as an ancient Sumerian goddess. Do you think he also believes that I'm this demon you've become convinced I am?"

I put some bills under my cup for a tip. "Yes, I think he believes you to be Inanna, daughter of the moon, goddess of love and war."

She tossed her head back and laughed. "You're both mad."

"Or we're both onto something you don't want to admit to yourself—or can't admit to yourself for some reason."

"Okay, let's just say for a moment you two are right. How can he trap me with Jessica in the mirror?"

I finished my coffee. "He's going to offer you a deal: free her for your services for life."

"Oh." Her face fell. "If I wasn't pregnant, I might have gone for that. Now, I don't know. I suppose it doesn't help that I'm not who he thinks I am; in the end,

I'd be offered the same bargain, and have the same choices."

I stood up. "Just remember, Drysdale doesn't know about you being pregnant."

"This is a hard choice: between the woman I love but can't have and the child I bear but never asked for."

"It is your choice."

She stood up and pushed her chair in. "Even though you're the father?"

"Yes, though I frankly think you'll have both."

"Yes, that's what I must fight for. Now, about that piece of paper?"

"Sure, let's take a look."

I pulled the paper out of my pocket, unfolded it, and held it up to the lamp. Sure enough, I found writing on it. "It's a note from Fred written in lemon juice. It says, 'The stuff Drysdale didn't want can be found in a St. Vincent de Paul at 525 fifth street. I'm sorry. He gave me no choice.'"

"Is that the one where we found my clothing?"

"Yes. When this is done, we should go there. We may still find the rest of your things."

"Go with me?" she asked in a small voice, pressing herself against my arm while she took my hand.

She was manipulating me again and, knowing this, I still said yes.

****

We walked to where we'd parked my car. Instead of a car, a Honda CL350 motorcycle was parked there.

"Can you ride?" asked Inanna.

Glad it was a dry day, I climbed on and inserted the key. It turned and the cycle roared to life. "Climb on."

Inanna climbed behind me, holding me by the waist,

and pushed her cellphone in front of my face. "He's still in his place on Pacific."

I glanced at the phone to get a sense of the route there and said, "Hold on tight."

She moved the phone out of my way. I kicked the bike in gear and rode up Stockton towards Pacific. I crested a hill to find the road blocked by traffic. I took a left and rode along Pine looking for a road where I could ride. Each seemed inexplicably blocked by cars.

"Time to break a few rules. Hang on."

I took the right, weaving in and around the vehicles, hoping no one would be so stupid as to open their door. A tractor trailer blocked the end of the street; I cut to the right to go around when six men with weapons drawn stepped in front of us. Why men and not more demons? Had we broken her remaining addictions? Or was his power over her running out?

"Go home, Johnny. Leave the whore with us."

"You ready?" I shouted back to Inanna.

"When you are."

I wheeled the bike around, weaving at high speed away from them. In my mirrors I saw Inanna let fly throwing stars as bullets swept around us. Anticipating an ambush on the other side of the truck, I accelerated. Sure enough a group of armed men popped out, but too late to block us, as I swept around them.

"Johnny, look left!"

A truck, barreling down at us at high speed. I swerved again, nearly flattening us against the pavement, but righting the bike as I zoomed up Mason. I heard sirens in the distance; someone must have reported the shooting. Hopefully they were not after us. I felt the ground shake and a large crack emerged in front of us. I hit the throttle and the bike leapt past a green scaly arm that reached out of the ground to grab at us.

"That was no earthquake!" shouted Inanna.

"Drysdale is throwing everything at us!" I yelled back over the roar of the bike and the wind. "He must be scared silly."

"Hope he shits in his pants! Look right!"

I swerved to avoid another stream of bullets. How many men did he have? Or was that the police?

For that matter, how was it I could see the bullets and react to them? No sense worrying about the imponderables.

I turned onto Clay and hit the brakes to avoid a woman pushing a stroller. She looked at us in horror as we skidded towards her and her child. My front tire came to rest but inches away from the stroller.

"Sorry ma'am," I said.

She morphed into a demon with flaming eyes, the stroller changed into another, shorter demon that slashed at the tires of the cycle.

"Damn you!" I powered off the cycle, stepped off, and drew my sword. Inanna was by my side in a moment.

"Ha! You fools! We're already damned, as is that bitch next to you! We're here to drag her back to hell."

I bit back the 'Like hell you will' retort. These demons had just confirmed my theory. These were NOT Inanna's demons.

"You think I'm damned?" Inanna challenged. "Well, boys, just try and take me."

They both rushed at her. I blocked the shorter of the two with my blade, drawing black smoke with the cut. The demon turned its attention and claws to me, slashing out furiously. Somehow, I matched the demons' speed, and the length of my blade kept it from getting to me, but I was entirely on the defensive. One slip-up and those claws would tear me to pieces. As I let myself become one with the blade, I found myself chanting the Hebrew inscription. The demon began to smoke, and then it disappeared in a sudden burst of flame.

Panting, I turned to Inanna, who was down on one knee, clutching her side.

"Thank you." Her voice was strained.

"Yours disappeared at the same time as mine?" I asked.

"Yes."

"Did it hurt you?"

"Yeah, but I don't think it broke skin or bone. I'll have one heck of a bruise though."

"Those two were different. I don't think they were summoned the same way as the others."

"I agree. He's taking bigger risks and trying to raise hell."

"I've been trying to avoid puns like that. Those were not your demons."

"That explains why I had so much trouble with them, and why my comb wasn't enough. I'll use my sword next time. Is the bike okay?"

"Damned thing shredded the tire. We're going to have to continue on foot," I said.

"Talk about bad puns. Will it be okay to leave it here?"

"Should be," I answered. "We'll come back for it when our business with Drysdale is done. If it turns back into the Torino, there is a spare in the trunk. I wonder why it's stayed as a cycle."

"I think it's because the poor thing is hurt. I'm

starting to think your car is possessed."

"I don't think so. Your clothing also changes, and I doubt something is possessing your yoga pants."

"You're right. I wish we could figure this out."

"Right now, we've got plenty of other things to worry about. My car has to be tomorrow's problem."

We sheathed our blades and started to climb the hill. One thing about San Francisco, you didn't get anywhere fast by foot.

"How are we doing for time?" I asked.

"We're still good. However, if his intent was to delay us, he's succeeded."

"Yeah. I wish I knew how he is tracking us and if there is a way to block it."

"We could try prayer," she suggested.

"Something like 'Dear Lord, make us invisible to our enemies so that we can undo the abomination of trapping a soul?'"

"Amen," she said. "I wonder if it will work?"

"If it doesn't, it means that the Lord wants Drysdale to know we're coming, and to know he can't stop us," I said. Somehow that thought encouraged me.

"Yeah, I want him to know that too," she said.

"You and me both."

"Take my hand," she said.

I took Inanna's hand.

She held it tight, and then said, "Lord, you know better than anyone that I am not worthy of your notice or attention. I've broken every commandment you lovingly gave to your people, and I now put my unborn child's life at risk. I do so to save the only person I ever loved from perpetual slavery to a man who treats with demons. If you give me strength to pass through his protections and stand once more in the presence of Sam Drysdale, I will give my all in trying to free Jessica from his intended doom for her."

I felt her body shake once; and her cold hands turn warm in mine.

Inanna smiled. "Carmen?"

"Carmen," I agreed.

"The perfect song for a whore to go to war for love," she said. "Let's go."

Chapter 20

Drysdale

Clay Street was relatively flat for San Francisco, so we headed for Lafayette Park. My plan was to keep going until we hit Filmore and make our way to Pacific on that well-traveled road, seeking protection from attack in the crowds. With each step I fought to keep the balance between vigilance and paranoia. After the mother pushing the stroller that turned out to be a pair of well-concealed demons, there was no one we could trust. Then again, if I was right, my client was actually a powerful goddess incarnate.

If I was right, could I trust her? The entire thing could be an elaborate trap. I'd spun an elegant explanation for everything except why Drysdale wanted her comb. That was the one part of the entire mess that didn't fit in with my explanation—or any explanation I'd been able to come up with. The comb seemed to be the key to the entire mystery about Inanna's identity, Jessica's freedom, and the truth to what was going on. I tried to ignore the pun that she kept her key in the comb.

We got to Lafayette Park without further incident, and the shrieks of delight from the children at play helped me relax. We skirted the north end of the park, not wanting any of the diligent mothers to have a chance to notice our concealed weapons and call the police.

Thankfully, our raincoats were far from atypical on this typical cool San Francisco day.

The fog started to descend before we got to the end of the park, and within a hundred feet it was thick, cold, and clammy. Something about this fog smelled odd. Almost as if she was hearing my thoughts, Inanna and I drew our blades.

Tendrils of the cloud whipped out at us, shimmering as if charged with lightning. Each time one touched me or my blade, I got a painful shock. Out of the corner of my eye, I saw that Inanna was leaping into the air as she swung, so I tried the same. The pain was less as the electricity of the tendrils could no longer pass through us to get to the ground. With each leap, we'd slice more tendrils to have yet more lash out at us. I leapt and sliced through a dozen to land and have a dozen more hit me until my muscles began to twitch uncontrollably. Not knowing what I had left, I leapt and suddenly found myself surrounded by a score of children squirting water guns at Inanna and myself.

I stumbled as I landed, sweat covered and panting.

"You guys were awesome!" said a black-haired boy.

"Are you a superhero?" asked a kid wearing a Giant's baseball cap.

"What was that you were fighting?" asked the black-haired kid.

"Are you her side kick?" asked a young blond girl.

"Can I try your sword?" asked an Asian girl.

"Where is your shield?" asked the blond.

"Guys. Guys. Not all at once!" said Inanna. "I'm not a superhero, and I've no idea what we were fighting. We're trying to free my wife from a bad man, so thank you, but we really must be running on."

"You must mean the slaver," said a thin black girl with beads woven into her cornrows.

"Yeah, he lives in a big house on Pacific with walls where the ivy grows in diamonds," said an Asian boy with black glasses.

"You know this house?" Inanna's voice rose about five octaves, mirroring my own amazement.

"Hell yeah, we all avoid it," said the black girl. The other kids nodded solemnly.

"One girl went to the door on Halloween on a dare and never came back," said a girl with freckles, wire frame glasses, and red hair.

"Yeah, that guy is dangerous," said a blond boy.

"Why do you call him the slaver?" asked Inanna.

"Sometimes you can hear what goes on in there," said the red head.

"He's got women in chains," said the blond.

"Yeah, naked women," said the girl with the beads in her hair.

"Naked women in chains?" asked Inanna.

"I saw one through the windows at night," said the boy with the black glasses.

"Is your wife his slave too?" asked the girl with the beads in her hair.

"Aren't you worried he'll put chains on you?" asked the girl with red hair.

"She's not worried, did you see her with that sword!" said the blond-haired boy.

Inanna smiled. "Do you kids know of any way in except the front door?" she asked.

They all seemed to think for a few seconds. "I think there is a garage connected to the house on Steiner Street," the girl with the beads in her hair finally said.

Inanna beamed. "Thanks, kids! We're going there to free his slaves and make certain that the slaver never harms anyone again."

The kids' responses were tumbled and came out all at once: "Awesome!" "Can we come?" "Yeah!" "Fighting that monster was so cool!"

She shook her head no and gripped her bronze sword. "The best thing you guys can do is to scout the area, look for people or things that aren't normal around here. We'll take care of the slaver ourselves," said Inanna.

"Awesome!"

The kids ran off in the direction of Filmore.

"Those kids were amazing," I said, breaking my silence.

"Yeah, I'm not certain how much longer I could have withstood those shocks."

We resumed our walk up the hill towards Filmore.

"I wonder why the parents didn't stop the kids from going after the monster," said Inanna.

"I don't know," I said, "perhaps to them it just looked like the kids were squirting their water guns at the fog."

Inanna said, "Do you think maybe the kids could see us but not the adults?"

"Well, that would explain why no one called the police on us," I said.

"Good point, although it makes no sense."

I chuckled grimly. "Has there been anything about this case that has made sense?"

We turned onto Filmore and Inanna grabbed my hand. "Johnny, there's a fortune teller over there! Do we have time?"

"You want your fortune told?"

"I've not seen a horoscope in days."

I glanced at my watch. "We've only got two hours left. We should skip it."

"It's important. Please."

"She's your wife."

Inanna smiled. "Let's run to make up the time. A reading will only take a few minutes."

"All right, let's run."

****

Breathless from our run, we entered a well-lit room with plants hanging in the windows and colored-glass sun catchers sending rays of brilliant color into odd corners. The place smelled of sandalwood, though I couldn't see any incense. An old, bearded man with olive skin marked by age spots shuffled into the room and bowed to us. Both his button-up pink shirt and gray pants were too large on him, held close by a leather belt at the waist. "I am Enlil. What is it you wish?"

"I would like a reading," said Inanna.

"Sit." He sat as well and placed a deck of cards on the table, spreading them out so that you could see the backs of each.

"Pick a card. This card will be how you feel about yourself."

Inanna picked a card and turned it over. The Magician.

"You feel a strong sense of purpose and have the will to accomplish it. Even if you are opposed, you should believe in yourself and work to achieve this purpose. Choose another card. This will be what it is you want most."

She chose the World.

276

"The final chapter is here. What you strive for is upon you. Now choose a card for your fears."

She chose the Sun.

"This is a time for renewal: an end of difficulties, and a time to celebrate. You are expecting a child, no? One you've longed for. Have faith, you will have that child. Now choose a card for what is going for you."

She chose Death.

"This is a time of absolute endings, brand new beginnings. You will be a mother. You can no longer be a woman who was not a mother. This will be difficult for you, but you will be free of your past if you push past the pain.

"Now choose a card for what is going against you."

Inanna chose the Devil.

"You are opposed by addiction to drugs and have an obsessive sexual relationship. These are things that will work against that great purpose, prevent you from having that child, and bind you in bondage. Now choose a card for the outcome."

Inanna chose the Hanged Man.

"The time for a decision is at hand, a time for passage from one phase of your life to another. You must make the hardest choice and choose rightly." He looked up from the cards and looked hard at her. "Choosing to overcome addiction is a choice you constantly make. It is hard, because it is also who you are, and who you are not. Keep this in mind: no one is beyond redemption, not even the devil himself."

I pulled out my wallet. "How much do we owe you?"

The old man smiled. "To have Inanna herself enter my place is payment enough."

I blinked. The old man was gone, though the cards still lay on the table. "Let's get moving," I said.

Inanna gathered the cards and shuffled them back together. "It would be wrong to leave things a mess."

"Was that as helpful as you hoped?" I asked as I held open the door for her.

"Yes, thank you."

We stepped back onto Filmore and resumed our walk to Pacific at a more measured pace. I must say that after the gun battle, the attack by demons, by the cloud thing, I was on edge, looking at every person passing us for any sign that they were not just the normal people they appeared to be.

We crossed the street next to a woman who was pushing a shopping cart filled with bags up the hill. From the look of her and the amount of stuff in the bags, this may have been her worldly possessions. As the hill was steep and she seemed to be struggling I said, "Could you use a hand in getting this to the top of the hill?"

"Thank you, my dear."

I put my hand besides hers and started to push. For a second, I felt myself pulled and then I was at the edge of a cliff, the heat of the boiling lava rising from the abyss.

A voice behind me said, "If you don't stop trying to help her, you'll find yourself thrown into that pit to be eternally burned."

I turned to face the voice. A beautiful woman stood there, light flowing through her white garments and wings.

"That is not for you to say. You are not my judge."

"I am concerned for the well-being of your soul. Too many have fallen because of her. Uncounted souls tormented by her opiates; uncounted souls defiled themselves for her," said the angel.

"Neither are you her judge. Both judgment and redemption are the Lord's. He is kind and merciful."

"You presume to lecture me on the Lord of Hosts? Do you know who I am?"

"I don't know your name, but I know what you are. I also know that we are charged by Him to forgive. She strives for redemption. I will give my life in her service. I have no fear of you, nor of the abyss."

"I am not threatening you. I am here to rescue you. This is your last chance. Let me rescue you."

"I put my faith in the Lord," I said, and the angel disappeared.

I stood in-front of a panic-stricken Inanna at the intersection of Pacific and Filmore. "Johnny! Thank God! What happened? Where is the woman you were helping?"

"This is the second time that I met someone who was trying to get me to stop helping you. This someone showed me a fiery abyss and claimed if I continued to help you, I'd be thrown into that abyss."

"You don't think it was an angel here to save your soul?"

"No, it was one of the fallen trying to tempt me," I said. "The first time they promised me things; this time they tried threatening me."

She looked at the sidewalk. "But what if they're right? What if in helping me you endanger your soul?"

I glanced where the angel had been and then back at Inanna. Her wide dilated eyes gave me the answer I sought. "When I stand before the Lord at the time of my judgment, if I did wrong to help you, He'll know that I am not perfect, and my mistake was not made to defy Him but in love for Him. I do not fear damnation for helping you. On the contrary, to turn from helping you out of fear for my own soul would be the most damning thing I could do."

She hugged me tight. I could feel her shaking in tears.

I returned the hug. "Look, behind you. It is his house. Your beloved waits for you in there. Let's go set her free."

She turned to look where I pointed, a large tan three-story mansion behind a wall where ivy grew in diamond patterns.

"Last I checked, his cell phone was still active in the place. Let's find a way in," I said.

****

I casually tried the gate to the yard. Locked. I didn't want to try to pick the lock in broad daylight. We walked the perimeter looking for another entrance, but the wall ended at the garage without further openings. We had three options: try the garage, hop the wall, or pick the lock on the gate. Unusual for San Francisco, the garage was large enough for two doors. Unfortunately, both were locked.

"He probably has garage door openers, so trying to pick the lock wouldn't help us. If I was a hacker, I could get the doors open, but I don't have either the skills or tools. Our best way in is for me to help you over the wall and have you open the gate from the inside."

She looked at the wall with her hand on her chin. "Okay. What do we do if I can't open the gate from the inside?"

"Then I risk someone calling the cops on us. As it

is, if anyone sees me hoist you over, we may have the police here in minutes."

"Think Drysdale would call the cops on us?" she asked.

"No. He wants you. The cops would take you away, and his leverage over you expires at the equinox."

"If he wants me so badly, why the attacks, and why the locked gate?"

"He certainly doesn't want me in there, and he's a sadist, he wants to drag you to him kicking and screaming."

"How about I hoist you then. This way, to get me in, he's got to let you in too."

"Can you lift me?" I asked.

"Let's find out."

Inanna squatted and linked hands. I put a foot into her hands and pushed up with the other. Unfortunately, her hands fell away under my weight.

"Damn. We're going to have to risk you going over first." I'd never regretted my weight more.

"All right. Let's do this."

I set myself. She placed a foot into my hands and held onto my shoulder as I lifted her. She was easily able to scramble over the wall. I heard a thump as she landed.

"Johnny, there's a problem."

"What?"

"Poppies. The garden is nothing but poppies. The smell is intoxicating."

"Hold your breath."

"Okay, I'll try. Meet me at the gate."

"Okay."

Not knowing how fast she'd be able to move, I walked as quickly as I could to the gate. I called her name—nothing, then the sound of steel on steel. She was fighting someone. Damn. I was either going to have to climb over myself or try picking the lock. I pulled my picks from my pocket and as nonchalantly as possible, I worked on the lock.

Unlike in the movies, where you jiggle your picks and the lock opens easily, most locks require more patience than I had right then. I fumbled a few times, took a deep breath, and tried to calm myself. I tried again, felt the lock give and I turned the cylinder. The gate creaked as it opened. The hinges must be little used; Drysdale probably came and went via the garage. I slid through the opening to see two large men with raven's heads trading blows with Inanna whose blades moved so fast they were a blur.

I stepped through the door and pulled out my gun. Glock in hand, I said, "Put the swords down and step away from her."

The raven men ignored me, pressing their attack on Inanna harder. I didn't wait to find out if that would be too much for her. At almost point-blank range, I didn't miss. The two monsters crumpled to the ground. We didn't have much time, as the sound of the shots might bring more of them, whatever they were. Or worse, the cops.

"Thanks for the help," said Inanna.

"Let's get out of sight."

The door to the house was thankfully unlocked. We entered and heard a sound like crying coming from a side room. We found a light switch and the light revealed an office of sorts: large oak desk and shelves, and a naked woman chained to the floor. She was gagged but made sounds like whimpers.

I found the gag wasn't locked on, so I removed it. "Do you want to be here?" asked Inanna.

"No. And if you're smart, you'll get out of here before the master or some of his demon servants come," she said.

"We're here to destroy your master and send his demon servants back to the hell from which they came," I said. "Give me a moment." Click. The lock chaining her to the floor came open. "There, you're free."

Inanna helped her stand. "Are all the women held against their will?"

"No, there are some who serve willingly. Most of us were simply strippers or prostitutes, women whose absence causes no alarm when we go missing. Can I help you?"

"Can you fight, or will you follow his command?" asked Inanna.

"I'd kill the bastard with my bare hands."

"You may need more than that. If nothing else, you'll need some protection." I took off my rosary and put it around her neck. "This should protect you from the demons."

She started to tremble, eyes went wide, and she let out a howl as the trembling increased. Beads of sweat poured down her face.

"Let her go!" said Inanna.

She started shaking uncontrollably and the howl became a growl and then a shriek.

"Let her go and go back to the hell from which you came!" Inanna shouted.

The trembling stopped. The woman collapsed, panting heavily.

"Thank you," she managed between pants.

"Can you manage a prayer?" asked Inanna.

The woman nodded. "Hail Mary, full of grace, the Lord is with thee. Blessed are thou amongst women and blessed is the fruit of your womb."

"Good." Inanna turned to me. "How did you know?"

I said, "Freeing her was too easy. It had to be a trap." I turned to the woman wearing my beads. "Let me guess; it wanted you to convince us to lend you a weapon and you were to kill me and take her?"

"Yes." She sat up. "I've no idea how many of the others have been possessed. He shoots us up with drugs that steal our will. The withdrawal symptoms are so bad that you beg for death and will do anything for a fix."

"How many others have you encountered?" I asked.

"There are about a dozen of us. There is a half dozen of the raven-men."

"Now there are only four."

"You killed two of them? Good. They love to use their talons to cut us when we step out of line." She stood up, though she had to use the desk for support. "I'm a bit weak, but I would like to help if I can."

"What we need is an understanding of the layout of the place. If you could draw us a map of what you know, that would be tremendous."

"I'd be happy to."

Inanna handed her a lipstick and she drew a rough map on the desk. The house had three levels above ground, and three below. Each level had six rooms in a ring around the main hall. She'd never been in some of the rooms on the lowest level. The women all lived on the first level below ground, two to a room. The next level down was where the raven-men lived. They were Drysdale's guards, fiercely loyal. Thankfully, we'd discovered that old-fashioned lead bullets did them in.

What she knew of the lowest level was that there were five rooms that circled around a central room. Those five she drew as pentagons, with the central room a five-pointed star. She'd never been in that room.

The upstairs had a more conventional layout. On the other side of the door we'd not come through was a large room used for the parties that Drysdale would occasionally host. She'd been the entertainment at one of those. On the other side of the house was a spacious dining hall, kitchen, and pantry. Upstairs was the library, Drysdale's private office, a billiards room, and the drug room. The top floor held Drysdale's bed chamber, and guest bedrooms, linen closets, and bathrooms.

"I'm a little surprised there are no secret passages," I quipped after reviewing her drawing.

"None that I'm aware of. Instead of looking to hide his servants, he loved to parade us in front of his guests. They had full access to our rooms and could select any of us to use in any way they chose."

"Do you remember where you were supposed to take me after killing Johnny?" asked Inanna.

"Yes. There." She pointed to the star-shaped room in the center of the lowest level. "I recommend that we pretend I've done my job. Hand me an empty gun. Johnny can follow at a short distance. This way we can perhaps catch him unawares."

"Sorry, no," said Inanna. "He'd expect me to have surrendered all my weapons. Last thing I want to do is walk into that room unarmed."

"Besides, I doubt that any ruse we can come up with will work. He must know where we are through surveillance equipment," I offered.

"I've never seen any," she said.

"That doesn't mean there isn't any. We should expect that he'll know where we are and plan to meet us with armed force. Let's get ready for anything," said Inanna.

I mused aloud, "Shall we go through the party room or back to the main hall?"

"The party room will be less expected. Let's try that," the woman said.

Inanna paused. "Wait. Before we go into battle together, what's your name?"

"I'm Laura."

"I'm Inanna and this is Johnny Talon."

"Pleased to meet you." She extended a hand. Inanna took it, and then so did I.

I took charge. "Let's get this show on the road. You two go to that side of the door, I'm going to go first with my gun at ready. Follow me closely."

I'd emptied my Glock on the Raven men, so I drew my revolver and stood to the one side of the door. Inanna stood to the other, with Laura close behind. With my free hand, I turned the handle and cracked open the door. A black claw slashed out at me and I fired. It screamed and fell back. I opened the door the rest of the way, striding forward with the gun at ready. One of the women must have found the light switch as suddenly the room was no longer dark. A winged reptile with a long beak lay on the floor in a pool of blood.

I gave the room a quick scan. Party room? Not my kind of party. Whips and floggers were hung on the black papered walls. Three women were chained so their arms hung from the ceiling, legs spread by yet more chains to the floor. One of the raven men dropped his whip as I entered the room.

"Those whores you are with belong to the master," it said.

"I am here to free all these women—and to destroy your master," I replied.

"Free them? They signed contracts, each of them, willingly. Trust me, they are simply misbehaving because they crave the punishment their master will dole out to them for their naughtiness."

"I am no longer drugged, fiend. What I crave is beyond your understanding. What I seek is your master's destruction," said Inanna.

"And you, slave?"

"I am no longer a slave. You will address me as Laura, if you address me at all."

It advanced at us, whip raised. "I will not be spoken to thus by my master's slave!"

My shot brought its hand down, a bloody mess, the whip falling harmlessly to the floor.

"You dare harm such as me!"

"I'll dare more than that," and I let my revolver finish the sentence and him as he dropped to the floor with a thud. "And then, there was one."

We untied the women and removed their gags. One confessed that she'd enjoyed being Drysdale's slave and provoked the punishments, but the other two were quite glad to be released. Even the willing slave was eager to leave the establishment; and understood why we were seeking to destroy Drysdale.

"It is one thing for him to keep those of us willing to serve in this manner, it is another thing for him to hold women against their will, drugged into the submission that I willingly entered into. I'll not stand in your way," said the woman who had self-identified as a willing slave.

"Good. Unless you're coming with us, feel free to leave the house."

"What should we do about clothing?" asked one of the women who had identified as an unwilling slave.

"Is there nothing in the house?"

"Nothing."

"Drysdale must have something for himself. Take from that."

"Steal from our—" said the willing.

"We'd be glad to. Come," said the unwilling.

The two who would be free each took an arm of the willing slave and left the room.

"Be careful, there is still one of the raven men alive, and we've no idea if Drysdale has any of his men about," I said after them.

"Even if we're not being watched, there are bound to be alarms," I reminded the women. "Let's get out of here. Laura, please take us to the stair."

****

We followed Laura through the other door in the main central hall and made our way unobstructed down the stairs to the lowest level. In front of a large door with handles in the shape of the elder sign stood the last of the raven men, a blade in each hand.

"Would you shoot me like a coward? Or fight me like a man?"

Inanna stepped forward. "I will fight you like the woman I am."

"The whore? You know I have orders to bring you inside alive to the master."

"That's your problem." Inanna's sword was golden

in its arc, to be met by the crossed blades. It tried to twist her blade from her hands, but she pressed and twisted, freeing her blade and causing it to stumble. She slashed again, it parrying this time while slashing at her with the other, cutting her arm.

"Think you, a *whore,* can best me!"

Her blade flashed and the raven head flew through the air, the body frozen and then collapsing, swords falling with a clang.

"Here, let me bind that arm," I said, pulling off my coat and tearing off my shirt sleeve.

Laura picked up one of the raven man's blades. "Do you mind if I use this?"

"Help yourself."

Inanna went to open the door.

"Stop," I said. "Laura, is there any other way into that room?"

"Not that I'm aware of."

"Damn. Opening that door, we're breaking an elder sign. We should be prepared for some unknown horror."

"Unknown or not, I'm going after Drysdale." Inanna thrust open the doors and collapsed as a gunshot reverberated.

"Talon, you forced me to do that to my whore. Get out before I kill her, and this worthless slave that dares to bare a blade in my presence."

"Drysdale," I replied. "Your life is forfeit. Prepare to meet your maker."

"Ha! At your hand? Hardly." He went to fire but threw the pistol down in disgust and drew his blade.

I tried my revolver and was equally frustrated. I'd used my last bullet on that Raven man. I'd have to try the sword. I drew it and advanced on him, dimly aware that

Laura was tending to Inanna. He calmly waited for me to be within reach and then slashed out. I barely caught his blade on mine. My sword hand shook in pain from the force of his blow.

"You think you can face me with a blade! You will regret the day you took that whore as a client."

Considering that each word was accompanied by yet another slash, each made with such a crushing force, I knew it was a matter of time before my own blade was knocked from my hands.

"And if you think I'm fast, try me now," he snarled.

My thoughts were a prayer for help as his blade became a blur that I parried and parried, stepping ever backwards until my back was against the wall.

He pointed his blade at my panting chest. "Talon, I will spare your life if you just walk away. The whore is mine. There is nothing you can do to save her."

I heard Inanna shout, "Then taste nothing." With a thud, a dagger landed in his chest, a field of scarlet growing around it. He staggered backwards, the wicked triumphant look replaced by confusion and pain.

"Talon, you will die with me!" He rushed me, swinging. I side stepped and thrust. His pommel hit my side with the force of a truck, and I crumpled as he fell with my blade through his chest.

Wincing, I pulled myself to my feet and stumbled over to Drysdale. "Where is it?"

"Fuck you, Talon."

I grabbed my blade and twisted until he screamed. "I can make this easy on you—or hard. Where is the mirror?" I pushed the sword up as his screams became less coherent until he fell unconscious.

I limped over to Inanna. Laura had removed

Inanna's pants, torn it into strips to make a makeshift bandage that she'd wrapped around Inanna's left leg.

"Can you help me up?" Inanna said, her voice strained in pain. "I want to help search for the mirror."

"And have you bleed to death? Forget it. He may have broken some ribs, but I'll manage." I glanced at my watch; we had half an hour. "I'll find the mirror."

"I'll stay with her incase Drysdale is able to try something," said Laura.

"Yeah, thanks," I said. "I'd hate this to become a bad horror movie where you can't kill the monster."

"Johnny," said Inanna. "Be careful. He's likely to have it guarded in some manner."

"Got it."

I went back to Drysdale's body and searched his pockets. Nothing. That would have been too easy. No keys either. His dead body was making this as hard as his live body had. I cautiously approached the altar at the center of the room. As expected, I found steel shackles where a victim could be bound, and a trough and bowl for the collection of blood. No mirror.

Reflection. To find the reflection required reflection. Time to think, if only I had time. The opposite of a mirror is a shadow. I needed to find the right shadow.

My gut instinct was that he had it near in one of the four rooms off of this one. I couldn't find any marks on the floor to indicate if one door was used more often than the others, and all were closed. I felt the handles; one was colder than the others. I'd try that one first.

I pulled it open and saw in the distance the twisted parody of Los Angeles Inanna and I had explored what seemed like years ago. The mockery of the Capital Records Building was in sight but getting there would not be a trivial task. If Drysdale went there often, his body might leave a trace on the path for me to follow. I took off my shoes and felt a path where things were warmer. I followed the warmth, the shadow of his life.

Ignoring the many-eyed thing that ignored me, and the moments when I found myself upside down or that my sword was suddenly on my left which I knew was still my right, I got to the building's entrance. Since I'd followed the warmth, I was lined up with the door and entered.

Chapter 21

A True Name In Blood

A naked woman was waiting for me on the other side. I recognized her as the willing slave we'd rescued.

"Fancy finding you here," I said, as I walked past her, glancing about the place for a mirror or shadow. Inanna's warning that the mirror would be guarded by a monster kept me wary; this girl was likely that guard.

"I thought that if you won over my master, you'd come here, and so I waited for you."

"How thoughtful." That was as good a lie as any and could even be a half truth.

"I can help you, if you agree to let me serve you."

There, the bribe. She was willing to betray her master. She was the shadow; the mirror must be near. "How can you help me? How can I help you?"

"You are looking for something. A mirror."

"Drysdale told you this?"

"I overheard him talking about it. I've a good idea where to find it, but it comes with a price."

She followed me down the hall as I traced his heat.

There is always a price you pay, usually damnation. "Name the price and I'll consider it."

"You let me serve you, in everything."

Like Faust let the demon serve him? "I'm not into that kind of thing." I wondered if she was the same kind of monster as I've met here twice before. The focus on service argued for it.

"Oh."

"Sorry to disappoint you." I wasn't really sorry, but it always paid to be polite.

"You won't consider it, even to find that mirror?"

"It would be making a dishonest bargain. You deserve better than that." Why not give her some truth.

"I don't follow."

The heat took me into a records room, and she followed me there. Bin after bin was filled with vinyl disks, most without labels. This case had as many puns as it did coincidences.

"If I said yes, you'd help me and then at the first opportunity I'd break my end of the bargain, dismissing you, and that is wrong."

"I've never wanted a man who cared about what was wrong in his dealings with me. I just want to serve."

Yep, she was the same kind of monster all right, yet she was offering to help me for a price. The price of using her as a servant. Damnation.

"You remind me of a young woman I met last time I was here." I started flipping through the albums. "She claimed to be owned by a scientist who she served. I asked her if there were others like her, and she said there weren't as many as there used to be. I wonder if you and she are much the same."

"How could you tell?"

I entered a part of the room so deep in the shadows I should have started there. I pulled my cigarette lighter from my pants. I used the thin light of the flame and stepped into the shadows. Sure enough, I found more crates, more records. I started to go through them one at a time while continuing to chat with the willing servant, hoping to buy some time.

"She told me she was created by the Old Ones to serve them, but there were no longer any Old Ones to serve. She served a professor, and you served Drysdale until just a few minutes ago."

"Is he dead then, as we surmised?" they asked.

The demon no longer tried to hide its reality. I'd guessed right. I just hoped it kept its current shape, I had no desire to face that horror again. "I left him dead, or as near to dead as one can be."

I flipped over the first disk of Carmen to find a silver rimmed hand mirror. Was this the one I was looking for? I picked it up and looked in it to see in its reflection a large glimmering blob with eyes that kept appearing and disappearing.

"Now that you know the truth of us, will you let us serve you? We must serve someone," said the blob which looked like the willing slave when I turned to face it.

Words were hard to come by, and I tried hard not to run, though I'd known the truth before the mirror revealed it. If they attacked, I was dead. I'd left my sword in Drysdale's house. "Yes, but in my own way. I need a new receptionist. Do you want the job?"

"Job?"

"Yes. The pay is okay, and the hours are mostly regular. My partner—"

"You want to pay us to serve you?"

"Yes, I'll pay you. You may serve me, but you will not be my slave. However, I could use a new receptionist. Are you willing?"

"Yes, master."

"Don't call me master, call me Johnny."

The demon beckoned for me to follow them. "Come, we'll have to hurry. We don't have a lot of time."

I followed the fading heat, jogging as fast as I dared through the twisted terrain. "What shall I call you?"

"Whatever you wish."

"Can I call you 'Tikilili'?"

"Do you speak the language of the Old Ones?" they asked. I wanted to ask why it called itself 'we' but didn't dare.

"No, but the 'I know this cry is the cry of the—" they didn't let me finish.

"Forgive us, but don't say it."

"The name of your species?" I asked. "Don't say that name?"

"It will bring others, others who will wish to do you harm because you've harmed the master."

"Ah, thank you. Why don't you wish to do me harm then?" I asked.

"You accepted us as your servant."

"Receptionist. If I hadn't, would you have tried to kill me?" Of course, they would have killed me, they just preferred to serve someone, anyone, and their former master was dead.

Silence. We reached the door back to the house. I hoped we were in time.

They touched my shoulder. "Yes, we would have tried to kill you. We would have followed our old master's last command. You gave us the truth; it is important that you know the truth about us."

"Thank you." I opened the door and stepped through, with Tikilili closing the door behind them. I ran to Inanna, who was sitting against a wall, Laura next to her.

"Here is the mirror. I found it next to a copy of Carmen."

"Thank you." She took the mirror and looked at it. "Jessica!" she said into the mirror.

"Inanna, thank God! Quickly, destroy it!" said Jessica.

"I love you."

"I love you too."

Inanna slammed the mirror against the floor. Nothing. She then took her comb out of her hair and smashed the comb against the mirror. The mirror broke into eight pieces. She picked up one of the pieces, muttered something silently, dipped an end in her blood and wrote her name in English.

Nothing happened.

"Are we too late?"

I looked at my watch. "No."

"Then why isn't she free? I did what we were instructed to do."

"Write your name again but do it properly."

"I know how to write my name."

"Do it in cuneiform."

"That again! How often do I have to tell you—"

"Inanna, do it. Every single time we've faced a barrier in Drysdale's warehouse, you wrote your name in cuneiform and the barrier was removed. Please, we're almost out of time."

She started with the eight-pointed star, working counter clockwise from the first line until all four lines were drawn to create the star. A bright light shown from within the star. "Hurry," I urged.

She drew the two pillars, the line that connected them, the V underneath with the line that reached down from the heavens to the V. Light bursting from her bloody name caught, reflected and refracted in the broken glass into the many colors of the rainbow. The earth shook. The glass shattered into dust that filled the air with all the colors fading into a glowing woman's form.

"Thank you, my Inanna. Now I can freely enter His heavenly mansions and wait for you there."

Her voice had the same joy I remembered from the cemetery. Tears welled up in my eyes as Inanna spoke.

"Jessica, my darling. I'm with child! If it is a girl, can I name it after you?"

"Yes."

Jessica faded into light that burst into a blinding brilliance. The building began to shake again, but this time, the shaking didn't stop.

"We've got to get you to a hospital. Can you walk?"

"Help me up. I think I can manage."

Laura and I helped Inanna stand. I put my arm around her, and the four of us made our way to the stairs.

****

Thankfully, my landlord had fixed the damage to my room, so I was able to live in my slum palace again. Over the next few days, I collected the remainder of her things from St. Vincent de Paul and brought them to her apartment. When her check cleared, I was able to catch up on my bills, and have a decent bank account again. My partner was surprised that I'd found someone to replace our receptionist, and Tikili (I'd already shortened it) was under strict orders to look and act human while on the job.

I dropped by to visit Inanna a few days later in the hospital. Tikili insisted on driving me.

Inanna beamed when I entered the room. "Johnny! Thank you for coming."

I moved to stand next to the bed. "How's the leg?"

"Getting stronger every day. They tell me I got lucky, that the bullet passed very close to the artery. How's the car?" She took my hand.

"It is recovering nicely, enjoying the new set of tires, but I've got no leads on its mystery as of yet. This is something I'm going to have to look into. I heard from Laura this morning. She asked me to convey her wishes for your speedy recovery."

"Kind of her. Who is this?" she stressed the last word to indicate that she knew who she was, but really was asking why I was consorting with a demon. I decided to play dumb for the moment and continue the fiction that Tikili wasn't demonic.

"This is Tikili-li," I said. "She was one of the women Drysdale kept enslaved. She needed a job, so she's now working for me as my receptionist."

Her voice raised an octave. "A receptionist? Are you certain you know what you're doing? Working with her *and* a possessed car?"

"Yes." I hoped she didn't ask me which question I said yes to.

"How is the little one?" I asked, to divert her.

"They did an ultrasound. It looks like a little bug." Her voice rose an octave, almost to a squeak.

"Sounds cute."

She squeezed my hand. "You don't have to do this, Johnny."

"Do what?"

"Stay in my life. I'll be okay. After I'm out of here, I'm going to rid the world of Murphy. Then I'm heading home to live with my parents. I'm going to get a more normal job and raise our child. I'll always remember you, every time I look in our kid's eyes, but I'm not in love with you."

"I know," I said. "I still thought it best to offer. I'll send child support if you want."

"I've seen the place you live in. You can't afford child support. I wonder how you afford your office and receptionist. You got my check?"

I took her hand. "Yes, I got your check. Thank you. I get by. Having a partner helps."

"Good. Tikili-li, can Johnny and I have a private word?"

"Of course."

She stepped out. Inanna motioned for me to put my face near hers.

"That's a shoggoth."

"I know, one of Drysdale's."

"And you've taken them as your—"

"Receptionist. Yes. I even pay her. Have you finally admitted to yourself who you are?"

"*Them,* not her. Get it right Talon, or you might wind up dead even faster. As for me, I'm me. No more, no less. However, yes, you were right about me. I can't deny what I wrote, the truth that freed my love. But why am I *her*? What does it mean to be the living incarnation of Inanna, goddess of love and war?"

"Why am I me?" I squeezed her hand.

"Are you making fun of me?"

"Only a little." I kissed her on her forehead. "It is a valid question that most of us never even think of asking, even though it is one of the most important questions to ask. I'd recommend that you keep asking."

"Speaking of truth and questions, tell me the truth, Johnny. Have I broken your heart?"

"Just a little." I kissed her again, this time on the cheek. "I do enjoy sleeping through the night now."

"They don't—"

"No. They have their own place. They're not happy with the arrangements, but then again, neither am I."

"How did you come to agree to this?"

I told the truth. "They made me an offer I couldn't refuse."

"The mirror?"

"No, worse. My life. I'm a coward, and therefore compromised my principles on the condition they compromised theirs."

"They have principles?" she asked in a whisper.

"Yes."

"Let me guess. The job, the fact that they don't live with you. Those are their compromises?"

I straightened. "Yes. However, now I have more than a receptionist. I have an assistant. They're going to try to help me find Jack the Fish."

"Take care of yourself, Johnny. Don't trust them, and don't trust that car of yours."

"You take care of yourself too, Inanna."

I stepped out of the room to find Tikili speaking with Father Donn.

"Johnny, it has been too long since you were in church, my son," he said with a smile.

"Father Donn, it is good to see you again."

"You know who she is?" he asked.

"Which one?"

"Ah, yes, that. The Lord works in mysterious ways. She now knows that the gifts she was so proud of—

301

poppy tea, prostitution, and war were problematic gifts at best. She's been humbled, in a good way, and is on the right road."

"How is it possible?" I asked.

"Not all the spirits who interacted with humanity and let themselves be called gods were malignant. Inanna saw only the relief from pain from the poppy tea, and frankly it was not due to her that people learned how to make it so much more potent and turned this real blessing into a curse. However, for those who suffer from cancer, it is still the best cure for pain known to humanity. Inanna only saw the joy of sex, its creative and healing powers, how empowering it was to women. It was not her fault that prostitution became a means to denigrate the practitioners. As for war, she'd only seen it as a way to increase her influence. Now she knows she can use that to rid the world of those who do harm, but it is more often used to do harm to the most vulnerable. She'd not understood what she'd done until now, how all of her gifts are dangerous and seductive."

"What made her come back?" I asked. "Sumer was such a long time ago."

"I don't know. Regardless, somehow Drysdale got wind of her. Thankfully you correctly deduced that he saw in Inanna a way to increase his hold over the demons he'd brought into the world. Thank you for helping destroy Drysdale and his operation."

"You know that she's going after Murphy, and she won't let me help."

"Yes," he said. "The Church will lend her and Edamame what aid it can. What Murphy is doing is an abomination and it would be a blessing to the world to rid us of it."

"You surprise me, Father Donn."

"How so, my son?"

"You're not praying for Murphy to repent," I said.

"Oh, I am. I am also no fool. Sometimes, when they won't seek redemption in this world, they must find their way to God in the next."

"And hell?" I asked.

"May it be as empty as the promises of the Father of Lies. One other thing, Johnny."

"Yes?"

"Word has gotten around what you did for Inanna, and for Tikili-li."

"Oh? Should I be worried?" I asked.

"Yes, but you can expect an active clientele."

"There are others whom the ancients called gods who have become people and are seeking help of one kind or another?"

"Yes. Inanna may have opened the door, but others have followed her example. And there are some who are still wandering the Earth the old way."

"Thanks for the warning, Father Donn."

"You're welcome. I look forward to seeing you in Church."

"And Tikili-li?"

"Of course. Redemption is offered to all."

****

Once again, I walked out of the theater without spying Jack the Fish. I felt in my pockets for a cigarette, but I had neither a pack nor a lighter. Their absence brought me back to the last time I'd smoked, and Inanna. Funny how we'd helped each other get over our mutual addictions. I wondered if she had some ghost habits like my looking for a cigarette when I was out of ideas and had no leads.

Tikili-li emerged from the fog, wearing a trench coat and fedora. "Where to?" They'd taken up driving as one of their many ways to serve. As a means to deflect them from the main way they sought to be of service, I'd let them serve in all the others for a good wage.

"The ballpark."

"Which one?"

"PacBell. I'm fishing for ideas, and somehow, I'm reminded that Dali believed that baseball contains the essential answers to life's important questions. Let's go catch a game. Where's the car parked?"

The End

A word about the author...

W. B. J. Williams holds an advanced degree in anthropology. He is an avid historian, mystic, poet, and author who manages an information security program at a prominent New England firm. He is noted for his bad puns, and willingness to argue from any perspective. He is endured by his beloved wife and two daughters, and lives in Sharon Massachusetts. When he is not at home or at his computer, he can often be found haunting the various used bookstores of Boston.

Thank you for purchasing
this publication of The Wild Rose Press, Inc.

For questions or more information
contact us at
info@thewildrosepress.com.

The Wild Rose Press, Inc.
www.thewildrosepress.com